To
Keith
Best Wishes
Phil

SETOPIA

by

Phil Cline

Acknowledgements

There are many people I would like to thank for helping me with this book, but I would especially like to express my gratitude to my fiancée Véronique for the countless hours she spent editing this book, to Richard for his editorial help, to Steve for suggesting changes, and to Eric for helping with the cover design.

Published in the USA by Amazon Digital Services.

ISBN 10: 1973340887

ISBN 13: 978-1973340881

CHAPTER 1
Flight To The Bahamas

Mayday, Mayday!" I shouted into the microphone. "This is JONATHAN CREWS aboard November 3794 Delta. Do you copy?" Only static came over the radio. The Piper Cherokee vibrated as we flew through a strange gray fog that appeared from nowhere. The plane's compass spun. Nothing seemed normal. A metal pen flew from my pocket and plastered itself against the windshield.

My voice sounded as though in slow motion. "Mayday, Mayday" I shouted again, but still no response. BOB McLEISH, my good friend of many years, looked like he was trapped at the distant end of a looking glass. Slumped over in the pilot's seat, he appeared to be unconscious. His canvas fishing vest cast an eerie greenish glow. I shouted to him, but the sound of my words seemed to go only to the edge of my lips before falling into the infinite space that lay immediately around us. Fear raced through every pore of my body.

Outside the aircraft, a ribbon of colors merged into a strange liquid that oscillated as if we were in an Aurora Borealis. Everything seemed to slow down and the movement of my arms and legs seemed frustratingly difficult. All objects distorted and the nose of the plane seemed to stretch into infinity. The longer we remained in the strange fog, the farther we advanced through pulsating walls of multiple colors. In the distance toward the distended nose of our aircraft appeared a silver ball that approached us with increasing speed and size until it threatened to destroy us.

Loud sounds like popping balloons filled the cabin and all about us was confusion. At the edge of it all was an immediate awareness of hopelessness. All seemed lost. Fear held me in its grip like a vise, and my heart pounded as though it would break through my chest. Then, in the distance, a bright ray of light penetrated a hole in the far boundary of our magnetic tomb. The hole increased in size as we approached. Then, the plane moaned as if it were a wooden sailing ship protesting the forces of the sea, and we were once again flying above the ocean. The instruments began working again and the altimeter indicated we were at 2,500 feet. The plane banked sharply to the left. Bob was unconscious, so I grabbed the control yoke and flew the plane. My few hours of flight training as a kid in upstate New York thankfully came back to me. The gas gauge showed we did not have much time left to be airborne. I looked around for Nassau, the destination for our fishing trip. In the distance lay a large island that looked like it might be one of the islands in the Bahamas. I flew in that direction and pulled back on the throttle to save fuel and to glide lower. I got back on the radio.

"Nassau tower, Nassau tower, this is November 3794 Delta, over."

Only static filled the speaker.

"Nassau tower, Nassau tower, this is JONATHAN CREWS aboard November 3794 Delta. We have a medical Emergency! Come in please. Do you copy?"

Again all that came from the speaker was static and a series of odd high-pitched sounds. We didn't have much time to find a runway. As the plane lost altitude, I could see more clearly the island in front of me surrounded by jagged cliffs and surf crashing upon the rocks. It looked like a tropical island with a lot of trees. We flew over the island at about 1,000 feet. The island lacked the pink and white sandy beaches or the Turquoise waters of Eleuthera. Clearly, it wasn't Bimini or one of the Andros islands. Several thoughts flashed through my mind as we circled the island, but my main thought was *WHERE ARE WE*?

Our fuel would run out soon and we would be forced to land. I throttled forward and gained altitude while crisscrossing the island in search of a suitable landing strip. In the distance, rose the highest mountain on the island and just beyond the peak, a pillar of smoke rose into the pale blue sky. Surely, if there is smoke, there would be people. As we circled the area, the engine sputtered, then quit. We had only enough time for one landing attempt and no more in this rain forest. Fortunately, not far away, a small clearing came into view, but it didn't seem to be large enough for a landing.

"If you crash land in a forest, put the nose of the plane between two large trees." I remembered my flight instructor telling me, "The wings will sheer off, but it will cushion the crash."

I approached with full flaps, and tried not to prematurely stall the plane, but to allow the plane to drop quickly past the tall trees into the opening. A sudden severe cross wind caused the plane to crab sideways and required pushing down hard with my foot on the right rudder to keep the plane straight. The wheels touched down and the plane careened forward toward two large trees at the far end of the clearing.

We hit the trees and I blacked out. When I awoke, the cockpit was in shambles and a limb was sticking through the windshield. My head ached. I shook Bob, but he didn't respond and he had no pulse. Blood poured down my forehead and obscured my vision. I unbuckled my seatbelt and attempted to climb out of the wreckage, but collapsed.

* * *

The next morning, as rays of the sun broke the chill, I awoke and looked dizzily about me and saw a lush forest of tall trees. To the right and left, as far as the eye could see was rain forest. Calls of a multitude of birds filled the air. A waterfall sounded like it was nearby. Carefully I moved my arms and legs to check for broken bones. My muscles were sore and bruised, but nothing seemed to be broken. I got out of the fuselage and walked toward the sound of the water. A short time later I stood in front of a huge waterfall that spilled out into a stilling basin.

A broad-leaf vine with a sweet and slightly sickening smell covered the ground near the waterfall. I knelt down, dipped my hands into the water and washed the blood from my face. The water felt refreshing and helped awaken my senses. Across the basin, a light purple moss hung from the trees. The water in the stream meandered down the slope a short distance, and then turned abruptly to the right and disappeared.

After a short rest, I returned to the plane. Bob would need to be buried as soon as possible. He had a physical exam scheduled upon our return. His wife had pleaded for him to take an EKG before he left for the fishing trip, but Bob had refused. He did not like heart medicine and refused to bring any on the trip. Heart failure was the most probable cause of his death.

An army trenching shovel in the baggage compartment proved useful. After a couple of hours of digging, the grave looked deep enough, so with all my strength, I pulled Bob's body from the plane and into the grave.

The only words from funerals I remembered were "Ashes to ashes, dust to --." Tears welled up in my eyes as I knelt at the side of my friend's grave and wept.

A little later, I placed torn pieces of aluminum from the plane's fuselage over his body to keep animals from digging it up and sadly filled in the grave with soil. A metal marker made from the plane's cowling stood at the head of the grave. It read:"Robert McLeish, age 47, Washington, D.C."

Bob had been a wonderful friend. Together we were heading to the Bahamas for a fishing expedition to get away from the hectic life of Washington, D.C. Bob was a well known lobbyist. We had been friends since college in upstate New York, and entered government service in Washington at the same time. I took the State Department examination and became a Foreign Service Officer. He went off to Capitol Hill to serve as legislative liaison for a prominent Senator. Those days seemed so long ago, and now they were over. Funny, how our lives could change so quickly.

Everything in the luggage compartment lay on the ground in front of me. Some of the items, such as the high-power rifle, canteen and survival kit were essential. The Hickey Freeman suit was not important and I put it back into the luggage compartment. There were enough emergency rations to last one or two days. Bob had a hunting vest and a back-pack that would be useful. I filled the pockets of the vest with a box of .30-30 shells, and strapped a hunting knife to my side. My thoughts returned to the days when two Marine Raiders and I were dropped into the Florida everglades with only matches, a first-aid kit and hunting knifes. The Marines considered these items sufficient equipment to survive for two weeks until our scheduled pickup. We survived on anything we could find. Swamp snakes turned out to be the tastiest meat we could find.

I strapped on my back pack, and looked at the compass from the survival kit. There had been smoke on the other side of the mountain and possibly people. My compass indicated the peak lay west by northwest from my present location. With my rifle slung across my shoulder, I set out.

* * *

The next four hours, I hiked up an incline and worked my way around to the west side of the peak. The mountains looked formidable. Climbing the steep cliffs seemed impossible. My feet ached as did my damaged muscles, but walking seemed to help loosen my muscles. Many times the pain was so great I wanted to stop, but continued up the slope. After an agonizing hike, I came upon a clearing and sat down to rest. In the distance, striped animals much like zebras grazed on nearby vegetation. They didn't seem alarmed by my presence. I hadn't eaten in several hours and walking had made me very hungry. I opened a package of MRE rations and ate. A small rodent resembling a squirrel with a bushy tail, but with the head of a small monkey looked down at me from a limb overhead. The strange animal was not indigenous to the Bahamas or anywhere else on the Earth that I knew. Strange place, I thought. The monkey crept closer, trying to figure out how to get my food. After a while he disappeared back into the forest.

After about an hour of rest, I set out again despite painful muscles that hindered my walking, but I hiked until late afternoon when I came upon a clear mountain stream. Several fish swam in the stream, and it seemed to me that one or two would make an excellent meal. The emergency kit contained a roll of fishing line and a hook, so I cut a limb from a nearby tree and fashioned a fishing pole.

Late that afternoon, I cut some branches, made a lean-too, and placed some soft pine needles on the ground for a mattress. A fireplace of stones and dry wood from fallen trees in the forest created an excellent camp fire. Catching fish proved to be an easy matter in this jungle paradise. The fish resembled small mouth bass and were about twelve inches in length. After catching several, I filleted and readied them for cooking. The metal container of the emergency kit worked well as a frying pan. Soon, the fish were cooking over the fire. The smell of fish brought out many curious onlookers from the jungle. The animals did not seem afraid of me. Perhaps they had never come into contact with humans.

* * *

The next few days I spent at this campsite. The days were relatively uneventful. A small squirrel frequently grabbed a piece of discarded fish and ran into a nearby tree where it got upon its hind legs to eat. In time, it became quite friendly and became like a pet. Drying fish into a kind of jerky occupied much of my time. On the morning of the sixth day, I explored the forest. After walking a few hundred feet into the jungle, I encountered a sweet mesmerizing scent that compelled me forward and seemed to overpower my muscles. Owing to my weakened condition, I stumbled and hit my head against a rock. When I awoke, the smell had disappeared, and I returned to camp with a large knot on my head.

On the tenth day, I slung the rifle over my shoulder and set out again. A formidable canyon surrounded me with cliffs that cast a purple hew as though composed of quartz. Getting to the other side of the island required going over the peak. A pass at the far end of the gulch looked like it led to the mountain peak.

Toward evening, I neared the summit. A group of boulders provided good protection from the weather. I collected fire wood and made another lean-too from the limbs of nearby trees. A warm fire blazed as the sun went behind the mountain. The temperature dropped very quickly at this altitude. Fish stew made from the dried fish and vegetables from the MRE cooked in the skillet. After a nice meal, I leaned back to relax and fell asleep.

* * *

In the early hours of morning, I awakened to the sound of breaking twigs. I readied my rifle and hid in the recess of one of the boulders. Whole minutes passed as my heart pounded. Then, again, the sound of breaking twigs. Adrenalin surged through my body. Soon, I heard a voice.

"Dio!"

I stood my ground and remained silent while adrenalin shot through my veins.

"Dio!"

The fire still burned bright enough to cast light upon an elderly white bearded man wearing a long white flowing robe and sandals who had entered my camp.

"Dio!" He called out again.

"Freeze!" I shouted, pointing my rifle. The man cried out in fright and stepped back, trembling. A thin man in his fifties, he looked intelligent, almost scholarly. We studied each other for a few seconds.

"Who are you?" I asked.

"Please," he replied, "do not take me to Latipac! I came here looking for my pet, Dio. I did not realize I had wandered so far from Seraphs."

"Who are you?" I asked again.

"My name is Faz. I did not intend to breach the Treaty. I am looking for my pet."

"Treaty?"

"Please do not arrest me," he pleaded.

"What is this Latipac?'

"What?" The man asked dumbfounded."Are you not a Set?"

"No, I'm not!" I replied, "who are these Sets?"

"But, the Gun! Only Sets have guns! You are a Set!"

"No." I said, trying to convince him."

"What is the name of this island?"

"Setopia," he replied.

"Setopia?"

"This island is Setopia."

"You do not look like a Set," he said after examining me in the light of the fire.

"I am not a Set," I said.

"You are not dressed like a Latipacian, and you are certainly not a Seraphian! Who, are you?" he asked.

"I am a citizen of the United States," I said.

"What is this United plates?" He asked, puzzled.

"No. United States." I said, but he looked even more puzzled.

"The United States is my country. Are the Bahamas near here?"

"Bahamas? I know of nothing of these Bahamas," he replied.

It became increasingly clear to me that this was a strange uncharted island. I asked Faz many questions, but he didn't know any more about the location of this island than I did.

"Where do you live?"

"In Seraphs, just over the mountain."

"How far is your village?"

"Half-day trip from here, but it is dangerous travelling at night," he replied, “you can visit my village, but you cannot remain without approval of the Supreme Council."

"Tonight, the fire will keep us warm and there is food. Join me," I said.

"I'm tired and hungry," he said.

"Then, join me."

He sat down, and I prepared another batch of fish stew. The eyes of my elderly guest grow larger as the stew boiled. Obviously, he hadn't had a meal in a while. After he had eaten, he fell fast asleep.

***

As golden rays of the morning sun lit the distant cliffs, I awoke to the sounds of many wild birds chattering in the nearby trees. I looked around and found my guest fast asleep. I nudged him and he awoke.

"It's morning," I said.

"Yes," he said as he stretched him arms outward, "shall we go to Seraphs?"

"Yes," I replied, "I need to find help."

We broke camp, covered the fire with dirt and left. Faz led me through the forest and to a passageway of carved granite steps that went steeply upward toward the peak.

"Be careful," he cautioned, "the morning dew causes the steps to be very slick."

"Where do these steps lead?" I asked.

"Up there." He pointed toward the peak of the mountain.

"What's up there?"

"It's sacred," he replied.

As we continued up the steps, he talked freely about astrology and told of ancient stories of stars in the universe. He talked about many things, but remained guarded and diplomatic when asked about the government. As we approached the top of the mountain, a large white bird flew past us.

"What kind of bird is that?" I asked.

"It's the Condor of Seraphs."

It was a huge bird with a wingspan of at least fifty feet across. Still, despite its size, it was graceful and sailed silently down into the valley below. Several times my feet slipped on the wet granite steps that led forever upward toward the summit. Fortunately, I was able to regain my balance and continue with Fez up the steps.

Stopping for a rest, I looked back down the canyon I had hiked up. As the golden rays of the sun fell on the cliffs, it seemed to excite the quartz and turned the cliffs into a beautiful radiant light purple. A haze filled the lower valley and hid most of the trees, except for their tops that protruded through the fog. The valley seemed alive with sounds of many animals that I had never heard before. After a short rest, we continued up the steps.

CHAPTER 2
Seraphs

After what seemed like a very long climb, we arrived at the top of the steps and the peak of the mountain. We stood on a broad plateau of pink and white granite. Before us was a city of indescribable beauty. The buildings were all constructed of light blue serpentine quartz. When the sun shone on the exterior walls at a certain angle, the buildings emitted a rainbow of colors that radiated out over the city. An ornate building with a huge golden rotunda stood at the center of the city. Other buildings were arranged around the rotunda symmetrically like spokes in a wheel. I stood on the plateau astonished at the beauty of this place.

"Come!" Faz said and walked toward the city.

We walked under a large clear quartz arch and down a path way leading into the heart of the city. The streets were composed of dark blue triangular stones that fit perfectly together. The first building we passed had an ornate courtyard with a flower garden of beautiful variegated colors. The courtyard had cultivated hedges, and marble statues adorned with precious stones. Every building we passed had its own unique courtyard with statues and fountains of various themes. The statues appeared to be carved by master sculptors reminiscent of Michelangelo or Donatello. Much of the narrative of these statues seemed dedicated to peace, harmony and serenity. None of the statues or monuments reflected warfare, heroes of war, or the agonies of existence.

Local residents congregated in small groups around fountains in the various parks we passed. The people were dressed in white togas, both men and women. The older men wore beards, but not the younger men who had closely cropped hair with no beards. All seemed happy. I felt awestruck by the beauty of this city.

"We must go to the Supreme Council," Faz said.

"Why?'

"To obtain a permit."

"Is that necessary?"

"Yes, you must have a permit to stay here," he replied.

We walked toward a large golden domed building that stood in the center of the village. At the uppermost tip of the rotunda stood a serpentine marble statue of a blindfolded woman holding a pair of golden scales. We walked at a casual pace, which gave me an opportunity to observe the beautiful architecture of the buildings. Many of their buildings were constructed of light purple quartz with exceptional artistry.

I stopped to speak with a scholarly looking gentleman, but the man looked at me with apparent fright. "*Set*!" he exclaimed, and immediately ran away.

“Why is that man frightened of me?” I asked. Faz raised his finger to his mouth and motioned for me to quietly follow him. Soon, we stood on the steps of the building with the golden dome. Near the entrance stood another very large white marble statue of a woman holding golden scales.

Ten giant pillars of light blue marble, each skillfully sculpted, supported the portico of the building. The pediment contained a variety of carvings in bas relief that seemed to signify the peaceful nature of the people here. The outer walls were reinforced with flying buttresses of black stone that contrasted with the white marble steps leading into the building.

The pedestrian traffic indicated to me that this must be an important building. The people who entered and left appeared to be government officials. We walked up the steps and entered the building through a large ornately carved wooden door. We walked across the vast lobby whose floor contained precious stones arranged in a mosaic depicting various historical events, but all of a peaceful nature. This city seemed to be what the Spanish conquistadores were looking for when they went in search of El Dorado, the city of gold, although all I saw here were precious stones.

We climbed a large circular stair case. By the time we reached the fifth floor, my legs were tired. The elderly gentleman climbed the stairs with an effortlessness of someone many years his junior. He agreed to rest, so we sat down on a highly decorated wooden bench alongside one of the busy corridors. All the males wore the same basic toga with sandals, and each had a well groomed beard, but of various length and sizes. The women wore blue togas of the same general style and had a variety of tasteful hair arrangements, some in buns, some in ponytails and some with elaborate braids.

"Who are these people?" I asked. Faz raised his finger to his mouth as he had done earlier, indicating for me to be quiet.

"Patience," he said. "You must be cleared by security before I can answer your questions. Stay here." Faz walked down the hall into an office. A moment later, he returned and sat down next to me.

"We must wait," he said.

We sat on the bench for about thirty minutes and I entertained myself watching the people going to and from the various offices that lined the hallway. Many of them gave me suspicious looks.

At last a tall lean young man in a smartly pressed tunic walked up to us and spoke. "Come!"

Faz and I arose and followed him down the hallway. We entered a set of large doors that opened into a room resembling a courtroom. Two guards met me and took my rifle, my backpack, emptied the pockets of my vest and took all my equipment. Normally, I would have protested their actions, but under the circumstances, I decided to cooperate. Then, they carried my things out of the chamber and disappeared.

The chamber walls were richly adorned with inlaid wood, and contained scenes of literary heros. Some of the intarsia fooled the eye with convincing illusion that made scenes in the wood look three dimensional. A large oculus at the top of the dome filled the chamber with natural light.

At one end of the room, a man with a well-trimmed mustache dressed in a white toga sat behind a large ornate well-crafted wooden desk. From the deference the others paid him, he must have been a person of authority. He had finely chiseled facial features and appeared quite intelligent. He motioned for Faz to sit down and for me to approach the bench. I did as instructed and stood before him although at a much lower elevation owing to the raised platform of the desk.

“Faz, who is this man dressed like a Set?” Asked the Magistrate.

"I met him in the mountains," Faz said.

"Why were you outside Seraphs?"

"I was looking for my dog."

"You know the rules!"

"Yes, your honor."

"You are excused. We'll discuss your indiscretion later." Faz arose and left the room.

"Who are you?" He asked, turning to me.

"My name is…" Suddenly, I could not remember my own name. I don't know why, but I couldn't remember. "Actually, I…" I stammered.

"You don't know your own name? Interesting! Did you forget the name Anil wanted you to use, or did you forget your given name?"

"Your honor, I had head trauma and--" I said, trying to explain.

"Silence!" He commanded, "why have you come here?"

"My plane crashed and I--"

"Don't lie to us! You are from Latipac!"

"I'm not from--"

"Did Anil send you to spy on us?" he asked."

"No sir. I'm afraid I--"

"You are a Set, sent to spy on us! Must we continually be infiltrated with spies from Latipac?"

"But," I pleaded, "I am not from Latipac and I am not a spy! I can show you the plane I flew and crash landed as proof."

"Enough!" He shouted, "Seraphs is sacred. Our laws are sacred. Anil has sent you and the others to subvert our way of life!"

"But, Sir."

"Guards!"

Two large burly men entered and stood at attention. They had purple sashes on their right shoulders and wore the ubiquitous white togas.

"Arrest this man! Take him to the prison!"

CHAPTER 3
Prison

The guards grabbed me and escorted me out of the chamber. They rushed me down the staircase, out of the building and across the street to another building. The guards said little as they escorted me other than to say I would be held until the Supreme Council scheduled an appearance date. They took me down a long corridor past a row of cells with steel bars and stopped in front of a small cell. One guard opened the door and pushed me inside. The cell was clean and sanitary with white marble walls. A bed stood to one side of the room. A quartzite window permitted the entrance of light, but did not allow me to see out. I sat down on the bed and waited. Soon,I heard footsteps in the hallway leading to my cell. A young muscular woman with dark hair appeared outside my cell and instructed the guards to let her enter. She placed a bright garment on my bed.

"Who are you?" I asked.

"The question is, who are you? You look like a Set to me. We get all kinds in here. Your tale is the most ridiculous story I've ever heard. Take off your upper clothing. I'm going to inspect your wounds."

I removed my shirt. She examined me but found only contusions, no fractures. She took some pills from her satchel and handed them to me.

"What are these?" I asked.

"Pills that will help heal your wounds. Take them with water. Guard, bring some water," she instructed. The guard momentarily left then returned with a metal cup of water. Reluctantly, I put the pills into my mouth while she watched. I swallowed the pills along with the water and handed her the cup.

"I'll step outside. Remove all your clothing and put on the toga lying on your bed," she instructed.

"What will happen to my clothing?"

"They will be burned." She left my cell and I removed my clothing. I was uncertain how to put on the dark-red toga lying on my bed, I attempted to put it on, but finally the guard had to demonstrate to me how to put on the toga.

"Put it on," the guard demanded. I put on the toga, and soon the muscular woman returned.

"You look better now," she said, managing a slight smile, "the pills will make you sleepy. Lie down and get some rest."

The guard locked the door. The sound made by their heels upon the marble floor echoed as they walked down the hallway and out of the building. I laid down on the bed and thought about many things, the plane crash, my wife, Emily in Washington, my boy and girl of 11 and 14. Then the pills took effect and I fell asleep.

* * *

Hours later, loud banging of metal upon the cell bars woke me up. A tray of food and a glass of liquid resembling fruit juice sat under the door. After hesitating, I ate the meal of meat and root vegetables and drank the juice that tasted like mango. After finishing my meal, I examined the cell, looking for a way to escape. After thinking that I might escape, the thought suddenly dawned on me that I was trapped on this island. What means would I use to go back through that strange mist? Any attempts at escape seemed pointless, so I decided to control my natural inclinations and befriend my captors. Perhaps then they would go easier on me if I cooperated.

***

That night, after the guards left our cell block, prisoners in the adjacent cells talked to each other. Bits of conversations came to me as whispers from my fellow prisoners. I couldn't understand very much of their conversations. Upon the approach of a guard, their voices turned to a whistle. Then, all became quiet, except for the footsteps of the guard upon the marble floor. As soon as the guard completed his rounds and left, the conversations resumed. During the night, I heard a sound from the next cell.

"Psst." Then, a short time later, I heard another, "psst!"

"Who's there?" I asked.

"Not so bloody loud! Want to bring the lot of em down on us?" The man whispered.

"What do you want?" I asked in a much softer voice.

"You one of Anil's men?"

"No," I replied, “who are you?"

"The magistrate mistook me for a Set, but I'm British."

"British? How'd you get here?"

"Long story. We were sailing my Pearson 44 from Southampton to Belize. When we were near the Bahamas we ran into some freak storm and were sucked into some kind of strange vortex. Next thing I knew our boat hit the rocks and I beached on this Island. Don't know what happened to the rest of my crew. They must have drowned. This island is not on any of my nautical charts. How about you, mate?"

"Plane crash. I flew into a bizarre fog that screwed up all the instruments in our plane. Next thing I knew, we crash landed on this island. How long have you been here?"

"Months," he said, "food isn't bad, but I don't think they will ever let me leave. They think I'm a spy for this bloke named Anil."

"Who are these people?"

"One of the fellows in Block C said the original people shipwrecked on this island several hundred years ago. Don't know where they're from or anything about them, but they seem to speak the Queen's English."

"Any idea of how we can get back to the real world?" I asked.

"This is real, mate. Trust me on that one."

"How can I get back to America?"

"Haven't the foggiest. About fifty nautical miles southeast of the Bahamas I sailed into a strange storm. Our compass spun like a top. Couldn't see nothing! Thick fog! Been thinking, if I sailed back into that area I might be able to get back to England."

"Anything left of your boat?"

"Don't know. My boat sank. There was a large hole in the hull. I swam ashore."

"Hey you!" Came a voice from across the hall.

"What do you want?" I replied.

"You from Latipac?"

"No. United States."

"Where?"

"United States," I replied.

"Is that near Detfar?"

"No," I replied, "it's near Canada."

"How did you get here?"

"I flew," I replied.

"Flew? Like the Condor of Seraphs?" He said laughing.

"Yes, like the Condor of Seraphs." I thought he could relate more to a bird than to a metal airplane.

The man stopped talking to me and talked with his fellow cellmates. They were laughing amongst themselves, and occasionally used the words *crazy*, *loco* and *madman* spoken in reference to me. They spoke a lot of someone named Treblam who seemed to serve some sort of diplomatic function between the divisions of Setopia.

Before long, we heard the clicking of boots upon the marble floor. All the prisoners stopped talking. At first, the footsteps were distant, but they quickly came closer. The guard walked the length of the cell block.

"All Quiet!" He yelled.

With these orders, the prisoners' conversations stopped. I laid down on my bed and fell fast asleep.

***

The next morning I awoke again with the sound of metal clanging on my cell door. A tray of food with a cup of the milk-like substance had been placed under the cell door. The food tasted good. After breakfast, a guard came to my cell door.

"You're scheduled for exercise!" he said.

"Exercise?" I muttered.

He escorted me down a long corridor with other prisoners going to a gym for exercise. Upon entering a large open room, he turned us over to another guard with one arm missing. Other guards stood around the room to discourage any resistance.

"Prisoners!" The guard ordered, "form four rows. I want twenty pushups. When I blow this whistle, begin." He blew a whistle, and the prisoners did pushups. Some were unable to do more than five or six but others seemed to be in good shape and could do twenty or more. Although my muscles were still sore from the crash, I was able to perform twenty pushups. However, the weaker prisoners who couldn't do the required number of pushups were hasseled by the guard who hit them several times with a baton. The one armed guard singled out for a beating one skinny man with limited muscular build. The poor man screamed with each blow of the guard's baton. Instinctively, I lunged for the guard, but a young blonde-haired man of athletic build grabbed me.

"Let it go, mate. You don't need more trouble. You're lucky the guards didn't see you."

"He doesn't need to beat the man like that!"

"Let it go, Mate. I'm warning you. Let it go!"

“You the Brit?”

“Yeah, that’s me, Ian’s the name.”

“Jonathan here,” I replied.

“Take care, they’re watching us.”

I got control of my anger and calmed down, but I swore to even the score with the one armed guard. We did other exercises for about an hour, and then we were returned to our cells. Two guards carried off the unfortunate man.

The first day passed slowly for me, but then the days began passing into weeks and the weeks into months. Each day our routine was essentially the same. I found the daily solitude intensified my focus on the strangest of things. One day, a fly entered my cell. He became an object of fascination for me and I closely observed his every move. The freedom he had to fly in and out of my cell at will I admired and envied. One evening I was sitting in my cell listening to the other prisoners talk when I heard the Brit.

"Hey mate,"

"Yeah," I replied.

"Got some information."

"What is it?" I asked.

"One of the blokes in the other cell block works in the minister's office. He said you're scheduled to see the Minister tomorrow."

"About what?" I asked.

"Don't know. You're scheduled to appear. That's all I know."

"Thanks," I replied.

"By the way," he said, "they're taking me away from here tomorrow."

"To where?"

"Don't know. I'll tell you one thing, mate. If I get a chance, just one chance, I'm getting off this island."

"How?" I asked.

"Don't know mate, All I want is one opportunity to get free, then I'm going to--"

Sounds of the measured steps of the guard rang out from down the hallway and the British fellow fell silent and didn't talk anymore. The guard walked past my cell and down into the far cell block. Then he shouted his normal order, "*All Quiet*!" and the cell block grew quiet once again.

CHAPTER 4
The Trial

The next morning a guard appeared at my cell door carrying a toga of white silk with a scarlet streak across the breast. A very attractive toga indeed, I thought.

“Put it on,” he ordered.

I did as instructed and put it on and he escorted me from the cell. We walked back across the street into the large building with the golden rotunda. As we entered, I could see several men sitting in the Chamber. The presiding officer sat behind a large desk upon a raised dais. A large guard grabbed my arm and stopped me from moving. The presiding officer motioned for the guard to release me and leave, which he did.

"Approach the bench," said the presiding officer. I did as instructed and stood in the well area before the bench. A man dressed in a very expensive toga joined me.

"May I, your honor," began the man, "use my diplomatic status to speak with the alleged spy from Latipac."

"The Ambassador from Latipac is recognized. You may have five minutes with the prisoner."

The Ambassador took me by the arm and led me to a secluded part of the chamber.

"My name is Trebnal. I'm the Ambassador-at-Large with the permanent delegation from Latipac. What were Anil's instructions to you?"

"There were no instructions, I--"

"Have you ever spied for Anil?" He interrupted.

"No!" I pleaded, "I know nothing of Anil and I know nothing of Latipac. Some freak of nature stranded me on this island. I am unfamiliar with the customs and ways of this land." The Ambassador took one step back and examined me with much amusement.

"But your manner of speaking is very Setish. Definitely not Seraphian and certainly not Seval. Why do you claim not to be a Set?"

"I am not a Set! I am an American. I come from a land far away called the United States."

"Well," he replied, "whatever you claim to be, I'm sure Anil has a reason for your denials."

"But--," I began.

"Silence! Walk with me," he said as we returned to the bench.

"Let me warn you of this place," he began, "they have a strange fascination for truth in whatever form they find it and they cannot tolerate the ways of the Sets. Sets are devious. Take my advice and plead guilty and appeal to their sense of justice and fairness. Perhaps we can arrange a diplomatic exchange and have you released. They love to convert people to the ways of the Seraphians and in so doing, save them from the clutches of the Sets. Perhaps we can arrange a swap." He stopped short of the bench and looked directly at me.

"I must leave now. Remember," he warned, "appeal to their sense of justice or suffer the onslaught of a mighty wrath. Good luck." He left and disappeared out the door. I looked at the Magistrate whose eyes were bearing down on me and approached the bench.

"Have you acquired a taste for the truth in your time in detention?" He asked.

"I have, your honor," I replied. My heart raced and my thoughts seemed to slow down so I couldn't think very quickly.

"So, are you ready to tell us what Anil's plans were for you here in Seraphs?"

"The truth is, your honor, I am not from this land. I am not from Seraphs, nor am I from Latipac, nor from Seval. I am from a far away land called America."

"Lies! More lies!" Screamed a man sitting to the right of the Magistrate. I looked at the Magistrate whose face had turned red with rage.

"Our most brilliant scholars," said the Magistrate, "have researched the whole of this globe and Setopia is the only body of land in existence. All the rest of the globe is water. Must you insult our intelligence with such cheap displays of imagination?"

The room grew silent. The Magistrate calmed down and shuffled papers in front of him. He thumbed through a sheaf of papers, pulled out three and laid them in front of him.

"State your name," he instructed.

"My name is Jonathan Crews," I replied.

"State your place of loyalty."

"It does not matter," I replied.

"Your province," shouted the Magistrate. Once again his face turned red. It became obvious I could not satisfy the Magistrate with the truth, and I wanted to end the interrogation.

"Latipac," I replied in a low voice.

"What? Latipac?"

"Yes, Latipac," I replied.

"Oh," he said with a smile, "so, we find that you are in fact a Set after all, and if not in fact a Set, you are most definitely representing the Sets. Is that correct?"

"Yes," I replied.

"So, we finally get to the truth." He wrote something on the paper and then looked up at a gentleman seated nearby.

"Sacram," he said motioning to a man sitting on a bench at one side of the chamber.

"Yes," the man replied.

"Approach the bench."

A tall elderly man dressed in a neatly tailored navy blue business suit stepped forward and stood next to me. The Magistrate then addressed us.

"Sacram, you will represent Mister Crews as his attorney," he instructed. "Mister Crews, I'm assigning Sacram to be your defense attorney. He is an honorable man and a fine diplomat. Your trial will be a few days. During that time, you will be released to Sacram. If you try to escape, the consequences will be severe. This hearing is hereby adjourned."

With that statement he hit the gavel upon a wooden plate. All arose as he walked from the chambers. My new host stood by my side in a stance similar to that of the military at attention. When all the council members had left, Sacram turned to me and extended his hand in friendship.

"You've had a trying time of it," Sacram replied. He was an elegant man with finely chiseled cheek bones, good complexion, and a healthy glow overall. He took a pipe from his suit coat pocket, filled it with something that looked like tobacco, and put it in his mouth. Before lighting the pipe, he removed it from his mouth and began.

"I heard what you said about being from another land. I know Anil's methods well enough to know he wouldn't have given such a preposterous directive to one of his envoys. You told the Magistrate you're from Latipac. Are you from there?"

"No," I answered," I admitted being from Latipac to keep from making the Magistrate even angrier. He wouldn't believe me when I told him the truth. What is the Magistrate's name?"

"Etat," he replied, "a good man, but highly suspicious of Sets."

"Do you know Etat well?" I asked.

"Yes, he is my son."

"Your son?"

"It's a long story. I'll explain it to you sometime. But, tell me. What is this land like you say you came from?"

"It's a wonderful place. It's a land of freedom for all, a land where even a poor man can one day lead the nation in its highest office. It’s a place where anyone can become wealthy if he has discipline and perseverance."

"Sounds like an interesting place. Where is this America located?"

"I don't really know. While coming here I got caught in some strange mist that brought me here. It seemed to carry me through to another dimension."

"Well, the location of America is not important. Our first priority is to work on your defense. We'll do that from my flat, but first let's get something to eat. I'm famished."

* * *

We left the Judge's Chambers and walked out of the rotunda building and through the marbled streets. There was a warren of small walkways winding between buildings that seemed to extend throughout the city.

"There's a little restaurant not far from here."

"What is it?" I asked.

"It's a place frequented by some of the more creative people in Seraphs. It's called La Travaille."

"Is it French? I asked.

"French? What is French?"

"The name sounded like something that might be found in a country called France."

"It is just a name," he replied, "what is France?"

"It's a country where the language spoken is French."

"Language?" Sacram said, seemingly confused, "what do you mean by language?"

"The words people use to communicate."

"Oh, we have but one language here, but there are very different uses of language. For example, in Latipac language is a tool for deception as much as a tool for communication of ideas."

"Where did your language come from?" I asked, "it's very similar to my own."

"Our language originated with the Sets long ago and all people of Setopia have been mandated to use it. Sometimes words are changed in meaning by the Sets. Often that confuses everyone. You say you're not a Set. Somehow I tend to believe your story."

"I'm glad someone does," I replied.

"Setopia must be experienced to be understood. Parts of Setopia are beautiful and models of excellence, while other parts are…" he said morosely, "we mustn't talk about that."

We entered La Travaille and sat at a small dark wooden booth. The interior of the shop appeared surprisingly European. As I looked around I saw many people engaged in conversation over cups of coffee or tea. There seemed to be an ambiance of intellectual curiosity.

"It's more interesting here in the evening," Sacram said. "I'll bring you back here in the evening sometime, perhaps tonight."

Sacram motioned for a waiter to come to our table. A young man came to the table.

"Coffees and two of your sandwich specials," Sacram said. The waiter wrote the order on a slip of paper and departed back to the kitchen.

"The waiter here," Sacram began, "originated in Seval. We, got him in a diplomatic exchange with a high ranking Set, Anil's lieutenant. Seraphs really came out well on that exchange. We got a good waiter and a group of fine talented people in the exchange. Overall, the people who came from Seval have made an excellent life for themselves here in Seraphs."

The waiter appeared with a very attractive presentation of sandwiches and a small plate of colorful hors-d'oeuvres.

"How did you end up here?" I asked. A sudden down pour of heavy rain pelted the streets outside and seemed to change Sacram's mood. His composure changed to one of sadness.

"I'm not at liberty to discuss my background. But I will say. When very young, my first job in Latipac was with the Treasury Department."

"What kind of work did you do?"

"I started out as a low level staff member in the economics section and worked my way up. Then I switched over to the diplomatic service and ended up here. That is about all I'm at liberty to say. However, we need to discuss your defense. You irritated my son with the strange tale you told about arriving in Setopia."

"I told him the truth," I said.

"He doesn't believe you. I question your story myself. It sounds a little preposterous."

"It may sound preposterous, but it is the truth. What do you say when you're telling the truth, but no one believes you?"

"The marshal told me your clothing looked strange, and the weapon you had with you was of unknown origin. We might be able to use those facts as evidence in your trial. But, I will tell you something, the spies Anil has sent here are clever and creative in their covers. Nothing that can be said would surprise the Seraphian officials. They have heard it all before."

"If I tell them the truth and they don't believe me, what can I say?"

"Sometimes, it is useful to tell small stories instead of fantastic tales. Even though it's untrue, it's more believable."

"So, what do you suggest?" I asked.

"I'll give it some thought. I want to spend some time talking to you and get to know you. Tell me more about yourself."

"Do you want the real story, or a small made-up story?"

"The real story."

"I grew up in Upstate New York, near Hamilton. As a kid…" Then, I went on to tell him some of the things I had done as a kid, like going swimming in Sandy Pond, and how with a group of friends we had encountered a pack of wild dogs one night while sleeping in a hay loft on an abandoned farm. How the severely cold weather in that part of New York made the hairs on my legs feel like needles when I sat down outside. Reminiscing about the old days made me homesick, but I continued to tell him about my stint in the Marine Corps and my involvement in activities in the Middle East. Then, I told him how I had spent several years at a university in Upstate New York, not far from my home with studies in government and economics. I told about the difficult State Department examination, and how relieved I felt to enter the Political Cone of the U.S. State Department. I told him about my friendship with Robert McLeish and how he had died of an apparent heart attack before we crashed on the island.

Sacram seemed fascinated by what I told him. After a while, he seemed content that I was telling the truth and our conversation switched back to my defense. During the remainder of our time at the restaurant that afternoon we discussed various small tales of intrigue that had a ring of possibility, that is, things that might be accepted by the Magistrate as true. I noticed the rain outside had subsided. After sitting in La Travaille quite a while, Sacram paid our bill with tokens, which is the medium of exchange in Seraphs and we left. He took me to his home in a section of Seraphs reserved for Sets with diplomatic status. The home had a wooden balcony that overlooked a well tended courtyard and garden. On the walls were paintings by well known artists of Seraphs. My bedroom overlooked a very pleasant courtyard.

"Make yourself at home," he said, "there are some togas in the closet that should fit you." He closed the door and left. I explored the closet, bathroom and balcony as well as the bookcase filled with many books. I sat on the balcony overlooking the courtyard, and thought about this strange island of Setopia. I picked a book from the library shelf and began reading, but soon tired and went to bed.

* * *

The next day I stayed in the house because Sacram did not want me to leave, so all day I entertained myself reading books I found in the library shelves. The more I read about Setopia, the more curious I became. It was indeed a strange island full of intrigue and conflict. Later that evening, Sacram returned home.

"I have a treat for you tonight," he said.

"What is it?"

"Get ready and you'll see."

We walked back to La Travaille. We entered and sat at a booth in the center of the room near a fireplace with a blazing fire. People in the room wore colorful jerkins as well as other forms of clothing, a pleasing departure from the normal toga. The smell of varied blends of coffee permeated the room. A waiter approached and asked for our orders.

"And how are my very special friends tonight?" he asked.

“Very well, Todd,” Sacram said, then he turned to me. “Johnathan, I would like for you to meet Todd.We saved Todd and several other people from the Sets.”

“And I am indebted to you, Sacram,” the waiter said,” What can I get you?”

“Coffee for me,” Sacram said.

"What would you like?"

"Do you have cappuccino?" I asked.

"Ah, an excellent choice. Will that be two?" He asked. We both nodded. "Two cappuccinos it is. You're just in time for the festivities."

"Are you reading tonight, Sacram?" Asked a young man carrying a clipboard.

"Not tonight. Perhaps another time."

The young man smiled and walked to another table. Sacram explained that the paper contained a roster of artists who would be performing.

"What kind of artists perform here?" I asked.

"Playwrights, poets, lyricists, essayists and performance artists."

The waiter brought two cappuccinos and placed them in front of us as the emcee announced the first contestant. A young man of average height and slender build walked onto the stage. His eyes were black as coal and piercing. He had sallow cheeks and unkempt hair and a somewhat neglected toga.

"I will tell you the circumstances that prompted the writing of this poem," he explained. "The morning rays of sun warmed the early mountains and lit the distant hills with its radiant beauty. Suddenly, the song of a lark broke the stillness with a heavenly song and awoke my consciousness. A vision appeared during which the gates of paradise opened. I felt at once infinite and omniscient. I do not know how long I remained in that state, but I could reach out and touch colors. Some of the color remained on my finger. I placed my finger into my mouth and could taste the color. Each taste carried me farther and farther into the presence of the infinite. I feel embarrassed that I am not able to describe the beauty that I experienced, but l will try with this poem: All is one. One is unity, all is unity. Thank you for listening to my poem."

Each person in the café meditated for a while upon the nature of his message. Then, they clapped and cheered for the poet. Next up on stage were two performers, one a playwright and the other a friend.

"The nature of Seraphs is truth," began the playwright, "and truth is the nature of wisdom and wisdom the nature of life. So it is with our brief skit that I will perform with the help of my friend."

"Two men, one a beggar in tattered clothing, and the other a wise man, meet on a mountain pass," he began. "One seeks truth, the other has truth, and so our play opens,"

Beggar: Excuse me, sir, but I have come a long way. I am looking for something. Can you help me?

Man: What is it you seek?

Beggar: Please tell me where I might find truth.

Man: (Becoming irritated) I've been told truth burns brightly in the fires of hell. Perhaps you should seek it there.

Beggar: But, surely you jest. I searched near and far. I sought ıt as the desert sirocco that stung my cheeks, and as steam curled about the sand on its airward journey. But I found it not.

Man: (Amused) Perhaps truth is a person. I have seen him in the corridors of our hallowed chambers sporting a beard and toga. I have seen him spread marmalade on his toast before his morning coffee. Did you know he was a musician?

Beggar: I heard him playing in the cacophony of sounds of seaward gulls frozen in blue-gray skies.

Man: And in the rustling of leaves?

Beggar: He played a mandolin.

Man: Then you did find truth.

Beggar: Only as a flute finds a note.

Man: A flute?

Beggar: One can often hear a note of truth without knowing from whence it comes.

Man: (Becoming serious) So, you found truth. Awaken the world to the beauty of truth."

With these words they ended their performance and thanked the audience. The audience applauded with hearty support. The performers walked off the stage and the manager called another performer to the stage.

"Next," the Emcee announced, "we have a well know essayist."

The essayist walked to the stage and lifted his hands to calm the appreciative clapping. "I have with me," he began "an essay dedicated to the treachery and deception of the Big 'A' of Setopia. We all know who that is." He held the document in the air so that all could see the print, then he continued. "What I have here is a treatise on the nature of Set law. It is a theory of Power, a theory of Economics and a theory of deception. I chose to call it, for purposes of brevity, '*Set Theory*'. It examines the ways the Sets control us: the Seval by direct and brutal ways, and us by more subtle but no less effective ways. We patronize the people of Seval and study their plight while we are victimized by the threat of Anil's military and police forces. One day Anil will no longer recognize our treaties. Last week Anil instructed Congress to give him a 15 percent increase in his defense budget. He made a speech to the Senate about the necessity of expanding his military. "

"Not allowed in here!" Shouted someone in the audience, and others joined him in opposition.

“Leave the stage!” Demanded the Emcee. The young man threw up his hands in resignation and walked away.

"Two things should never be presented in an environment catering to the arts," Sacram told me, "are religion and politics. Either is likely to create heated debate. Second rate novelists, as an example, burden their work with political themes. That young essayist built his work on political emotionalism and raised fears of a military presence in Seraphs. Such a thing is dangerous and unwanted here. I think we should leave."

The mood in the café became somber, so we paid our bill and left. We walked in the cool brisk air back to Sacram's home and talked for a while before turning in for the night. I opened the window of my bedroom and heard people talking as they walked past the courtyard below. The scent of flowers in the garden wafted into my bedroom as I took in the ambiance of my new home. My bed with a silk canopy looked very inviting. I laid down on the bed and fell asleep.

***

The next morning, I awoke refreshed. A welcome ray of sunlight came through my bedroom window. The birds chattered to the vibrations of the rising sun, enlivening the morning. Below the balcony and outside the gate came sounds of shuffling feet, of sandals upon stone streets. It was the sound of the people of Seraphs going to wherever people in Seraph go at that hour of the morning. There was a knock on my door.

“Yes,” I said, sitting up in bed. The door opened and a servant appeared in the doorway.

“Breakfast would be served soon,” he said and left as quickly as he had arrived.

I took a quick shower, dressed and headed down to the breakfast area. A steaming cup of coffee awaited me.

"Sit down and join me," Sacram said as he sat reading a morning paper. He wore a blue silk dressing gown and seemed perplexed about something.

"Something in the news?" I asked.

"An article about Latipac," he said, "how did you sleep?"

"Good," I replied, "the guest bed is very comfortable."

"Glad you slept well. We've got a lot to do today," he replied "you're appearing before the Magistrate again today."

"Oh," I replied, "you just ruined my breakfast."

"Don't worry," he said, "I have a deal in mind."

"What should I say to the Magistrate?"

"You're going to plead guilty."

"What!" I said, my heart pounding, "you want me to plead guilty to a high crime?"

"Yes, enjoy your breakfast," he said as he got up and left the table.

I ate a tense breakfast of cereal, goat's milk and fresh fruit while thinking about going before the Magistrate and pleading guilty to a crime. A short time later, Sacram returned to the breakfast table. He was dressed in a blue pen-striped business suite, black patent leather shoes, and a two-toned blue and red silk tie. He carried a brown leather briefcase which he placed on the breakfast table. Snapping the briefcase open, he removed some papers.

"You might want to read these," he said, handing me the papers, "it lists the counts against you. It contains an apology and places you at the mercy of the Court."

A large knot suddenly developed in my stomach and I felt ill. As we prepared to leave, a very beautiful young woman entered through the courtyard door. She paused to put some books into a bookcase near the doorway. She was very pretty and her golden hair fell loosely across her bare shoulders. It wasn't polite to stare, but I couldn't help myself, she was beautiful!

"Her name is ALITA," Sacram replied, observing my interest, "she is temporarily assigned to my staff. Her father is a well regarded intellectual here. Come, I'll introduce you."

We walked over to Alita who was straightening items in the bookcase. She turned and smiled as we approached.

"Good morning, Sacram," she said.

"Good morning Alita. I'd like for you to meet Mister Jonathan Crews."

"Nice to meet you," she said, flashing a smile.

"My friends call me Jona," I said.

"Nice to meet you, Jona."

"We were just heading down to the Municipal building to see the Magistrate," Sacram said.

"Tell your son hello for me," she replied.

"I will. Sorry we can't stay."

"Later," she said.

"Nice meeting you," I said to Alita. She smiled. We left through the gate at the far end of the courtyard. As we stepped into the cobblestone street, Sacram turned to me.

"So, now it's Jona!" he said.

"A nick-name."

"I don't like surprises before I go into court!"

"Sorry, I didn't know my nickname was important."

Angered at the revelation of my nickname, he walked without speaking. The last thing I wanted to do was anger my host who had gotten me released from jail. I felt terrible that my nickname had caused such a problem. After a while, Sacram lost his anger. Then he spoke.

"Alita's father thought a short stint on my staff would give her a more rounded education. She's very bright. I've known her since she was a toddler. She used to wear pigtails with bright purple ribbons. As a child she always skipped as she walked with us."

"Alita grew up here in Seraphs?"

"Yes, but she spent an internship in Latipac. She became one of the darlings of Anil."

"How old is she?" I asked.

"You're not supposed to ask the age of a young lady."

"Just curious."

"She is twenty-five, thought quite mature for her age. She spent a little time in Seval, but came back quite disturbed and depressed. She's gotten over that now. Sacram paused to look at his watch. "We're due in court in fifteen minutes."

We walked through a warren of narrow cobblestone streets before arriving back at the Municipal building. Entering through a side door, we walked up marble steps leading to a gallery full of artifacts representing an earlier period of Setopian history. Behind glass enclosures were glittering golden statuettes and well crafted swords. I stopped to examine one well crafted sword with serrated edges, but Sacram nudged me forward and reminded me of our court appearance.

A huge double door of dark oak about fifteen feet high and eight feet across stood before us. Sacram used a golden knocker on the middle of the door to signal our presence. After a brief moment, the doors opened and we entered. To my surprise, we were not in a courtroom, but in the chambers of the Magistrate. The room was tastefully decorated. At the far end of the room was a granite fireplace with decorative carved fruit and a stem of pea pods that wound its way up the sides of the fireplace. The pea pods stood open as though the peas had fallen out. Other men sat in chairs near the Magistrate who sat in a large chair behind a large desk with gold and silver inlay. The intarsia in the wood on the front of the desk gave the illusion of a condor with volant wings. Sacram later told me the condor is the symbol of justice, equality and fraternity for the people of Seraphs.

The Magistrate leaned back in his chair and motioned for me to stand in front of his desk. For a long time, he steepled his fingers and stared at me. A cold chill ran through my spine as he continued his silent stare. After what seemed an eternity, he spoke.

"At the request of your counsel, I have agreed to make this an informal hearing. I assume you have had the benefit of counsel?"

"Yes," I replied.

"You have been charged with high crimes against the people of Seraphs. Do you wish to enter a plea?" My thoughts went blank and I could barely utter the words.

"Yes, your honor."

The Magistrate picked up a folder from his desk. He opened it and removed a sheaf of paper. He then read from the paper listing the counts against me to which I would be pleading. After he finished reading, he turned to me.

"You many enter a plea."

I was perplexed by the Magistrate's request and wrestled with myself to force myself to speak. I felt I had committed no crime against these people, and pleading guilty went against every fiber in my body. Sacram noticed my anxiety and arose to speak.

"Your honor, may I speak with opposing counsel?"

"You may," replied the Magistrate.

After being granted permission Sacram walked across the room and spoke with Trebnal, who was seated. Their conversation quickly turned into an argument and threatened to turn violent. Finally, they seemed to come to terms with each other and gave the Latipacian sign for agreement which was very similar to the handshake in my country. Sacram arose and walked to the front of the magistrate's desk and stood at my side.

"My client wishes to enter a plea of guilty on all charges and throw himself upon the mercy of this court," he said.

The words struck me as liquid lead. My whole body ached and my legs felt wobbly. I looked at the Magistrate. He smiled at me and continued.

"By entering a plea of guilty to the charges of Treason against the state of Seraphs, you have acknowledged your connection with Latipac, with the leadership of Latipac and with the Sets of Setopia. In so doing, you have thrown yourself upon the mercy of this court. I accept your plea of guilty and acknowledge your attempts to destroy the institutions and traditions of Seraphs. Your offense is grave. It is an offence that strikes anxiety into the souls of all who cherish freedom and have abandoned the ways of materialism and power. Fortunately, your subversive actions were apprehended before irreparable damage occurred. To that our citizens are thankful. While aborted, your mission was designed to destroy the very liberties on which this community was built. I therefore grant you a conditional pardon and transfer you into the custody of your counsel, Sacram, in exchange for the release to Seraphs the lives of twenty-five Seval."

"No!" Screamed Trebmal."Our agreement was for fifteen!"

"Twenty five," yelled the Magistrate.

"Fifteen! Fifteen! No more!" shouted Trebnal.

"Then I will order the immediate decapitation of this prisoner!"

I gasped at the thought of losing my head over a few people from this place called Seval. I watched in amazement as the Magistrate and Trebnal wrangled over the numbers. Finally they agreed to the release of twenty Seval, but with the condition that they all be from a class of people designated as immediately dangerous to the stability of Setopia.

"Agreed!" shouted Trebnal who angrily left the room.

"Could I have lost my head?" I asked.

"That is within the powers of this court," said the Magistrate. "I only hope that the freeing of twenty Seval will somehow compensate for allowing you to remain free." He then turned to Sacram, "I suppose you want the prisoner granted diplomatic status!"

"Yes, your honor, we have already applied," said Sacram.

"Then, not only will you be allowed your freedom, you can also use your spying eyes to see all sorts of treasures here in Seraphs."

"I have no intention of spying, your honor. I am not a spy."

"An encouraging sign," replied the Magistrate, "but, we often have encouraging signs from Anil's spies. Very often they return to their former ways."

CHAPTER 5
Special Envoy

Sacram took hold of my arm and led me from the room. We walked back past the gallery of artifacts, down the long marble hallway and out of the Municipal building. All about us were people dressed in white togas busily going about their activities. Most knew Sacram and nodded to him, or said hello. All of the people seemed to be in good physical shape. I never saw anyone who did not look fit. All seemed to have good muscle tone and seemed to be in very good health. Their well tanned faces were no doubt the result of being out in the sun at this high altitude.

"I'm glad that's over," I replied with relief.

"My son has a flare for the dramatic," Sacram said.

“It’s odd,” I mused, “that I’m being tried for treason on this unchartered island when I was supposed to be fishing off the coast of the Bahamas.”

“So you say.”

"Where are we going?" I asked.

"To the Embassy to pick up your papers."

"Papers?"

"For diplomatic status. You will need an identification card and papers to carry with you at all times."

We walked down the winding narrow passageway leading from the Municipal building to another government building a short distance away, and up a flight of stairs to the second floor. On the door in gold lettering were the words:*"DIPLOMATIC PROFILES."*We knocked and entered.

"May I help you?" asked a middle aged woman with blonde hair.

"I dropped off some paperwork yesterday for Mister Jonathan Crews."

She shuffled through a stack of papers on her desk, then got up and looked in a nearby file cabinet. She retrieved a file, opened it and examined the contents.

"Here is it," she said, "Mister Crews?"

"Yes," I said.

"Your application has been approved by Trebmal. You are officially a diplomat with the permanent delegation from Latipac," she replied.

"Thank you,"

"You will be given a title and a salary," Sacram said.

"A title? What will be my title?"

"What do you want your title to be?"

"Don't know. Are there different kinds of titles?" I asked.

"Oh, yes," he replied, "as many as the winds have currents and eddies."

"Are titles important?"

"Very. Some Latipacians work exclusively for titles, even with no other compensation. Generally, the longer the title attached to an occupation, the more Set-like it becomes, and the shorter the title, the more non-Set it is. Thus, poet is an occupation that services the poor, whereas the title entrepreneur, by the length of its title establishes a connection with the Sets. The humanistic occupations tend to be shorter, such as poet, artist, writer, etc. This is a rule which applies generally to all of Latipac. A person is known by his occupation and his occupation determines his status."

"Why is that?" I asked

"People in various occupations are rewarded by how close they are to those in power, so they tend to have longer titles. However, the title of banker is a misnomer for the most part. The title is short and beckons to the lower ranking Lats. It places them at ease and they bring their money into the banking institutions. Bankers are swift to take advantage of people, and they disparage the Seraphians who do not believe in banks."

"How do the bankers take advantage of people?" I asked.

"They take money from the Lats and loan it back to them

while charging high rates of interest. To the depositor of the money, they pay hardly any interest. Then they began making rules that will exclude the Lats from being able to collect interest on their savings. They begin saying that they will only pay interest if it money is kept in the bank for a certain length of time, or, they will not pay interest below a certain level of savings. There are many other devises just as odious but I will not mention them here. They live well using other people's money."

"How about diplomatic envoy charged with exploration?" I asked after a fanciful thought.

"Very long, isn't it," Sacram asked.

"Should it be shorter?"

"Longer titles are usually assigned to more senior members of our mission. The longer the title, the greater the prestige, as a general rule."

"How about just special envoy?"

"Very good. Special envoy it shall be," Sacram said.

The lady behind the desk filled in a blank on the application form. Then she took a small official looking card with a raised gold emblem from her desk, wrote on it and inserted the card into a small box near her desk. Soon a laminated card came out the side. She handed it to me.

"It's a little warm. Might want to let it cool," she said with a smile.

"Thank you," I said. I examined the card. In raised letters, it said "Embassy of Latipac" and had a gold Condor embossed at the top. In the center of the card was my name, Jonathan Crews, Special Envoy. Below that were the words "Permanent Delegation to Seraphs."

"Congratulations," Sacram said as he shook my hand.

***

Later that day we returned to Sacram's home. I opened the windows to my bedroom and felt the refreshing afternoon air from the courtyard. I enjoyed the afternoon air, but a question kept popping up into my head. Had these Seraphians originated in ancient Europe and somehow slipped through the same space-warp that I went through? We had much in common, but at the same time we were very different. I wanted to find out more about these people. Suddenly, a thought crossed my mind. I rushed downstairs to speak with Sacram who was in his office.

"Would it be appropriate for someone with diplomatic status to have a guide?" I asked.

"Guide," he replied, "what do you have in mind?"

"I could learn about Seraphs much quicker if I had a guide."

"I'm listening," he said.

"I'm thinking of Alita."

"Alita?"

"Yes, she could show me around and act as my official guide."

"Alita is working at the Embassy today. I'll speak with her father."

"Thank you. In the mean time, if it's all right with you, I would like to go out and explore Seraphs."

"Okay, but be cautious," he warned.

"I will."

* * *

After leaving the house, I let my footsteps meander as they might. A topiary garden with a large bronze fountain of a nude mermaid with a beautifully complex patina of mottled browns and greens stood at one edge of town. Water shot forth from her mouth and breasts, and was captured in a small basin which provided water that spilled from the mouths of three fish into a larger scalloped basin. Sitting around the fountain were a group of people listening to an older man.

The man's voice was melodious. He had a long flowing white beard with grizzled hair. His parched face looked as though he had been in a desert for a long time. The older people in Seraphs lacked wrinkles and had ageless faces, but this man had a harsh weather-beaten face.

His eyes, dark and ablaze, were the most prominent part of his countenance. All his mental powers seemed to pour through his eyes. The frayed sleeves and knurled dirty fingernails complimented what remained of his torn leather sandals that were bound by twine.

"All is one," he said, “and all is unity. I am you and you are me. Nothing exists apart from itself, not I from you, nor you from me." He spoke in a loud voice that echoed across the garden park. "Man must look within himself for truth."

His dramatic use of body language emphasized meanings that could not be conveyed in words. His arms stretched toward the heavens and his long hair blew backward in the wind, giving him the appearance of a prophet summoning his followers. The logic of his thoughts was as a magnet and he mesmerized everyone ın the park. He possessed such charisma that I felt at once alone but not-alone, unique and not-unique, a person but not a person. After a while, he stopped and grabbed his head in his hands. His body trembled and his charisma disappeared. He began babbling, and walked away from the group talking about something that mortals would only guess. I watched him walk through the archway on the other side of the garden. The intensity of his presence remained and several people remarked that such an event had never happened within, Seraphs, though they said it happened often in the mountains.

"Who is he?" I asked an older man dressed in a red toga standing next to me.

"His name is Gloy. He's a prophet. Lives in the mountains."

"Do you know him?"

"Not really. I know something about his past."

"Tell me about him."

"Well, it's a long story. Gloy was an instructor in our university. He was a physicist by training and a philosopher by inclination. He was the cherished prize of our university. In his earlier years, he had been both a splendid scholar and a brilliant researcher. He was also just as brilliant as an instructor, which is no small accomplishment. He loved learning and research. He loved his students and was liked by all. He wrote two excellent books that today are used as general textbooks in the university. Many of his theories laid the foundation for modern thought in Setopia. Then, one day, something happened."

"What?" I asked.

"No one knows quite why, but it happened nevertheless. It was a quiet fall day. The golden leaves of the aspen were falling and the air was brisk. It was the type of day when one feels warm and cozy inside heavy clothing, when cold air stings the cheeks and the hills are alive with variegated colors. I happened to be in President Schmidt's office when Gloy walked in. His general appearance was one of strangeness. His eyes were glazed and somewhat vacuous. His hair was ruffled and his clothing disheveled. '*I know the truth*,' he announced to us. We looked at him in amazement, for in front of us stood the most respected of men. '*I must leave the university*!' Gloy told me and a stunned President. '*Why?*' Asked the president, to which he replied, '*I must go to the mountains. My destiny lies there. All my life I dedicated myself to the search for truth, but all my life it evaded me. Facts I learned, and knowledge I acquired, but truth never. Truth lies up there,*' he said pointing to the mountain top in the distance. '*What has happened to you*?' The President asked, alarmed by Gloy's aberrant behavior. Gloy did not answer. '*I must leave now*,' was all Gloy said. With that comment, he left the university and a startled president." The man paused and sighed.

"Then what happened?" I asked.

"No one heard from him for many years," the man said, "then one day we saw a purple glow on the highest peak of the mountain range. Over there," he said pointing into the distance. "A few citizens and I decided to investigate. Most citizens never leave the city, other than to go into Latipac, so it took a lot of courage for us to leave Seraphs. However, we put our fears behind us and climbed up the steep remote mountain peak. After several hours of climbing, we came upon Gloy's camp. '*I'm so happy to see each of you again*!' Gloy exclaimed. He greeted each of us as a dear friend. We camped with Gloy that night and questioned him about the strange purple haze that had been reported in the area. Gloy was puzzled for he said he knew nothing of such an occurrence, but he told us of an experience he had the previous day, while he was meditating. He said he felt the presence of a pleasantly soothing force. Suddenly, he said, he knew many things he had not known before. Advanced truths that had long evaded him were suddenly revealed, and he was in bliss for an amount of time that seemed like a few seconds but also like an eternity. We were puzzled by his ramblings and attempted to ask him questions, but the brevity of his answers and the subtleties of his statements left us more confused. '*Nothing is distinct and separate unto itself*,' he told us, '*for all things are united and parts of a greater whole.*' He made these statements with a certain aloofness, but with a warmth that was most human, a warmth that at put us at ease. Gloy tried to convince us of the need to make all men free and equal, but, that was very dangerous talk in Setopia because Anil and his units are never far away. Suddenly, there appeared around Gloy a bright pure light accompanied by low murmurings and soft madrigals. When we saw and heard this, we fled back down the mountain. The ensuing rumors that circulated in Seraphs created a legend that most citizens believe so wholeheartedly that the very name of Gloy elicites fear and reverence. After that encounter, he became known as the Wildman of the Mountains. Knowing that the Wildman was aging, the village council decided to allow Gloy to enter the village and speak his mind as a final salute to show their gratitude for his former service to the university. The council dedicated the topiary garden where you stand with the mermaid fountain and renamed it Gloy Park to serve as neutral ground from which he could speak without fear of retaliation. That's all I know about Gloy."

"Interesting man, this Gloy," I said.

* * *

After the others left, I sat down on a stone step near the fountain and watched the cool water pouring from the sensuous figure of the mermaid. Myriad thoughts poured from my mind. Much of the subtleties of what Gloy had said eluded me, but somehow it had changed me. By the time I arrived back at Sacram's office, word of the incident in the park had preceded me.

"What happened in Gloy Park?" Sacram asked.

"Gloy spoke to some people in the park. He's very charismatic."

"He was my advisor in the old days," Sacram said as he picked up a pencil from his desk and examined it, a distant look in his eyes. For many minutes, Sacram toyed with the pencil, oblivious to my presence. "They say Gloy is insane," he said finally, breaking the silence. "A brilliant mind, but insane. A local scarecrow to be mocked and belittled." He arose and walked down the hallway.

* * *

Later that night, I entertained myself by reading a popular book about financial manias in Seraphs. The first two chapters told of a flower mania that once swept Latipac where whole fortunes were spent and lost on a single flower bulb. Another concerned stock companies that sold worthless paper to an eager group of Latipacians who bid up the price to exorbitant levels, then the "*bubble*" popped. The people realized that the shares of stock they had purchased lacked value. Several chapters recounted crazy ideas and sayings that seemed to find fancy with a large group of people. One such saying was "*What a shocking bad toga you have.*" For some reason this saying caught the fancy of Latipacians. As I was reading, Sacram knocked on my door. "I spoke to Alita today," he said,“ she will meet you at the Embassy tomorrow at two.”

CHAPTER 6

Alita

Early the next morning when I awoke, a variety of birds were singing outside my window. I opened a window and saw an animal resembling a squirrel with wing-like appendages sailing from tree to tree. I watched it for a while, then showered, dressed and walked downstairs. When I saw Sacram, he no longer displayed the sadness from the previous night.

"There's an artist studio near here that you might enjoy seeing," he said, "one of the most impressive in Seraphs. There's a map of how to get to the studio on the table. I must leave now for a council meeting. We'll talk later." He replied as he walked out the door.

I studied the map as I finished breakfast, tucked the map into my pocket and left. When I arrived at the studio, I saw many artists working their crafts. Some chiseled away at marble and granite blocks. They didn't notice me. Near the door was an old man with a noble forehead, a grecian nose and a receding hairline. He had a beard and mustache and a magnificent set of blue eyes. Each time he brought his wooden mallet down upon the metal chisel it made a high pitched note, much like a musical instrument. I watched him work for a while. The artists didn’t talk much as they chipped away. Every so often, a sculptor would step back and examine his work, and then, continue chipping away.

Some of their finished works were displayed along the inside wall. I was amazed at the skill and artistry of these sculptors. They had created beautiful works of art, including nude statues of noble looking men and women as well as mythical figures. I introduced myself to an older artist who had taken a break from his work. He beamed with pleasure and told me about the symbolism represented by his Madonna, whose torso was partially sculpted down to her breasts.

"How do you know where to chip?" I asked.

"The form is in the stone. I chip away all the excess until the form reveals itself," he said.

"How?"

"It’s the duty of the artist to find the form that’s imprisoned in the stone and set it free."

"Are all the sculptures in Seraphs so beautiful?"

"Not all, but each work must meet certain standards, otherwise, it will not qualify to be placed in Seraphs."

"What happens if the work is not perfect?"

"It's tossed over the cliff over there," he said pointing.

"Come, I'll show you." The cliff of which he spoke was not far away. When we reached the cliff, we stopped and looked down at the marble rubble below.

"Down there," he said, pointing, "the works have flaws. Some are natural flaws from defects in the material, and others are from an inexperienced hand."

"They can't be used?"

"Perhaps," he replied, "the artisans of Latipac use our imperfect statues as models."

"Are there artists in Latipac?"

"No, they're not artists. They're too interested in making money to become master sculptors," he replied, "thankfully, we have standards of excellence."

"What about painters?" I asked."

"Oh, painters!" he replied with derision, "I don't care much for painters. They're inferior artists."

"Why?"

"It takes no skill to splash paint onto canvas. They place a blank canvass against a wall and throw paint at it. Horrible! Horrible! Painters are vulgar people who lack talent!"

"Oh," I replied.

"I must get back to my work now. Please excuse me."

A clock in the studio showed I was late for my appointment with Alita. I ran from the studio and raced along a small winding pathway.

* * *

When I arrived at the Embassy, Alita was waiting outside in the courtyard.

"Thought you were never going to get here," she said. "I’ve been waiting almost an hour. Did you forget our appointment?"

"Sorry," I replied, "I was watching the sculptors at the studio, and lost all count of time."

"Oh well, I want to show you some of my favorite places," she said, somewhat irritated. "We should go before it's too late." She grabbed my arm and we walked down the marble steps. Her perfume was sensual and her clothing clung to her frame revealing a perfect figure.

"Have you seen the painters' gallery?" She asked.

"No I haven't," I replied, feeling a warm glow.

"I often go to the painters’ studio."

"You like painters?" I asked.

"Yes, paintings speak to me."

We walked down a winding path and passed by La Travaille on our way to the studio. She paused to show me her favorite view of the city. I looked into her eyes as melodious chimes sounded from the clock on the municipal rotunda.

As we walked, Alita asked me many questions about my past and the reason for my being in Seraphs. She listened intently as though every word were important. We walked slowly.

"The studio is not far from here," she said, "it's just on the other side of this courtyard."

The painters' studio was in a building at the far end of the courtyard with a large open door. We could see numerous artists at work. As we entered the studio, we stopped momentarily in front of a young painter who was applying paint to his canvass. "This painter used the subtleties of light to delineate a theme," she said. "Now the other painter, over there," she said, pointing to a red haired painter, "uses dramatic contrast of light and dark to highlight his subject. We call the process Chiaroscuro. The painter, over there,"she said as walked over to a third painter, "layers the oil paint to give it a luminescent effect."

"You seem to know a lot about painting."

"When I was a young girl, I dreamed of becoming a painter"

"Why didn't you?" I asked.

"I secretly longed to be a painter but didn't have the discipline to master such a difficult craft."

“I talked to a sculptor earlier who said painters were inferior artists to sculptors,” I said.

“That was probably Scoro. He dislikes anything that he has not yet mastered. He tried painting when he was younger, but failed. Now he is bitter toward painters.”

Alita continued showing me around the studio and pointing out different styles of painting and introducing me to some of the painters. After about two hours, I grew weary of observing the painters.

"Why don't we go back to La Travaille and have coffee?" I suggested.

"Don't you want to see the rest of the studio?"

"We can come back later. Besides," I said, "I'm getting a little tired."

"So am I," she smiled.

We left the studio and headed for La Travaille. The sun was setting behind the distant mountain as we arrived at the restaurant.

“Nice place. Sacram and I were here one evening,” I said.

“It’s my favorite spot. I meet my father here often.”

“What does your father do?”

“He used to teach at the University. He was a highly respected intellectual in Seraphs, but for the past few years served as an administrator in Latipac. Anil admires and respects my father. He gave my father several choice assignments."

She took a bill of paper scrip used for money from her purse and showed me how she could make a swan by folding it in many different ways, then manipulating the tail to make the wings go up and down. She told me Anil himself had taught her to make these swans. She had a very fanciful mind, and at times I was drawn into her fantasies.

She told me of her past and of the things she liked to do. She continually amused me with colorful tales of past events in her life. She had a spirited and lively imagination, but I detected beneath the facade of amusing imagery was a lonely girl who desired to be noticed.

"I usually order a special coffee that is not on the menu, one that I call baby-blue."

"What is it? I asked.

"It's a special coffee bean that is harvested at an altitude higher than the regular robusto or Arabica beans. I'll order it. You'll see."

"Two baby blues," she said to the waiter who returned in a short time with two cups of baby blues on a tray. He sat them in front of us and walked away.

"My favorite!" She exclaimed,"try it!"

"Very good," I said, after taking a sip. The coffee was full bodied and interesting.

"I never cared much for the standard coffees," she said. Like the mochas, the cappuccinos, espresso, and the others. They're too bland. So one day I spoke to the waiter. He told me he sometimes goes into the mountains and harvests the wild beans himself, picking them just before they're ripe. He says they are his Baby Blues. Ever since I tried his coffee, I've ordered baby blues."

After a while, the waiter came by and refilled our cups. The second cup of this special brew was more than my stomach could take. I excused myself while I went into the men's room. I washed my face with cold water. After several applications of cold water to my face and neck, I felt a little better and returned. Alita smiled devilishly.

"You don't like baby blues?"

"Little strong," I replied, "I could use some fresh air."

"Perhaps we should go," she said.

It was a short walk to the Embassy, but it seemed we arrived much too quickly. I enjoyed the evening and wanted it to continue. I walked her up the steps of the Embassy and paused at the top.

"I'll show you more of Seraphs another time, if you like."

"I would like that," I replied. She gave me a warm smile and disappeared into the Embassy. I walked back to Sacram's home. He was reading when I entered.

"Enjoy your afternoon?" Sacram asked.

"Very much."

"Learn anything?"

"Yes."

"Alita is a special person," Sacram said.

"Beautiful too," I said.

"Seeing her again?"

"No definite plans."

"She's been staying with a friend on the other side of the village. Her girl friend is an artist who works in lithographs. She's well known in the village."

"Sounds like she has interesting friends," I said.

"Alita is very strong willed. She knows how to control people."

"What do you mean?"

"She gains control of her boyfriends. She begins acting like a nice sweet young thing, and before you know it her boyfriend is under her control."

"I should be on my guard, then?"

"You should be aware," he said.

"Thanks, but I think I can handle her."

"Other men said that very thing," Sacram replied.

"Well, I'm tired," I said, "I think I'll go to my room and

rest."

My room was filled with a heavy fog that had rolled into the room. It had a scent of soft coal that brought back memories of long ago in another world. I could scarcely see the nightlight by my bedside. When I closed the window, fog swished outward like a fine powder. It took several minutes for the fog to disappear, and when it did, the smell of soft coal remained. My thoughts turned to my family and friends at home as I lay down on the bed and fell asleep.

***

After breakfast the next morning, I strolled out of the courtyard and headed for the centre of town to observe whatever caught my fancy. I walked by a large building with ionic columns. In front of the building was a courtyard with marble statues of noble looking men stationed near the entrance to the building. At the base of each statue was inscribed the name of the person and a brief quotation from his works. At the top of the building was a series of Gargoyles with water spouts stood along the edges of the roof.

As I entered the building, my footsteps reverberated down the beautiful blue serpentine corridor. Faint voices seemed to be coming from behind a huge oak door about halfway down the hallway. A slight push on the highly polished brass door knocker and the door swung opened into a room of about fifteen people sitting on blocks of stone and looking at a blank screen on the wall. The room was perfectly quiet except for the occasional gasp from the audience. When I entered the room, a young man of slight build and red hair motioned to me with a bony finger.

"Would you like to enter this session of Deep Think?" he asked.

"What is 'Deep Think'?"

"You haven't been to Deep Think?"

"Never," I said.

"That is most unusual," he said, with one eye brow raised.

"Actually..." I stammered.

"Well, why don't you sit here and listen to this session. It just started," he said as he led me to a seat.

"I prefer standing."

"You can't hear the lesson unless you sit," he said.

I sat down on a hard granite chair that was surprisingly comfortable. Somehow the audio came through the stone seat, and through the medium of my body. It presented a nation of supermen intellectuals who lived on a mountain plateau and served as functionaries to a vile and cruel dictator. Each morning they hiked down the mountain to the fortress of the dictator bearing offerings of honey, milk, bread, and delicious fruits to appease him, forever fearful the whimsical dictator might decide to destroy them as he sometimes did to the slaves of the lower valley. Each morning they returned to their homes in the mountains, and shook with fear when they saw the armies of death maneuvering in the valley below. Their fearful moans filled the air and were as madrigals to the ears of the Tyrant. All this they saw, yet they retreated more and more into their scholarly studies to hide.

One day an unknown messenger delivered the idea that all men are born equal and have the same rights under universal law. The message spread throughout the land, but when it reached the dictator, his eyes flew open and white frothy saliva poured from the sides of his mouth as he paced about the room in a fit of rage.

“Who dared said that!”

“We don’t know,” said one of the generals.

"Find the ones responsible, and kill them!" The dictator ordered. “Kill them one-by-one until you find out who passed that message!"

The whole mountain reverberated with the frightened cries of the intellectuals. The dictator wanted to punish the race of supermen, eventhough they declared themselves innocent. He nevertheless sent his armies up the steep banks past the marble talus into their village. Thundering hoofs of soldier’s horses echoed throughout the mountain valley. The soldiers selected men, women and children at random and marched them at sword point to the edge of an enormous cliff that overlooked the fortress of the bloody dictator. With a slight push from their sharp swords, the men, women and children were forced over the steep cliff. Their terrified cries could be heard for miles as they fell the two thousand feet to the bottom of the ravine.

The dictator sat on his throne at the base of the mountain. His excitement began when he heard the first screams of the helpless victims. As he saw their stiffened bodies come into view, his pleasure increased. As their torn bodies bounced from the jagged rocks along the cliff and exploded upon the rocks of the ravine, his pleasure turned to ecstasy. The scene unfolding before him was the source of his pleasures. He felt himself to be an artist, for he was the divine creator, and these drippings of fresh blood brought to his eyes the most fervid beauty imaginable. His ecstasy mounted with each new wave of torn bodies and exploding flesh. The screams from the victims and the wailing put him into a heightened state of bliss. Their terrified cries became as music to his ears because the scene before him was a masterpiece of deathly expressionism.

"Pop big! Pop Big!" He shouted, but his desire for blood and power and orgasm was not satisfied. Afterwards, he sat in his fortress thinking of ways to tear people apart in bouts of sadism. Screams of his victims were delicate madrigals to his ears, and whole symphonies played in the dungeons of his castle.

One day his generals informed him that they had found the person who passed the treasonous idea.

“Bring him to me!” Ordered the dictator.

In anticipation of the traitor's arrival, the tyrant ordered built a most efficient torture rack that his engineers assured him would make anyone talk. Later that same day his generals arrived bearing the prisoner.

“What is the meaning of that message you sent?” The dictator demanded.

"That all men are born free and equal and have equal rights under the laws of the universe," replied the man. His statement sent the dictator into a fit of rage.

"Blasphemy!" He screamed,"treasonous blasphemy! I and only I have the power of the law, and of life and death!" His bellowing voice resonated throughout the caverns beneath the fortress.

"Put him to the rack!" Ordered the dictator. The unfortunate prisoner was placed with his back to the rack and tied down. Slowly he was stretched on the rack.

"Take my life. Tear apart my body, but my idea you will never destroy," he said calmly as he was very slowly pulled apart. He did not scream, nor did he cry out for mercy. The prisoner departed the world without so much as uttering a single cry of agony. His silence drove the dictator absolutely mad and he swore to destroy the idea if he had to destroy all intellectuals.

The next morning he sent his armies up the mountain, and once again positioned himself quite comfortably on his throne below the cliff. Terrified screams once more filled the air, but when bodies exploded on the rocks, the sight did not send him into fits of ecstasy, instead he became quite bored. In a fit of utmost anger, he ordered his army to find the idea and destroy it. However, hunt as they might, they could find the idea even though they looked high and low. So great was his obsession that he ordered his army to search night and day until it was found. Search they did but they did not find it. Slowly his army dissolved for they dropped dead one by one from exhaustion, and the remaining tattered men of his army returned to find their dictator stark raving mad.

A shadow of the idea followed him around in his insanity. He sought to outwit the idea and hide from it, but was unable to do so. In time, it assumed the form of a hideous monster that stalked him day and night. In his fear he walked backward up the long flight of stairs leading to the crenels on the uppermost battlements of the fortress, trying to escape. Once on top, he backed up shouting for the idea to leave him alone, but it would not. He backed up one step too many and fell from the highest battlement. The scream that accompanied him on his deathly journey was true music to the race of supermen. They shouted with joy that the idea of freedom had been so strong, but they all knew that an idea could only be as strong as its defenders. At this point the vibrations from Deep Think stopped, and those present arose to leave.

"We're having a special Group Think in the other room about the old prophet Gloy, if anyone would like to attend," said the young red haired man.

"Are you referring to Gloy, the madman of the mountains?" I asked

"One and the same," he added.

"Yes, I would like to see it."

"Follow me."

We walked through a set of large oak doors and entered a pretty blue room of oak parquetry with ornate furniture and crystal chandeliers. Another group of people were sitting on similar concave seats and, like the previous group. They were watching a translucent screen, but this time with an image of the mountain prophet. The image showed him as a much younger man with a full intelligent face and a well kept beard. He wore a finely textured toga of blue silk with a red embroidered emblem to show rank. Setting on a concave seat, I listened as he spoke on the nature of wealth. He lectured on the methods by which the controllers of wealth are at liberty to set rules and guidelines for less fortunate people. He told us that all Sets have the same manner of speaking, walking and dressing. Gloy told about the means by which the Sets control people by making them adhere to rigid guidelines. The non-Sets, on the other hand, are taught from early life non-Set values and ways of speaking so they become unqualified to attend the university or attain high positions in Setopia.

As he continued, his countenance bore an unmistakable sadness that I had previously witnessed. His voice was wonderfully melodious, and his spirit captivating. Suddenly the image disappeared from the screen, and the voice of the Chief Diplomat Trebmal boomed across the room.

"Everyone, stand and follow me!" Trebmal demanded.

We arose and followed him through another set of large oak doors and into an antechamber. Standing before our group were cruel looking soldiers wearing gray uniforms standing at each side of the entrance. Everyone was fearful. Whispered fears spread throughout the group. I didn't know what was going to happen, but my instincts told me it wasn't going to be pleasant.

The young man who had asked me to attend the session stood in front of us. He was quite pale and shaken. His face was graven and lined and his eyes red and full of tears. I felt sorry for him. As soon as all we were all in the room, Trebnal, the chief diplomat, excused himself and left. We were in the presence of soldiers of the Latipacian army. They wore heavy black boots, gray uniforms with gray caps that contained the insignia of a bird. They looked menacing and fully capable of the most horrifying of tortures. We stood unified in fear. The commanding general, a large burly man with many ribbons on his uniform walked from behind a large oak desk, and stopped in front of us.

"Just what the hell is going on!" He shouted. The very walls of the room seemed to vibrate. "What kind of crap are you jerks trying to pull?" He yelled as he walked through the group, eyeing each person. He stopped and got into the face of one man in a tattered toga and shouted.

"What the hell you trying to do? Answer me!" He yelled. Terrified, no one said a word. The general's face turned red as he shouted at one young man.

"Answer me you little bastard! You want me to take your damn tongue out and feed it to my dogs?"

"No sir."

"What!" Shouted the commander. “Whose idea was it to show that damn video!”

"I cannot tell you."

Incensed, the commander hit him in the stomach, folding him over. He cried out in agony. He then pushed him down to the floor with his boot. The general remained standing with one foot on the unfortunate man and looked at each one of us with a mean sneer. I felt adrenalin racing through my veins and I wanted to do something to stop the general, but my instincts told me to stand down. They outnumbered us and resistance would be futile.

"You, come here!" he said stepping off the unfortunate man and pointing to the young red haired man who had invited me. He did as directed and stopped a few feet short of the commander. In a quieter voice the commander motioned for him to come closer. The man did as directed. The commander put his arms around the young man and in a soft voice said, "I don't want to hurt you or anyone here, but I need to know whose idea it was to use Gloy in the group think session today? I need to know. Do you understand?"

"Yes sir," he said, trembling.

"Then, tell me boy, who put that treasonous bastard into the group think session?"

"It was my idea," he confessed.

"Your idea?" The general put his hand to his chin. "Your idea, you say?"

"Yes sir. It was my idea."

"This man says this event was his idea. What do you think of that?" He laughed. His soldiers responded by also laughing, but the laughter of the commander was loudest of all. "So this man is responsible for playing the image of Gloy. I find it amusing, that this man is the only person responsible for committing treason." He paused and studied the faces of the people quaking in front of him. He weighed his words and studied their impact on the huddled mass of people in front of him.

"Committed treason alone...all alone...all by himself. Indeed! Do you take me for a fool?" He shouted so loudly that each of us jumped.

"Who else is willing to step forward and accept responsibility?" He looked at each of us examining each person for a look of guilt or a facial tick or anything else that might show duplicity. I had to fight myself to remain calm and take no action.

"Sir, no one else is guilty," the young man said.

"Wrong! You are all guilty. You all know that lectures by Gloy are expressly forbidden except in Gloy Park! You all know that! Yet, each and everyone stayed and listened to that villainous snake knowing that in doing so you were committing treason against Setopia to which every one of you owes your very existence! You there!," he said pointing to one small man who wept from sheer fright.

"You are not a native Seraphian, are you?" The commander demanded, "answer me!"

"No sir," he whimpered. "No sir, I'm not from Seraphs."

"We have here a man who is not a native," the general announced to the group. Then he continued. "This man is living in Seraphs because of the goodness and mercy of our leader in Latipac. Yet! He engages in treasonous actions against us."

"I didn't--," began the man

"Silence!" shouted the commander

"Where you from boy?" he inquired, but before he could answer, the commander continued, "You're from Seval, aren't you? You're a lousy son of-a-bitch from Seval and you're polluting the atmosphere of Seraphs and trying to get these good people to engage in treasonous acts, aren't you?" The commander looked the red haired man directly in the face. "Answer me!" He shouted. Sobbing, the small man fell to the general's feet. The general kicked him. The man cried out in pain. The general stood above him and continued.

"We give these people good jobs in our factories and we even permit some of them to live the good life here in Seraphs and what do they do? They try to over-throw our government!" He shouted. "You little swine! Arrest this bastard!" the commander ordered. Two of his soldiers dragged the bleeding man from the room. His screams echoed down the halls.

"General…" I began, but the savage way the he turned to address me made me reconsider my protests. I had been around such men before, and I fully knew what they were capable of doing. My self preservation instincts made me clam up.

"What?" he demanded.

"Nothing sir." It was difficult to get the words out of my mouth. I wanted to fight him and his men, but they outnumbered us and they were armed. We wouldn't stand a chance.

"I'm glad we found the culprit behind this treasonous act," the general said as he addressed us. "I will make a report and mention that you good people helped me apprehend this man." The Commander then left as his soldiers followed him out of the room. We were afraid to leave until the last echo of their footsteps disappeared.

We rushed down the long hallway leading to fresh air and sunshine outside. The fresh air felt wonderful. I rushed home as quickly as I could. I arrived panting for air and rushed in to tell Sacram.

"What's the matter?" Sacram asked.

"Group Think with Gloy," I gasped.

"Did you go to Gloy Park?" He asked.

"No! It was Deep Think. Gloy was in the video."

"That's illegal!"

"I know that now," I gasped, "the Latipac army took one of the men in our group."

"What! That's a violation of our Treaty! What is the army doing in Seraphs?"

"I don't know, but they are here."

"This is not good. I need to talk with Trebnal."

Sacram grabbed his portfolio, and we departed for the Embassy. When we arrived at his office, Tebnal did not seem surprised to see us.

"You know the Army is here in Seraphs!" Sacram said.

"There is nothing I can do," Trebnal replied.

"There must be something."

"No, there isn't," Trebmal said. "The man from Seval was executed a few minutes after his arrest. He was thrown over the cliff at the edge of Seraphs."

I felt a sick sensation deep within my stomach to have witnessed the arbitrary arrest and execution of an innocent man whose only crime was to have been born a Seval.

"Are the soldiers in Seraphs?" Sacram asked.

"No. They are on their way back to Latipac. I'm lodging an official complaint with Anil. The Army overstepped its authority."

"A complaint indeed!" said Sacram."They just killed an innocent citizen of Seraphs, and you can only lodge a complaint?"

"'What do you think I should do?"

"Have the commander arrested!"

"That general is Anil's right-hand man. Anil would rather arrest me! Do you take me for a fool?"

"The Latipacians have broken their agreements with us!"

"I know. I'm going to Latipac. I'll speak with Anil," Trebnal said.

This sort of thing can not be allowed to continue!" Sacram said.

"Yes, yes," Trebnal said, "don't worry. I'll handle it."

“Fine,” Sacram said as we were leaving.

* * *

We walked down the hall to Sacram's office. He threw his briefcase onto the desk and sat down.

"I'm sorry if I created a problem for you," I said.

"It's not you. They should have known better than to show Gloy. That is strictly forbidden! The Army must have been just outside the city, waiting for an excuse to enter Seraphs.” Sacram took a sheet of paper from a file in his desk, filled out a form and put it into his brief case.

"I want you to go with me to Latipac," he said.

"Latipac?"

"We'll need to clear the trip through Trebnal."

"Trebnal said he will speak with Anil," I said.

"Trebmal lacks back-bone. He won't be forceful enough."

"But, he’s your boss," I said.

“Yes, I know.”

We returned to Trebmal's office. Sacram knocked and a young man with blonde hair, blue eyes and fair skin opened the door.

"Please enter," he said.

"Ivan," Sacram said, "this is Jonathan Crews. He's a member of our delegation."

"Nice to meet you," Ivan said.

"Ivan is my son." Trebmal said, from behind his desk. "What can I do for you?"

"I have a proposal," said Sacram.

"A Proposal? For what?"

"I want to speak personally with Anil."

"What!"

"Don't get upset," Sacram said. He handed Trebnal the forms. He took it and read.

"Preposterous!" shouted Trebmal "Are you trying to commit suicide? One Treaty breach is not a major event. They won't come back."

"But they will," warned Sacram.

"Do I need to remind you that you are part of my mission. I'm your superior. I will not tolerate nsubordination!"

"I don't intend to be insubordinate," Sacram replied in a softer tone, "perhaps we could handle this differently."

"'What do you mean?"

"I could take Jonathan with me on a training tour of Latipac. While there I could speak with Anil informally. He might respond better if it’s not an official visit."

"I am quite capable of handling Diplomatic missions without help from my subordinates!"

"I think a training exercise would be excellent," said Ivan.

"Stay out of this, "warned his father.

"But, Dad, such a trip would be better than having the Army come back. After all, how many Seval do we have here in Seraphs?"

"I don' know the exact number," responded Trebmal

"Exactly! The army hates the Sevel. They could make a bloody sport of any Seval we have living here. No one would be safe. Not them, not us."

"It would be risky."

"It will be risky to ignore the Army," replied Ivan.

"Anil has a fiery temper. If either of us got on his wrong side, he can have us both put to death," Trebnal said.

"Anil has known me since I worked at the Treasury Department. I know him well. If I told him I was on a mission to train a new Diplomat, he might be more receptive. He may not know that his general has broken the Treaty."

"Trust me! He Knows! There isn't anything he doesn't know. He has spies everywhere," Trebnal said.

"The future of Seraphs depends on our going to Latipac."

"I don't know," Trebnal said as he pondered the idea.

"It's important, Trebnal, if we don't go, we'll live to regret it, and so will all the people in Seraphs." Trebmal paced back in forth a bit while shaking his head. Finally, he paused and turned to Sacram.

"Against my better judgment, I'm going to agree to let you go."

"Good. We'll need transit visas to Latipac."

"You'll have all the paperwork you need," Trebmal said.

"Thank you."

"Good luck to both of you. And you, Jonathan, be circumspect. Listen and observe, but talk as little as possible. Do you understand?"

"Yes," I replied.

"Take my words to heart. They will serve you well."

"I will. Thank you for your advice," I said.

"Have a safe trip," Trebmal said. Sacram and I left and walked back down the hall to his office. When we entered, Sacram threw his briefcase on his desk and started pulling files from a cabinet.

"How long has Ivan been in Seraphs?" I asked.

"He grew up in Latipac. He also went to school there and learned the Set ways."

"So why is he here in Seraphs?"

"He grew tired of his life in Latipac and wanted to travel. He was allowed to travel to Seraphs under special arrangement between Latipac and Seraphs. Once in Seraphs, he felt he had found paradise. The rarefied atmosphere of the people appealed to him. After Several weeks in Seraphs, he met a girl with whom he fell in love. He defected and sought asylum in Seraphs. That infuriated Anil. He ordered Trebmal to force Ivan to return to Latipac. Anil then appointed Trebnal as Chief Ambassador to Seraphs in order to be in a position to get Ivan back. Try as he might, his father could not get Ivan to return. Trebnal made many excuses to Anil because he knew that his son would be better off in Seraphs than with an angry Anil. In time, however, the issue was forgotten."

"That's quite a story. What do we need for the trip to Latipac?" I asked

"Before we leave," Sacram said, "there are briefings for you to attend, books to read, and lectures about the culture of Latipac. There is also a list of tasks that are given to all who are assigned to Latipac," he said handing me a list. "You need to start first thing tomorrow morning. Mark off each item as it is completed. The vaccinations," he warned, "are not without side effects and can cause nausea. You might want to save the shots for later in the evening. The shots are given with an air gun under very high pressure that forces the vaccine fluid through the flesh. It's very quick and efficient." A slight shiver ran down my back when I thought about needles entering my arm. I don't like needles, and I was not looking forward to the next day.

***

The next morning I studied the list of tasks. All thirty three items would need to be completed before making the journey. After breakfast, I left. My first stop was an early morning briefing in the municipal building on the twelfth floor. Several people were seated around a large oval table when I entered the office.

"Come join us," said an older man wearing an expensive white toga.

As soon as I sat down, the briefing began. The general topic was the proper conduct as a visitor to Latipac, and, the nature of "*Culture shock*" for those who had lived all their lives in Seraphs. The man briefing us informed us that there existed a great difference in living styles between Latipac and Seraphs.

"Many of the Sets," he began, "care little for people who live by their intellects. The Sets have derogative terms for us. They say our ideas have little value because we do not have our feet on solid ground. They say we live in ivory towers, and knew little of the real world. Furthermore, we lack common sense! The Sets, manner of dress is also very different from ours. You may not see any actual Sets because you will not work at the highest levels of government. You'll mainly be in contact with the officer workers, referred to as Lats. If you're going to live among the Lats, you must dress like a Lat. That means, the beard and long hair must go."

"I have never had my hair cut,"objected one attendee, "and I have never shaved my beard, and I'm not about to start now! You're telling us all people in Latipac dress like that?"

"No, not all people in Latipac shave their beards and and dress in business suits, but those who do not arc ostracized. If my instructions are not followed, you will stand out among the wolves as a lamb ripe for the sheering.

"You must understand how the mind of a Set works. They think in terms of weakness, while we think in terms of strengths. When we meet someone here in Seraphs, we examine a person's strong points. The Sets, on the other hand, make a habit of trying to find a person's weakness and using it to their advantage. If you want to get along in Latipac, you must change your clothing and methods."

"We're academics, we're not in business like the Lats in Latipac," said another attendee.

"Most of you at this briefing are going into Latipac as policy specialists. Your task is to conduct specialized policy studies. It is your task to work backwards on a problem. You're highly skilled logicians, you can make white seem black and vice versa. Anil's aides will give you the conclusion he wants and then you are to do as much research as possible to find supporting data. Then, you are to write reports that will be used by Anil's executive branch. Anil is especially pleased when Seraphians use tight-fisted logic on their assigned problems. The more rarified the argument, and the better the obfuscation of the real issues, the more you will please Anil. Obfuscation is considered a high art form in Latipac, and you, my friends, are considered by the Sets to be *Eristic Logicians*."

"So we work backwards to prove that white is actually black, or two and two equals five, or perhaps another number. Whatever Anil wants," said another attendee.

"That's right. I'm going to hand out a list of key words and phrases that you are to memorize and use. For your information, the people here in Seraphs use of the word Set to refer to all people in Latipac. However, use of the word Set in Latipac refers to a select group of very wealthy and powerful people. Try speaking their language and fitting in. That is my final advice. Thank you for attending this briefing."

* * *

Outside the briefing room, I felt as though I had been in a pressure chamber. My temples throbbed and my mouth was dry. I looked at the long list of remaining tasks, and made my first check mark next to "*Briefing*".

Next came a Strategy session. In this session we were told not to reveal anything about life in Seraphs, or, if pressed, to reveal as little as possible. We were told Anil has a special hatred for Gloy, and under no circumstances were we to mention anything about him or what he talks about while in Gloy Park or elsewhere. The briefer warned us that each of us would be taken into an isolated room in Latipac and interrogated.

"If you say the wrong thing, you might be imprisoned. If pressed, deny knowing anything about Gloy. Just say that all you know is he is a raving madman who lives in the mountains. Say nothing more," he warned, "use your intelligence to outwit them. Remember, they will be watching for signs of weakness. The safest thing for you to do is to reveal no weakness. Show weakness and they will hound you continually throughout your stay. If they feel you are hiding information, they may not permit you to leave Latipac."

With that concluding comment, we left the room. I paused outside, took out a pen and made the second check on my list. During the remainder of the morning, I went to various offices to obtain supplies and to check off other items on the list. Late that afternoon, I went to the clinic wherein I was to have my physical checkup, and the dreaded shots. The physical went well enough, but the shots were horrendous. I was barely able to walk back to Sacram's house owing to soreness and pain. Sacram had a very hearty laugh when he saw me hobbling into his house.

"I was going to tell you how painful the first round of

shots would be, but I decided against it."

"How many more shots?" I asked.

"Four more tomorrow, but the remaining injections are not as bad as the ones you had today."

"That's reassuring," I replied, "but how am I going to get to sleep tonight? My whole left side aches!"

"I have some pills that will help." Sacram went into his room and brought out several small red pills. "Take two of these before going to bed. Take another two if you wake up during the night. Also, I left some cotton slacks and shirts to wear when we leave Setopia. Togas aren't designed for the jungle."

"Okay, I'll wear them tomorrow."

"Try them on first, to see if they fit."

I returned to my room and found the clothing that Sacram had set out for me. The slacks were similar to denim jeans I used to wear and the shirt was of fairly heavy cotton. I tried them on and they were a reasonable fit. I took the pills, and prepared for bed. Then, I read for a while before lying down and falling fast asleep.

***

The next morning, I awoke and rushed into the shower, dressed, ate, and ran down the hall. Outside, I stood on the steps of the house waiting for Alita. A little while later, she walked through the courtyard.

"Good morning," she said with a warm smile, "how do you feel?"

"My arm is still sore and my leg hurts. Other than that, I feel fine."

“How far did you get on your list?”

“I checked off about half the items on my list. Today there are three places left to go. The first two will not take long, but then there is the clinic and the remainder of my shots.”

“Walk with me to the Municipal building.”

“Okay, I’ll go with you.”

Alita went with me to the Municipal building where I filled out yet more forms for my visa to Latipac. The visit to the municipal building took most of the morning and then we walked over to the clinic where I received the remainder of my shots.

Around noon, Alita and I decided to have a picnic in the park. We went into a small shop and purchased sandwiches, then walked to Gloy Park where I had heard the prophet speak. With Alita near me, the park seemed more beautiful. We picked a nice place beneath a splayed tree and spread a table cloth on the ground. Then, we ate the sandwiches.

“Tell me about Sacram,” I said.

“What do you want to know? Like, how did he get here?” She asked

“Yes,” I said,”I’m interested.”

"I'm not supposed to say."

"Why?"

"I was told not to."

"You can trust me," I said, pleading.

"It's a long story."

"I have time."

"Okay, he was born into a very poor family."

"In Latipac?"

"No. Not in Latipac."

"Then, where?"

"Oh, I shouldn't say."

"Please, I must know."

"He was born in Seval."

"Seval?" I asked, astonished.

"Yes, it's in the lower valley. Sacram's father was a worker in one of the factories making small balls of clay that are used as a medium of exchange in that province. He told me his mother was a kind woman but died in her twenty fifth year, leaving him motherless at an early age. He was left responsible for his three younger siblings, two brothers and a sister. His life was one of starkness, lacking the basics of life. Every day he arose at five o'clock to help his father pack a lunch for work. His father worked at the clay factory every day of the week from six o'clock in the morning until ten o'clock at night for seven clay balls per week, scarcely enough to pay rent and buy food. In the land of Seval, all land, housing and commercial stores are owned by citizens of Latipac who the locals referred to as Sets.

"One day, Sacram told me, one of his neighbors didn't return from the factory at ten o'clock in the evening, as was his habit. At eleven, soldiers of the Sets showed up and informed the neighbor's wife that the husband had been arrested for trying to steal clay balls. They told the wife that her husband had been tried by a court and found guilty. The weeping wife knew the rest. He was sentenced to Detfar for rehabilitation."

"What is this Detfar?"

"It's a place…I'll explain it later, but the wife knew she would never see her husband again. In her grief she exclaimed '*why! He works hard. Why not he be paid more. He no want steal.*' But the Set soldiers told her that was not in accordance with Set law. They told her rent would be paid for two weeks and the company store would give her provisions for one week. After that, she would have to make do. From that day on his neighbor's condition only grew worse. In desperation, the wife, trying to feed her hungry family, took some bread from one of the storage units, a flagrant violation of Set law. She was apprehended and sentenced along with her children to Detfar."

"Terrible," I said, "So what happened to her?"

"One day the soldiers took away the family. Sacram never saw them again. Sacram said his father never spoke much about work at the factory. All he said was he lost many friends. Every time the Sets raised taxes, he lost friends to Detfar. The managers of the factory, those loyal to the Sets, always seemed better off after the tax increases. The managers were the ones most loyal to the Set owners."

"What about Sacram's family?"

"Well," she continued, "as his younger siblings grew older, he was eventually relieved of his responsibilities because under Set law, all children must spend a minimum of four years in a place called a Looh where they are taught to be useful citizens."

"A Looh? What is this Looh?"

"It's a place where they learn the Seval vocabulary and grammar which is composed of words containing at most six letters, which is in sharp contrast to the colorful language of the Sets who use elegantly seductive rhetoric. The vast majority of the Seval language consists of four letter words. When they were of the appropriate age, the younger brothers and sister were sent to the Looh. While they were in the Looh, he amused himself by trying to write words he heard spoken by Set soldiers who patrolled the streets. He said it was very difficult at first, but then he perceived a certain logic to their language. At first their language seemed awkward because he was accustomed to using six letter words and longer words seemed too long and complex. Finally, he was able to understand much of what they said. But, he had to be careful to keep his new vocabulary a secret. In time he acquired an acceptable Set vocabulary. It was his Set vocabulary that was the basis of his later mobility into the ranks of the Latipacians."

"Please, tell me more about the Looh. What was it like?" I asked, fascinated by what she said about Sacram's past life.

"Oh, the Looh," she continued, "the Looh was broken up into special classes. They were taught ditties containing a few Set words containing no more than six letters that helped instill in them total obedience to Set customs. Though the children in Seval could not understand many of the words in these patriotic ditties, the very flow and rhythm made them feel a fierce loyalty to the nation of Setopia. The Looh also served to separate children into three categories. Do you want me to continue?"

"Yes, I'm interested. What are the categories?"

"Group One is assigned to the brightest students who possessed independent natures and are inclined toward questioning of convention. This category is broken up into four subdivisions ranging from 1-A to 1-D. People in the latter group, the 1-D's, are the most rebellious and are promptly sent to Detfar for retraining. The others are usually sent to Detfar within the first year."

"How about the other groups?"

"Group Two is assigned to bright students who lack independent natures, are sycophantic and willing to be dominated. This group is also divided into four categories, from 2-A to 2-D. This group usually ends up in the province of Seraphs as apprentices to a master. The final Group Three is assigned to average students who are further broken into subgroups of 3-A through 3-D based on their potential rebellion toward Set law. Those in group 3-D are usually eliminated by placing them in factories and keeping their pay steady while increases in taxes or inflation force them through necessity into some violation of Set law. These workers eventually turn to some form of crime and are sent to Detfar. Well, I don't know if I should go on."

"What was Sacram's life like in Seval?" I asked when she paused. I felt sorry for Sacram, an elderly man, who had suffered so much during his life.

"While his younger brothers and sister were at the Looh," she said, "he studied the habits and demeanor of the soldiers who patrolled the streets. He listened to their conversations whenever he got a chance. Eventually his siblings finished the Looh. His brothers went to work at a clay factory while his sister went to work in a seamstress factory. One day his father received a demotion in his job and the next day a tax increase was levied. The financial pressures on his father were enormous. Because of his families' dwindling finances, he felt himself to be a burden on his family. He knew he must earn a living and bring in money, but was very suspicious of life in the factories because he knew it would mean eventual death."

"Then, what happened?"

"One day after his father and siblings left for work, Sacram left home. He was determined to speak with the famous Anil about his father's demotion, an unheard of act in Setopia. He left home and avoided the soldiers patrolling the streets. He walked through the forest, and came upon the body of a Latipacian who had apparently been struck by a broken limb from one of the tall pine trees. He thought for a while as to the best thing to do. He knew it would be foolish to report the dead man because that would mean certain death. As he pondered what to do, an idea popped into his head. He could assume the identity of this man. As fortune might have it, the clothing was a perfect fit and what's more, the man had papers of transfer into a clerkship at the Treasury Department in Latipac."

"What was the dead man's name?" I asked, my curiosity aroused.

"The dead man's name was Sacram."

"So, Sacram is not really a Latipacian?"

"No he's a Seval. He exchanged clothing with the man and started out for Latipac. From that moment everything seemed to go in his favor. He told me when he entered the city of Latipac, he was awestruck at the incredible beauty of the city. The granite buildings had huge pillars that seemed to rise to the heavens, and the people were so well dressed. As he passed through the city he used the Set language he had taught himself. To his surprise, he could pass himself off as one of them. He said he was almost shocked at first that he was accepted as one of them. Finally he came to a white marble building with tall columns."

"That was the Treasury Building?"

"Yes. At the entrance were marble steps that led down into a garden area. In the middle of the garden was a marble statue of a man standing on a pedestal. On the pediment of the building were inscribed the words, The Department of the Treasury. He was terrified as he stood at the entrance of the Treasury Building, but he gathered his courage and entered. A guard stationed inside the building just beyond the brass doors asked for his papers. He handed him the transfer papers. The guard examined them and told him to go down the corridor to room1003. So, he walked down the corridor and entered the room. A receptionist took his papers, smiled, and asked him to be seated. A few minutes later a young man appeared, and introduced himself. He led Sacram to a small office where he would work for the next two years. The job he got was at a fairly low level, so it wasn't demanding and he wouldn't be high enough in the organization to be noticed."

"Amazing! How could he conceal his true identity?"

"The first year or two he kept to himself and observed those around him. At first his coworkers though him to be rather stupid because he kept to himself and didn't say much. They seemed to think of him as a pleasant enough sort of fellow, though a little odd. He learned fast and well, and became very adept at bureaucratic infighting and strategy, so he quickly won promotions. After a few years, he was appointed by Anil himself to head the permanent diplomatic delegation to Seraphs."

"And, what of his family?" I asked.

"He wanted to send them money, but had no way to get it to them. He had to be very careful not to betray his true identity." She dropped her head, "He never saw his family again."

"I had no idea he had been through so much. I assumed he had come from a wealthy family somewhere."

"That's what everyone thinks, but, now you know the truth."

We picked up our sandwich wrappers and deposited them in a nearby trashcan. Then, we walked back to the Sacram's place. Along the way, Alita fell silent. When we had walked about half way back, I noticed her crying. I wiped the tears from her eyes.

"Why are you crying?"

"I don't want you to leave," she said.

"I'll be back," I said.

"You will not return,"

"Of course I will."

"Many go to Latipac, but few return."

She broke into tears. I tried to comfort her, but I also felt like crying. Leaving was always a sad event and I had grown fond of her. After a tearful moment, she collected herself and asked if she could iron anything for me, or help me in any way to prepare for the trip. She tossed her head to one side and studied me.

"Race you to the top of the stairs," she said.

She ran up the stairs and I followed. She won by one step, but I didn't care. I grabbed her and kissed her. We kissed as though we would never see each other again. Then, we entered the house. Sacram seemed surprised to see the two of us.

"Alita offered to help me pack for the trip," I said.

"Splendid!" he replied, "why don't the two of you go upstairs and pack. I'm going to the Embassy."

We went upstairs into my room. Fortunately, I had very little to do to get ready. My suits and other clothing I had been issued were already packed. What few papers I needed were in a black leather briefcase. Instinctively, we moved toward each other. Our body chemistries spoke and we became locked in a mutual exchange of emotion. I was transfixed by her hot firm lips and her warm cheeks spread fire to mine. Suddenly, she broke away from my embrace and walked to the door.

"I must go!" she said.

She kissed me and then departed. All that lingered behind were nice memories of my time with Alita. As I was absorbed in reverie, Sacram knocked on the door.

"We leave in two hours," he said.

"I'll be there shortly," I said, more to myself than to Sacram. I felt torn apart as though my world was coming to an end. On the very foundation of my new world stood Alita. She had beauty, lively manners, and intelligence. My mind flashed back to the short time we had together, but I knew that we must now depart.

CHAPTER 7

Journey to Latipac

We left Seraphs before sunrise. We reached the cliff, and I stood with Sacram overlooking the Imperial Valley that lay between the mountain estate of Seraphs, the lower valley of Seval and the plateau country of Latipac. We began the descent down the 8,000-foot cliff by way of a crudely constructed dumbwaiter. The hand-operated elevator would only accommodate three people at a time, so two trips were needed. Each trip took more than an hour. After each descent, the ropes needed to be inspected, in case frays developed that might weaken the ropes. At last, all six members of our team were at the foot of the mountain. Three mule drivers awaited us when we got to the bottom. One was tall with red hair, the second had a gimpy leg and wasn't so tall and the third was medium height and missing his left hand. We decided to call them Red, Gimpy and One-hand. They helped us load up the mules with our provisions and baggage and then we set out. Besides Sacram and I, there were four other members of our delegation, including one person named Sutraps who was young and fairly tall. The four tended to stay together and didn't interact very much with us.

We travelled many miles through murky darkness because the dense forest did not permit the entrance of much sunlight. Disturbing cries from wild animals came often from the forest interior. Our guide, a stout red-haired mule driver, assured us the savage animals would not attack. "It's their way," he said, "to tell us to stay away. It's the law of the jungle."

We journeyed for hours through the dense rain forest. It was sultry and at times the heat was intense. My shirt was wet with sweat after only a short distance. At times we were forced to hack our way with machetes through thick foliage. Red said our path was used often, but the swiftness of growth and the thickness of the underbrush soon obscured the path. We would not have found our way were it not for markers implanted in the trunks of selected trees. These markers were painted with bright red luminescent paint so that they glowed in the darkness of the forest.

One vine we encountered called a Quintec grew so fast that I could actually see a cut branch reproducing its cells. It had broad leaves that grew out of the stem at five inch intervals. The forest floor was covered with this problematic Quintec vine. Fortunately, the absence of sunlight prevented the vine from entirely engulfing the forest.

Ten hours into our trip, we set up camp at a spot often used by travelers. We found old fire pits constructed out of rocks, water reservoirs, and other accommodations. After we set up camp and pitched canvas tents, Red and I set about gathering fire-wood. About two hundred feet from the camp, we found limbs on the ground, but most of the wood was too damp and rotting, unfit for campfire wood. Nevertheless, we gathered enough dry wood from a large tree lying in an open area. When the tree fell it made an opening in the forest canopy that permitted sunlight to penetrate and dry most of the wood.

Several trips were necessary for us to gather enough firewood. Gimpy was in charge of building the fire. He did so gladly because the darkness of night had descended, and the chill of the evening was upon us. By the time I carried my last armful of wood into our camp, Gimpy's campfire was glowing and cast a bright light over our encampment. The fire proved a treasure for I shivered from the cold. Gimpy served as the cook. He handed me a cup of warm coffee. It tasted delicious, and warmed me up.

"Why is it so cold here?" I asked, "This is a rainforest."

"The wind blows cold at night," Gimpy replied.

Red and One-hand returned to camp carrying a small deer and two pheasant. The mule drivers prepared the game and put the meat on skewers above the fire. The skewer turned slowly until the meat was thoroughly cooked.

"Come and get it!" Gimpy said, as he dished out the food.

I received a small portion of venison and a leg of pheasant. Both were delicious. After everyone had eaten his fill, Red produced a bottle of fine brandy.

"Latipac Brandy!" Red said.

We drank and told tales. The mule drivers told of their homes and things that happened in their village of Seval. Sacram, however, remained silent throughout. When asked about his background, he told that he was born in Latipac, and how he had received an appointment in the Foreign Service of Anil's government. He said he knew a few people in Seval, but didn't mention their names. Sacram put down his food and departed our company, complaining of tiredness. As he turned to leave the camp, the campfire illuminated his face. He looked sad.

I remained with the mule drivers. Ours was a merry lot. Their wild tales of adventure were entertaining as they were splendid storytellers. Each told a strange and fascinating story of dangerous conquests. Gimpy showed his scars with great pride. The best storytellers told tales of bravery. Each man had his story to tell and he did so with graphic detail. Each told of his many loves and often went in explicit detail of each encounter. I felt very at ease with these men and I began asking them questions, which they gladly answered. When I asked them about wars or battles, they fell silent.

"We cannot speak of such things," Red responded, "it's Set law. I'm sorry."

I tried to gain their confidence, but I could not get an answer to any military related question. The only thing they would say is that the subject of Detfar is banned to them and they could be imprisoned for discussing it. I found they were especially suspicious of Sacram, being a Set representative, but I managed to quell their suspicions. They told me Sets had laws that prevented them from getting the education and skills necessary to qualify for management jobs in Latipac, but they were resigned to their lot and accepted their social stations.

"It's our fate," said Gimpy.

Their aspirations were for simple pleasures. To seduce the most attractive woman in Seval, and to appear to be the most brave. It was difficult for me to understand their language at times because they had a very specialized language of at most six letter words, but most of the conversations were with four letter words. Some of the words they seemed to have as many as three different meanings within the same sentence, so I found their language confusing. But their physical gesticulations conveyed well enough what they meant, and when they discussed voluptuous women, their eyes become quite large because they enjoyed the subject of sex.

At last we grew tired, and decided to turn in for the night. Sacram was sound asleep in his sleeping bag when I unrolled mine. I examined the sleeping bag for bugs, snakes, or other critters, but found nothing, and crawled inside. I awoke in the early hours of the morning because I was not accustomed to the strange sounds of the night coming from the forest. Our fire had turned into ambers and our camp was quiet. After what seemed like two hours or more, I finally fell back asleep.

***

The next morning came too soon. The only discernible differences, between night and day in this forest were the piercing sounds made by birds and wild animals during the early morning. I got up and put more wood on the fire. The cold morning air made me shiver, but soon I had a blaze going and I put on the coffee pot. It didn't take long for the water to boil and I added coffee grounds from the cook's supply cabinet. The coffee tasted superb and eased my shivering.

Soon the others awoke. They were surprised that I had awakened before them, and took my getting up so early as a sign of excellent outdoor skills. They thought of me as a natural man of the forest, a great status symbol to these mule drivers. Forest men were without a doubt the boldest and most robust of any of the mule drivers.

Gimpy prepared breakfast. I helped him by slicing the

bacon. One-hand found fresh eggs from wild birds in the forest. I had never tasted anything as good as the breakfast I had that morning. After breakfast, each driver belched loudly as was their custom after a good meal. We broke camp and set out once more on our trek through the forest. We marched about four hours before reaching the main trail in the forest. As we walked with the mule drivers, Sacram cautioned me about wandering off the trail.

"The poisonous vipers in this area are lethal," Sacram said,

"That's no lie," Red said, "lots of snakes."

"The most beautifully colored snakes are the most deadly," Sacram continued, "One viper, called the Piz Viper can strike within a fraction of a second, and its venom will bring death within two minutes. But that is not the only peril out here. The quicksand is thick and with such a strong vacuum that any unfortunate victim will be pulled under. Quicksand is certain death."

"Any other things we should know about?" I asked.

"The forest has many perils. Some of the plants are also lethal. One plant, called a Yellow Snapper, has a large oval shell which opens and shoots out a multitude of tendons which have an adhesive fluid on their tips. If one of these tendons gets near enough to attach itself, you will never be able to get free before the other tendons close in and begin pulling you into the main pod. Once inside, digestion takes only minutes. Even the bones are dissolved. Anyone who is caught by these plants will completely disappear. I've been told it's a painful death. Death comes slowly, but you're partially dissolved before death comes."

"Yeah," Red said, "real painful!"

"You're making me leery. What clsc is out there?"

"Vines! Tell em bout the vines," Red said.

"There are equally lethal flowers and vines in the forest. One vine, the Whipsaw, lies in wait like a snake. It has a heat sensing device on its tentacles which detects the presence of living animals. When the victim gets too close, the Whipsaw sends a whip-like apparatus into the flesh of the victim. The victim is immediately paralyzed from the chemicals injected from the tentacles. The victim remains in a catatonic state, conscious of what is going on but unable to move a muscle. The plant then sends its tentacles out to the flesh and they slide themselves into the body being very careful not to harm the major organs so that the blood will remain warm and fresh for several days until the victim finally dies from a lack of blood. The whipsaw can live on a small quantity of blood. That seems to be why it prefers to keep the victim conscious and alive for many days, so it can enjoy small quantities of fresh blood daily without having to search for new prey. Animals don't generally venture into these regions. The Whipsaw has adapted itself quite well to its environment."

"You're giving me cold chills," I said, thinking of the many deadly things about me. "How can you detect the presence of these plants?"

"It's really very easy," he said, "The most deadly plants emit a very pleasing--almost intoxicating—odor. The chemicals in its pods are used as a perfume that is used in Latipac as an aphrodisiac. Enterprising people from Latipac collect the chemical. Of course it is very expensive because not many of those men sent out to collect the potent chemicals ever return. They are caught by one plant or another eventually. If we pass one of the plants, I'll point it out and you can smell the scent. It can be smelled from only a short distance, but it is potent"

“I'm not certain I want to get that close,” I replied.

"Don't worry," he said, "the plants can be spotted easily, but the closer you get to them, the more the perfume entices you to get closer and closer until it's too late. So don't be taken by the deadly scent."

“Sounds like an old myth,” I said.

“It's not,” he said, “Follow me.” We walked off the path and through thick vegetation for a short distance. Then, he stopped.

“Smell the air,” Sacram said. I did so and noticed a most

marvelous scent. It had the consistency of the most pleasantly scented roses combined with jasmine. It was the most potent and attractive scent I had ever smelled. We followed the scent. The closer we got, the more powerful it became until I felt the scent pulling me and gaining control of my muscles. I felt as though I could float along on the trail of this scent.

"That's close enough," Sacram cautioned, "I learned long ago not to be enticed by its fragrance because I know what lies at the other end. There," he said, pointing to a gigantic yellow flower. Its petals opened wide and exposed light purplish hairy fibers covering the central portion of the petals.

"That is the giant Nosrewolf. It doesn't have long tentacles to snare its victim. It relies entirely on its scent. If we were to walk only a few feet closer, we would no longer have control of our muscles, and we would walk into the flower with open arms, only to be engulfed by the petals which would quickly cover us. The small purple fibers you can see in the center of the flower emit an acid which quickly digests tissue. The NosRewolf can consume an entire man in thirty seconds. It needs to feed only about once a month. The hungrier it is, the more powerful its scent. That's why this plant is among the deadliest in the forest."

We walked further until he pointed out another very colorful flower. "That plant over there is called the Yellow Snapper. It too had a very pleasant but distinctive smell. Again, don't get too close." Yet, I was close enough that I could tell that its scent affected my thoughts. I found it difficult to think. It was as though my thoughts were being blocked out by the effects of this powerful scent.

"The scent of this plant is lighter than that of the Nosrewolf plant," Sacram said, "however, it's no less deadly."

As we observed the Yellow Snapper, a small deer ambled past. A tendon shot out and attached itself. The animal twisted and fought for its life, but before it could free itself, other tendons shot out and dragged the deer twisting in agony into the center of the pod which immediately closed. A rancid odor emitted from the plant and the pleasant smell was replaced by a putrescent revolting odor. When the pod opened a minute or two later, only a single bone dropped to the ground to join a pile of bones at the base of the plant.

"Anything else you should warn me about?"

"Yes, on occasion there is a mysterious miasma," Sacram said, "a kind of fog that suddenly appears and will cause you to lose your sense of direction. The miasma and the plants are well suited for one another, one acts to feed the other."

"I think I've seen enough of this bog country," I said, "let's get out of here."

We returned to the main body of men who had been resting on the pathway. As soon as we returned, the group began marching again. After a while, we were out of the swampy country and walking through a safer part of the forest. The long trail we endured left most of us tired and somewhat irritable. The men were constantly complaining about the thick vegetation. When Red tripped over one of the vines, he let go a string of abusive words which I had not witnessed before. After a long march, we reached an open field. We were elated to see sunshine again, and rested a while basking in the golden rays of the sun.

I lay at the base of one large tree and stared upward into its tall branches that seemed to climb forever upward. Small squirrels and birds inhabited the lower branches. The upper branches were splayed so as to extend over a wide area and covered the tops of smaller trees. A perfect canopy to envelope the light of the forest and prevent rays from reaching lower vegetation. A flock of large white birds took flight not far away in another part of the forest. They honked like geese as they flew over us.

"We leave this area," Red said, alarmed.

"Why?"

"Soldiers! We must go now!"

We followed a dry riverbed through the lower reaches of the valley which made our progress much easier. Red and the other two drivers nervously studied the nearby woods for any signs of soldiers. Finally, they seemed content that there was no longer a threat, so we stopped and rested. I kept looking for movement in the woods that might signal an ambush. After a brief rest, we returned to the forest and once more chopped our way through the thick vegetation. Several hours later, we made camp in a clearing. Later that night, we were sitting around the campfire, when we heard rifle shots in the distance.

“Soldiers,” Red said.

“What?” I asked.

“How close are they?” Sacram asked.

“Not far.”

“Do they know we’re here?”

“Don’t know,” Red said.

"Gimpy!" said Sacram, “Hang our flag from that tree over there." He pointed toward a very tall tree. Gimpy limped to the tree, unfurled the cloth and attached it to a limb. The flag had red and white stripes with a large Volant winged Condor in the center.

"That's the official Set Flag," Sacram said. “We need to build up the campfire to illuminate the flag, and make sure the fire is kept going all night. We don't want our camp invaded, or we will all die tonight.”

"Why the flag?" I asked.

"Anil's soldiers have orders not to kill anyone camping under the banner of his flag."

We were all edgy with imagined threats from all around us. A slight wind had come up and the flag flapped in the breeze with an eerie pop like an exploding firecracker. It looked surreal. I didn't like the feeling of being watched and the forest seemed to have eyes everywhere. Every sound, every call of a bird, every ember popping in the fire alarmed me. We were all a little jumpy. I wished I had my rifle, but the authorities confiscated it, that would have been some protection. I found a branch that I fashioned into a club that I kept with me.

The wood in the fire popped on occasion and sent burning embers into the air. That the embers might set off a fire in the forest concerned me, but we were in an open area and fortunately nothing caught fire. Smoke from the fire seemed to seek me out because it changed direction each time I moved to avoid it. But the scent of the burning wood was pleasant and smelled like pinion. The crackling fire and the sky full of stars brought back memories of my days in the other world, as I began recalling my previous life. I remembered the days we went on vacations to Martha's Vineyard and how the kids loved the cottage of their Aunt Violet, and how they loved to swim in the ocean. I must have had a look of sadness, because Red asked.

"What’s wrong?"

"I miss my family."

"You get home one day," One-hand said.

"Don't know."

"We make you family in Sevel," Gimpy said.

I knew I was stuck here in this strange new world with only a remote hope that someone, perhaps the Wildman, might know how I could return home. Though tired, I remained awake with the mule drivers. They warmed themselves by the fire, but said little. Every sound sent shocks of fright through them.

Despite the risks, we were tired from a long trek and we finally turned in for the night. My sleep was fitful and I kept waking up. It was during the dark of midnight that a blood curdling scream shattered the quietness of the forest. I bolted upright in my sleeping bag. I had heard similar screams when a pack of coyotes killed a rabbit. It was a sound I will never forget. Then, there were several more horrible screams.

"What are those screams?" I asked.

"Not an animal. A man, a Seval," whispered Red.

We heard a lot of laughing and whooping coming from men not far away. I walked a short distance from our camp and saw the distant red haze of another encampment about a quarter mile to the south. After a while, the screams stopped and the laughter faded. When I arrived back at camp, the mule drivers were in good humor, which puzzled me, especially after just witnessing the death of one of their own.

"Come, my friend, join us!" said One-hand.

"Why is everyone so cheerful?"

"No fear now. They had their fun. Not bother us tonight," Red said.

The mule drivers laughed and told stories as they had the previous night. Gimpy brought out a bottle of homemade liquor. It had the smell of sulfur and did not taste good, but was very potent. Soon, we were all in good spirits and laughing. I fell into the mood of the moment. They wanted me to tell them more stories of my life in the forest. I had already gotten myself in deeper than I would have liked, so I began making up yet more tall tales. Again they hung onto every word of my stories of intrigue and daring.

"Once I rescued a baby ape," I began and told them a fictional tale of a baby ape I had rescued and how I had fostered it until grown, and how it had later saved my life from a band of ruthless cutthroat pirates. My tales of pirates and cutthroats especially pleased them and they became fearful of these fiendish people who lived aboard ships and marauded upon the high sea.

"Tell us more," they pleaded.

Their growing interest prompted me to continue with further stories of the pirates and marauders. With each new story they grew more afraid, yet still they wanted to hear more. It was late and we decided to get some sleep.

* * *

The next morning, Sacram awoke me for breakfast to the aroma of cooking meat and coffee. When I got up, the other members of our delegation were eating breakfast, but the mule drivers were nowhere to be seen.

"Where are the drivers?" I asked

"Gone."

"Where?"

"It isn't safe for them to travel farther into the forest," Sacram said. "They bid you a farewell. You gained their respect with your stories of pirates."

"Did they take the mules?"

"All but one," he said.

"What happened to the fellow in the other camp?" I asked.

"Gimpy, Red and I went into their camp after the soldiers left and buried the unfortunate Seval. Not a pleasant sight."

***

Later that morning, we broke camp and started out again. We climbed a series of rugged foothills that led to a broad plateau of pink granite. Sacram, old and tiring easily, had trouble keeping up with the rest of us, especially when we started up the hills. However, he was in surprisingly good shape for his age of 70 years. Our remaining mule sometimes refused to climb the hills, but a firm twist of his tail forced him to be obedient. Once on the plateau, our group of six stopped for a much needed rest.

"Latipac lies over there," Sacram said pointing into the distance, "it's a long walk from here."

As we travelled, the sun beat down upon us. Swarms of small black flies were a constant nuisance. Our mule was especially annoyed by the flies and swished his tail often and bucked occasionally to get rid of the pests. I continually brushed them off, but it didn't help much. Their bites were painful and left red welts on my skin. It seemed that the more sodden with sweat we became, the more those flying devils swarmed us. The plateau soon gave way to another series of foothills that sloped upward toward the blue haze of the mountains. As we climbed higher, the air became cooler, and the flies disappeared.

"Finally, the damn flies are gone," I said, relieved.

We stopped for a brief rest and then continued. In the distance was the faint outline of a large cathedral glistening white in the afternoon sun. As we got closer to Latipac, we saw a medieval city of Gothic architecture.

"That's Latipac," said Sacram.

***

Later, we arrived at a large very old door about twenty feet high with an arch in the center. The wood, now cracked and weathered, had obviously been very attractive with ornate rococo designs in intaglio relief, though now heavily weathered with images that were no longer distinct. A long cord hung from the center of the door with a large knot at the bottom. Sacram pulled the cord that rang a bell. A small rectangular window opened in the center of the door, and an old man with spectacles appeared through a small opening.

"What do you want?" he asked in a gruff voice. Sacram showed him our identification papers. He quickly examined our papers, and then handed them back to Sacram.

"Wait," he said, "a guide will show you to the hotel. But stable that blasted mule in the stalls! That smelly beast is not coming in here!"

We unloaded our bags and led the mule away to a stall a few yards away. Once the mule was secure in the stable with sufficient hay for him to eat, we returned to the entrance and waited. A few minutes later the large doors swung open on squeaky hinges. A young man dressed in a dark three piece suit stood in the entrance.

"Come," he said, "let's go." We picked up our bags and followed. People walking past us were similarly dressed in business suits. Each person had a quick determined walk. We followed our guide a few blocks to an old hotel called the Arbor House that was used to house visitors. Arriving at the hotel, we registered. I had a posh room with pastel blue walls, beautiful wool rugs, and a firm but comfortable bed. We showered and dressed in business suits, as was the custom in this city.

CHAPTER 8

The Dictator

After a brief rest, we regrouped in the lobby and walked across the street to the Fuchsia Palace. We stopped at a guardhouse surrounded by a wrought-iron fence. Sacram disappeared into the guardhouse while we waited. He soon returned. The heavy iron-gate swung open, and we walked down a gravel pathway that led to a bright fuchsia-colored palace.

Sacram pulled a silk rope beside the main entrance. A servant in a black tuxedo opened the door. The interior was astonishing in its opulence and beauty. On the highly polished marble floors lay beautiful rugs whose designs reminded me of Persian patterns. Ornately carved tables contained red and green precious stones. A huge chandelier of diamonds in the center of the lobby radiated sunlight in variegated colors, like a prism. On the wall opposite the entrance hung a huge portrait in a golden frame of a man wearing a regal looking blue suit with a red sash across his chest. A golden condor was embossed on the sash.

"That's Anil," Sacram said.

"Impressive," I replied, "he looks very regal."

The Butler ushered us to a large ornate brass door, and stopped. "This is the Blue Room, his majesty is expecting you." the Butler said. He pulled a gold and silk chord that rang a single melodious bell. The door opened and a military officer appeared.

"Please, enter," he said.

As soon as we were inside, we were met by a very handsome middle aged man with a pleasant smile and a solid gold tooth on his upper incisor. He was of medium height with light brown hair and wore a gray military uniform. On the pocket above his heart hung a huge gold medal that looked like an eight pointed star. He had a lively and pleasant disposition and seemed determined to please us. He exuded the power and grace of high office.

"Sacram, so good to see you again," said the man.

“Good to see you again, your excellency.”

"Please, be seated."

We sat down on plush chairs woven out of threads of pure gold and silver. Anil clapped his hands, "refreshments!" Two servants appeared carrying a silver tray of hors-d'oeuvres with pitchers of fruit drinks. They served us drinks in golden goblets. The drink tasted like mango. The other servant offered us various snacks from a highly polished golden tray.

"Eat to your heart's content!" Anil said. "You are now, in the great city of Latipac, land of opportunity for all. I welcome your delegation to my humble home." He paused to see if we were receptive, then, continued. "Make yourselves at home while in Latipac. We are here to serve you in any way we can. You have the key to my city, all I have is yours."

He smiled, showing a golden tooth in his upper incisor. Then, a strange thing happened. His hands became deformed and his fingers swelled in size. The fingernails, coarse and thick, projected too far past the flat ends of his fingers. The thumbs were the most hideous of all. They were too thick for his hands and truncated with thumbnails that extended past the thumbs on all sides that gave a ghastly appearance. His teeth were out of proportion to the size of his mouth. When he laughed, some of his teeth were three times larger than normal. One tooth in the front of his mouth looked like that of a saber tooth tiger. His lips were heavy and his eyebrows grew together with thick dark hair. His eyes were set far into his head and his eye brows hung over his eyes. He had the look of a beast. I glanced around at the others in the room, and was astonished to see them carrying on as though nothing unusual was happening. I was puzzled.

Then, in an instant, his large fingers became slender and tapered. His fingernails no longer hung beyond the fingertips, but were well manicured. His teeth were no longer too large for his mouth, but were perfectly straight and of the correct size. He was once again handsome with, strong eyebrows, high-cheekbones and a high intellectual forehead. Affable, with an attractive twinkle in his eye, he now looked normal. I looked around again at Sacram and the others, but no one seemed alarmed. Perhaps this was a normal event, I thought.

As the meeting progressed, Sacram and Anil talked about many trivial pleasantries, but the presence of his Army in Seraphs was never discussed. It quickly became obvious to me that his presence was bewitching. He was obviously a dangerous man who made full use of his skills. He now looked like the picture I had seen in the central hallway of the Palace. Every member of our delegation, except Sacram and I, fawned and fought for his attention. Like moths drawn to a flame, they fought to get nearer to the prodigal son.

"How is it that I have such a group of brilliant minds," Anil said, "and me such a simple man. I'm sorry, but I must get back to business. I enjoyed our visit. Please come back again."

The military officer ushered us out. I was the last to leave the room. I turned to shake Anil's hand, and I again witnessed the metamorphosis. He had that wild canine look that I had seen earlier, and his smile was that of a beast. I excused myself and quickly left. The door closed behind me and I caught up with the others who were waiting in the foyer.

"What a wonderful man," said one of our delegation.

"I had no idea he is so clever," said Sutrap.

"Brilliant," said a third.

I was surprised by their comments. It occurred to me that they had come under the influence of Anil's charm, like so many before us who had been bedazzled by Anil's power and wealth.

CHAPTER 9

Night Life

We returned to the hotel. I was resting in a very comfortable chair reading a book when I heard a knock at my door. Opening the door, I saw Sacram.

"We're going to a pub a little later if you want to join us," Sacram said.

"When?"

"After dinner," he replied.

"Mind if I explore the area first?"I asked.

"Not at all," he replied, “but don't go far from the hotel. Flash your diplomatic status card if you get into any trouble, and don't say too much."

The lobby was filled with activities and the smell of ladies' perfumes. The room smelled of excitement and adventure. Slot machines lined the wall in the hotel lobby and men dropped handfuls of coins into the slots. Outside, well dressed people walked by, men in expensive suits, women in furs and sleek outerwear. An older man walked by accompanied by a much younger woman. He had a large diamond ring on his little finger, and a cigar in his mouth. He had the air of pomposity, she of innocence. I walked a few blocks from the Hotel when a young man approached me dressed in dark slacks and a hooded jacket.

"Want to buy a nice diamond ring – cheap?"

"Sorry," I replied, "I only have two scrip."

"You jiving me?" He asked.

"No, that's all I have, two scrip."

"Man, that stuff is useless. Don't you have no real money?"

"Sorry.

"Ah, man, you can't do me no good!" With that comment he left me and continued down the street looking for another customer. I walked past a newspaper stand and looked at a local newspaper called the Latipacian and a competitor called The Daily Standard. Both had Anil on their front covers dressed in formal military attire.

"Man! You don't want to read that. It's fake news!" said a young man walking by with his girl friend.

A plethora of retail stores of various kinds lined the street. Most of them sold upscale clothing and jewelry, but a few sold tobacco products. After a brief exploratory walk, I returned to the Hotel. The evening meal was in a special room devoted to

V.I.P.'s. The meal was superb, considered one of the best in the land, according to Sacram. Beef and vegetables from the fields of Seval were presented with great artistry. After we finished our dinner, Sacram turned to me. “Jonathan, would you like to join us? We’re going to a pub called ‘*The Place*’, a very popular night spot in Latipac.”

“Where is it?”

“Not far from here.”

“Okay,” I said.

We left with other members of our delegation and walked a few blocks from the hotel. When we arrived, the place was already crowded. We sat at a table near a round stage in the middle of the room. The waiter brought a liquor menu. I examined the menu briefly and chose a drink that sounded exotic: "Hermes Tango."

"Excellent Choice!" Sacram said.

I must admit, the Hermes Tango tasted very good! We enjoyed several drinks before the floor show began. By then we were a bit tipsy from the effects of the drink. When the act began, girls came out on the stage and did a strip teae while dancing to music played by a live jazz band. As the young women removed most of their clothing, some of the men in the audience moved closer to the stage. One middle-aged man climbed onto the stage and danced with one of the lovelier nudes.

He removed his clothing as he danced, and soon they began having intercourse. The appreciative audience threw money upon the stage while yelling for more. Other men, mostly younger, joined the middle-aged man on stage and also danced with the nude women. Before long a sexual orgy erupted on stage.

“This often happens here,” Sacram said, “the women are from Seval and were brought to Latipac because they are especially beautiful. The girls, by decree, cannot refuse the advances of the men. They are prohibited from denying a patron a dance or sexual favor. It is their duty as workers from Seval to do whatever is deemed necessary by their employer. Here, they are participants in sexual orgies.”

As the night progressed, more men climbed onto the stage. Soon a long line of men awaited their turn to enter upon the stage while others grunted and squirmed upon the stage. I felt torn between my sympathy for the women, and the animal instinct within me to partake of their bodies as the others were doing. I could understand why the club was so popular. It seemed to me that all who came on the mission changed when they entered the swinging city of Latipac. No longer were they solitary intellectuals who though only of their research and policy papers. Here, pleasures of the intellectual life changed to thoughts of sensual pleasures. The more the participants squirmed and squealed, the more other men joined them. Drinks flowed from the bar and more cigar and cigarette smoke filled the room. Before long, the room filled with the stench of smoke and spilled drinks.

"Don't be upset by what you see here," Sacram said, "I brought you here to show you the culture in Latipac. This," he said, pointing his finger about the room, "is the mentality of the Latipacians."

“I think I’ve seen enough of the night life,” I said.

I excused myself, left the pub, and walked on for many blocks along the streets on a cold dark night in the city. After an hour of more of walking, I was somewhat confused as to my location. I knew the general location of the hotel. As it happened, the hotel was on the other side of a large mansion that stood between me and the hotel. The mansion had a wrought-iron fence about eight feet high with spikes at the top. Beyond the fence was a thick row of hedges with a well manicured lawn. Night lights along the fence illuminated the fence area. The fence presented no problem for me to climb because two horizontal sections of metal fence holding the vertical pieces together made excellent steps. I decided to take a chance and climb the fence.

Once over the fence, I walked across the wet lawn in the general direction of the hotel. A thick fog hung in the low areas of the lawn. The grass contained a pleasant though heavy smell of an organic fertilizer. When I was near the great house, a siren rang out and lights flooded the area. Two large security guards ran out of the house and grabbed me.

"Who are you?" they demanded.

"Name's Jonathan Crews, I have diplomatic status," I said, showing them my documents.

"Come with us," one of the guards demanded and they forced me to walk with them into the house.

"Who is it?" The owner demanded.

"An intruder," said one of the guards, "he has diplomatic status."

"Means nothing when he's on my land," stated the owner, "guards, come with me."

The guards looked at me with cool disdain, and followed the owner into an adjoining room. They talked briefly. I heard enough of the conversation to know that they intended to make sport of me by turning me loose on the grounds and hunting me down like an animal. This idea excited the guards. I heard them checking their revolvers and spinning the cylinders. Adrenalin rushed through my veins and I looked for an escape route.

The front door was open. I quietly walked to it and. glanced outside. I could not see any additional guards. Then, came a familiar sound of a bolt slamming shut on a rifle. I immediately ran out the door into the heavy fog near the fence.

"He's loose. Get Him! Kill Him!" The owner shouted. I

dove into the low lying fog.

"Which way did he go?" shouted one of the guards.

"I don't know," responded another guard, "check that fog bank in front of the building."

"Right."

At that moment I felt a cold chill go up my back because one of the guards walked toward me, his footsteps coming closer and closer. The guard fired two shots in my direction. Both were too close for comfort. The adrenalin in my system must have helped me because as soon as the guards walked to the other side of the house, I vaulted over the fence and ran down the street. Two police officers in blue uniforms with their pistols drawn stopped me before I got very far.

"Why are you running?" One asked.

"Exercise," I replied.

"Do you have identification papers?" Asked the second.

"I have Diplomatic status. Here is my card," I said, handing my papers to one of the officers. He examined my papers and gave me a suspicious look.

"We'll need to take you to headquarters," he replied.

"Why?" I asked.

"Procedure. These papers can be forged. If you're legit, you'll be released."

They ushered me back to the downtown area where we

went inside a local police station. They turned me over to some kind of diplomatic officer who examined my credentials and smiled.

"Your papers will have to be verified." he said, "Sit over there until we check your papers. We just arrested another Seraphian a short while ago who claimed to have diplomatic status."

From where I sat, I could see a man sitting on a wooden chair in an adjacent room. A bright lamp was shining in his face. He was sweating profusely. I recognized the prisoner as Sutraps, one of the men who made the trip from Seraphs with us. The three inquisitors ask him questions, some facetious, some not, but they were obviously interested in gaining information about Seraphs.

"What's your name?" one inquisitor demanded

"I told you, Sutraps."

"Birthplace!"

"Seraphs."

"Every been to Lactipac?"

“Several Times."

"The nature of your visits!"

"To advise on policy issues."

"To advise whom?"

"Anil and his staff."

At this point the interrogators paused. They cloistered together and talked a bit and then continued their interrogation.

"Who is Gloy?" One asked.

"Don't know him."

"Don't insult us! Who is Gloy?"

"Don't know."

The interrogators were irritated. One of them walked around the table and slapped Sutraps who cried out in pain. Every so often, the interrogator slapped and cursed him. Finally, Sutraps cried out for the interrogator not to hurt him anymore. Both interrogators smiled as though pleased.

"I'll start again. What is your name?"

"Sutraps"

"Birthplace."

"Seraphs."

"Who is Gloy?"

"A madman, but I never met him. Only heard talk. He's, insane. No one listens to him. He's mad."

"But people do listen to him! The park is crowded every time he visits Seraphs. Is this your idea of no one listening to him? "

"People only listen to him for entertainment. The madman entertains them."

"Entertains? Is it entertainment in Seraphs to hear a man

say treasonous things? Is it entertainment to hear Gloy speak of overthrowing the nation of Setopia? Answer me!" One officer screamed.

"No one listens to him!"

"So, Gloy speaks treasonous things for hours, yet no one listens?"

"I mean--"

"Silence! Do you take us for fools?"

"No Sir," Sutraps replied.

"Then why did you tell us the people in Seraphs listen to him, but no one hears what he says?"

"What he says is taken lightly, as a joke," said Sutrap.

"So, it's a joke to speak of treason?"

* *

"Your papers are in order" an officer said as he tapped me on the shoulder, "you should leave now." As I was leaving, I saw an officer wheeling in a strange looking machine. They told Sutrap to remove his clothing. Another officer brought in a chair with canvas straps. I knew they were going to torture him. Muffled screams echoed down the hallway as I left the building.

With the aid of one of the policemen, I returned to the hotel. I told Sacram about Sutraps and his being tortured at the police station. He grimaced and said there was nothing we could do until morning.

CHAPTER 10

An Encounter

We left the hotel to inquire about the unfortunate member of our delegation. The jail was located on Piraeus Street near a large concrete channel used for carrying storm runoff during periods of heavy rain. Piraeus Street was the most important East-West corridor in Latipac. The Poros building, the name of the jail, was an ancient structure with stark walls containing small slits for windows and red ceramic roof tiles. There were two main prison buildings in the complex with a third building serving as headquarters that was somewhat taller than the others. We entered the Police headquarters building.

"Who is the officer in charge?" Sacram asked.

"Chief!" shouted a policeman behind the desk. A middle-aged man walked into the room.

"What do you need?" he asked.

"You arrested a member of my mission last night," Sacram said.

"What is the man's name?" The Chief asked, an eyebrow raised.

"Sutraps," Sacram replied bluntly.

"I'll check my records," he said. He picked up a large ledger, flipped through the pages of the log, and then looked puzzled.

"I have no record of a Sutraps being arrested. Is he from Seraphs?"

"Yes,"

“According to the night records, no arrests were made."

"Let me see that log!" Sacram demanded. The officer handed him the log which he inspected. "Did the night shift question a member of my mission?"

"There isn't a record of any questionings," said the officer.

"Are you certain you saw Sutraps?" Sacram asked as he turned to me.

“Most definitely," I said.

"Unusual," Sacram replied. "My aide here told me Sutraps was last night in this very building."

“So?" replied the guard.

"Why is there no record of his being here?"

"My log does not show any arrests or interrogations last night."

"Perhaps you would like to talk to my general officer."

"I would like that," Sacram replied curtly.

The officer disappeared and soon reappeared with a uniformed officer of general rank. The general wore the usual gray uniform with gold inlay on the bill of the cap along with the normal amount of ribbons and other decorations for an officer of his rank.

"May I help you?" Asked the general.

"One of the delegates on my mission was arrested and interrogated here last night."

"Did you explain your problem to my Officer in Charge?"

"Yes, but he said there are no records of an interrogation," Sacram said.

"If there are no records of an interrogation, then no interrogation took place," the general said slamming the log book shut.

"I have a witness who says there was an interrogation," Sacram said pounding the table.

"Who is this witness?" The general demanded, his face turned red and his mouth twisted with mounting rage.

"Standing beside me!" Sacram said, pointing to me.

"Did you see this Sutraps?"

"Yes," I replied, and told him what had happened. When I described the electro shock equipment, the general was outraged.

"I cannot help you!" He slammed the log book down on the

desk. "Perhaps you were mistaken as to where you were. Perhaps you were not at this station last night, but at some other!"

"This is the only police station in Latipac!" Sacram said,

"Is it possible for the prisoner to have been transferred?" I asked.

"Possible," the general replied, giving me a piercing look "if it is a political case."

"Please check," Sacram requested.

"Wait here," the general said, glaring at me. He left the room for ten or fifteen minutes, and then returned.

"The political wing interrogated a prisoner last night."

"We would like to see him," Sacram said.

"No!"

"I have a right to see a member of my delegation!"

"You have no rights here!" screamed the general. "What the hell do you think you're trying to do coming into my station and making requests?" The general and Sacram glared at each other.

"The prisoner became ill during the interrogation and was sent to a hospital for political criminals."

"Thank you for the information!" Sacram stated. He turned away from the general and motioned for us to leave. We walked outside.

"What does this mean?" I asked.

"It means Sutraps is considered a threat to the state and will probably be executed."

"What happens to the political prisoners?"

“They're usually placed in Detfar."

"Detfar?"

"You will learn more before you leave Latipac.”

We walked to the Fuchsia Palace, a distance of about fifteen city blocks. We checked in at the front gate and were cleared through to the Palace. We entered and the butler asked us to be seated. We waited a short time and were soon met by one of Anil's adjutants, a man of noble-features and an educated demeanor. He asked for the nature of our visit. Sacram explained the mysterious disappearance of Sutrap whom I had witnessed being interrogated the previous night. He told the aide that he had been told by the general at the police station that Sutrap had been transferred to the state prison hospital.

"In what way can we help?" the aide asked, frowning.

"I want Satrups released!"

"Please wait," the aide said. He left, but soon returned.

"You have Anil's permission to visit the hospital."

We left the Palace and walked to the prison hospital a few blocks away and were cleared to see Sutrap. We found him sitting on a small metal cot in a concrete cell surrounded by large steel bars. The guard opened the door for us.

"Sutrap, can you hear me?" Sacram asked, but Sutrap was unaware of our presence. His eyes were glazed and vacuous. The movement of his arms and head were slow and jerky. One look in Sutraps vacuous eyes told me he was as trapped inside his body as I was on this island.

"They tortured him," Sacram said, scarcely able to control his emotions, "One day!" Sacram said suppressing his rage, "But now, we must leave. He's beyond our help,"

"What will happen to him?" I asked.

"He is dead. Only his body remains alive," Sacram replied, a hitch in his voice.

"Will they release him now?" I asked.

"No,"

"Why?"

"Because he's an enemy of the state,"

"Did he say too much during the interrogation?" I asked.

"Too much, too little," he replied, "it doesn't matter. Men's lives do not matter here, only money matters. We need to arrange a meeting with Anil"

"How?"

"Senator Dennick, a friend, is very influential. We'll talk to him at the Capital."

CHAPTER 11

The Legislators

The Capital building stood at the opposite end of Piraeus Street from the Fuchsia Palace. It was a large imposing building with a huge dome and fluted columns supporting the overhanging precipices that were decorated with reliefs of various historical moments of note to the Sets. It too was Fuchsia in color with gothic architecture, like other buildings in Latipac. It had a great flight of steps leading to the entrance, with a highly ornate lobby directly below the dome. The interior was magnificent with beautiful mosaics made of marble chips that covered the entire area of the lobby floor. Above the lobby were three levels of floors, each with a balcony from which one could look down upon the great mass of mosaic below. Great chandeliers of the finest crystal hung on golden chains suspended on beams in the uppermost part of the dome.

"You'll see scenes up there in the stained glass dome," Sacram said pointing toward the ceiling, "scenes from our stock exchange which is a bastion of tradition and the basis of much Set history." The stained glass scene depicted men on the floor of a stock exchange. Their faces expressed great excitement as they executed orders from their Set customers.

Several members of the legislature spoke to Sacram as they passed by while others simply nodded. Those who spoke to Sacram did so in a warm manner with sincere respect. One smartly dressed young man in a finely tailored business suit walked up to Sacram and pulled him to one side. "Senator Denneck's bill is up for a vote in about fifteen minutes," said the aide, "if you hurry you can watch from the visitor's gallery." He handed Sacram two visitor's passes.

A circular staircase wound upward toward the center of the rotunda. At the top of the staircase, we walked across marble floors to the visitor's gallery. We handed the guards our passes and took our seats on the first row. From our seating position, it was obvious to me that the man who had given us the passes had high rank.

"Who gave us the passes?"

"An aide to Senator Denneck," Sacram replied.

"This chamber will come to order!" stated a man with a boyish voice. He pounded a gavel on his desk. A hushed silence filled the room.

"The Clerk will read the bill being considered by this chamber," instructed the Speaker who sat in a high-back leather chair on a raised dais. The clerk walked to the desk of the presiding officer and picked up the bill. Then read it out loud, but before he could finish reading, a member arose to be heard.

"Mister Speaker," interrupted a member who arose to address the chairman.

"The Gentleman is recognized," said the speaker.

"I request the clerk refrain from reading the entire contents of the bill because each of the members already has a copy and can read the whole bill, if in doubt, as to its provisions."

Another member arose to speak. He was tall and slender with a full head of silver hair. "Mister Speaker," he began, "this bill should be read to the floor in its entirety. This is an important bill."

"Mister Speaker," said the first gentleman, "it is not necessary to read the bill in its entirety. We all have copies."

"Mister Speaker, I object," said a third member, arising from his chair.

"Overruled," replied the Speaker, "We'll take a vote. All in favor of not reading the bill say aye." From the gallery below came a series of ayes and nays. "The ayes have it. The Clerk will return the bill to my desk. The floor is now open for debate."

"But, Mister Speaker," objected a member.

"The ayes have it, your objection is overruled," said the speaker. Sacram excused himself and said he wanted to get a copy of the bill to see what was being debated. He left and returned a little later with two copies of the bill. He handed me a copy. I glanced over the bill which concerned inherited wealth. There was a lot of heated debate over the bill. The majority of the members were for shelving the bill.

"Mister Speaker," began a member in a white suit and a drawl in his speech

"The member is recognized,"

"Mister Speaker, I move that we change the word *'and therefore'* in the first sentence of the second paragraph to '*and henceforth*'."

"Change noted," replied the speaker.

"I object, Mister Speaker," stated another member, "the wording of the bill should not be changed. It's important that this bill pass without change. The passing of wealth from one generation to another serves only to create a permanent elite and stifles initiative and innovation."

"I object, Mister Speaker," said the gentleman in a white suit, "The job creators of Setopia should be able to pass their wealth to their kids. They earned it and they are entitled to give it to their children without interference from the government."

Another man rose to be recognized. "Mister Speaker," he said, "I move that we substitute the middle paragraph on page fifteen with the last paragraph on page twenty one and reverse the wording in the last sentence of the middle paragraph on page five."

Other members offered amendments and motions during the floor debate which lasted over an hour. Then, the Speaker announced a vote.

"All in favor of the amendments say aye," said the Speaker to which the chamber erupted with many ayes. "All in opposition say nay." From the floor of the chamber came only a few nays. "From the sound of it, the ayes have it. The amendments are approved. Clerk, make changes the bill, then read it to the assembly."

"Yes, Sir," replied the Clerk.

The Clerk left the chamber and returned about an hour later. The resulting bill was so incoherent that when it was read by the clerk, no one in the room could make heads or tails of it. The speaker asked if any more motions were on the floor, but there were none, so he suggested that the chamber vote on the bill. The bill passed overwhelmingly and was enacted into law.

"In its present form, that bill is incomprehensible," Sacram explained, "this is a common tactic to make a law so ambiguous that it could never hold up in any court in Setopia."

The next bill that came up in the chamber was to protect consumers from merchants who prey on their unsophisticated buying habits. The members modified that bill as well until it too was totally incomprehensible.

Many of the members were elegant speakers. In fact, many were brilliant and used superb language. They were obviously well trained in their use of rhetoric and were able to deliver with polish and persuasion. That is not to say that the words uttered by these polished rhetoricians fell on unsympathetic ears. As Sacram explained to me, most of those in the congress were either wealthy or were very anxious to become wealthy.

That day, I heard great orators engaged in meaningless rhetoric and treacherous bombast that began as seductive rhythms that drew the listener into a labyrinth of falsehoods to protect the interests of the wealthy while ignoring the interest of the Lats who elected them into office.

"Nothing is obvious in politics," Sacram told me, "If it weren't for fake news and propaganda, people would revolt. A person must be very perceptive to understand. Unfortunately, being perceptive eliminates the majority of Lats because their education prevents them from understanding. "

I enjoyed listening to these members of the legislature. Each had a distinctive style and possessed elegant language coupled with a high native intelligence. However, after a ong period of silence, I became curious. I leaned over the rail of the balcony and saw the majority of the members of congress asleep in their chairs. Meanwhile, the gentleman in the white suite continued speaking, but his speech had lost its meaning. What he uttered were words without the connecting fabric that makes the words logical. I looked at Sacram. He seemed about to fall asleep. I shook him. He told me if we didn't leave he would soon be asleep, so we left.

"I want to go to Senator Dennek's office," Sacram said. We walked, out of the visitor's gallery and to the marbled hallway of the third floor. The doors of the offices were constructed of red oak, and were about ten feet high. The moldings on either side of the door were carved wood with various fruit and vine designs. We entered and were greeted by a young woman who acted as the personal secretary to Senator Denneck.

"Please wait, I'll see if the Senator is available." She went into the Senator's office.

"Of Course!" The Senator said from inside his office.

“You may go in,” She said when she reappeared. We entered the Senator’s office which was festooned with pictures of him with various important people in Setopia.

"Glad to see you again, Sacram!" exclaimed the Senator.

"I’d like you to meet an associate of mine, Jonathan Crews."

"Any friend of Sacram's is a friend of mine," he said as he shook my hand. “Glad to meet you.” He was a tall man with a thin frame and silver hair. He had a ruddy complexion and dimples appeared when he smiled. His bearing elicited grace and confidence.

"What have you been doing these past months?" The Senator asked.

"I've been assigned to Seraphs."

"Great place, Seraphs. I enjoy taking my holidays there."

"Yes, it's a great place, but there's a problem."

"Oh, what's the problem?"

"Military troops were recently in Seraphs in violation of the Treaty of Bodiglioni."

"When did this happen?" The senator asked, his smile disappearing.

"Last week. They killed a man from Seval, one of our trainees."

Senator Dennick sunk back into his leather chair. Lines of worry creased his forehead as he rubbed his chin. For a long moment he was silent.

"How can I help?" he asked finally.

"We need to speak with Anil in private. I was there yesterday, but didn't find an opportunity."

"I knew this was going to happen one day," he said with a sigh.

"I didn't think it wise to lodge a formal complaint about the matter," Sacram said.

The Senator thought for a minute. "I sometimes have lunch

with Anil at the Palace. That would be a good time to talk."

"We need to handle this matter gently," Sacram said, "Anil has a quick temper."

"I'm well aware of his temper," replied the Senator as he leaned back in his chair, "Where are you staying?"

"The Arbor House."

"Nice place, we call it the VIP hotel. I'll arrange a meeting with Anil. I'll get back with you when we get a time set up."

Sacram and I walked back down the circular staircase that led to the floor of the rotunda and out through the front entrance. Outside, dark gray clouds hung over the city and flashes of lightening illuminated the sky. A sudden crack of thunder sent people on the streets scurrying for cover. Following another blinding flash of lightening was a deafening roar of thunder.

"Pick up your pace," Sacram said, "we need to get to the hotel before this storm hits."

Rain pelted us with large drops of water when we were short distance from the hotel. By the time we reached the hotel, we were drenched. For a short time, we stood under the marquee of the hotel and watched the downpour. Soon, the rain changed to hail that bounced upon the pavement. I returned to my room and took a hot shower. The warm water felt good. I dressed and met Sacram. Then we went downstairs and sat in a booth next to a window. Outside, the streets were filled with runoff from the storm. I touched the glass window, felt its coldness, and watched droplets of water running down the glass. I felt at peace sitting inside a warm building while the storm raged outside. It reminded me of my former life.

***

The next morning, I felt unusually tired and discovered that I had contacted a head cold. A knock on the door forced me to get up. Sacram was standing before me fully dressed.

"Not ready yet?" he asked

“No, just got up.”

"Meet me in the coffee shop. I'll be waiting there."

Right.” I jumped into the shower, dressed and hurried downstairs.

"Glad you could join us," Sacram said. I recognized the man seated with Sacram as the aide to Senator Dennick I had seen earlier at the Capital building. The aide excused himself and left. I ordered breakfast and enjoyed a meal of eggs, bacon and coffee.

"Senator Denneck has arranged a meeting with Anil." Sacram said. "The Senator doesn't think you should be in the meeting. Anil doesn't like to lunch with anybody he doesn’t know. But, first, I want to take you to a special club."

CHAPTER 12

The Setro Club

We finished breakfast and left the Hotel. The air outside was cooler than the previous day. Perhaps the rains had caused a cool front to move through the area. But it was pleasantly cool. Sacram took me through the busiest streets in Latipac. We walked up to a large mansion with a wrought-iron gate. Inside the gate was a topiary garden similar in style to the one I had seen in Seraphs in Gloy Park. We walked up to a large stone house that looked somewhat like a castle because of the crenellations and battlements. The large door to the building was open, so we entered. The interior was richly decorated with colorful hand woven rugs hanging on the walls. There were several high backed leather chairs in the lounge area. Many oil paintings hung from the walls, and the lamps were of fine porcelain with jade bases.

A butler entered the main room and greeted us. "Follow me," he said and led us to a large room in which many people were gathered. All seemed quite well off. They each wore expensive suits which were of subdued colors as though the wearers did not want to draw attention to their clothing. Sacram nodded to the gentlemen in the room and they nodded back.

"Only the very top Sets are allowed membership in this club," Sacram said, "they're powerful people who control industries and banks."

In this room were gathered the most powerful people in Setopia. They seemed very educated and cultured. Sacram seemed to know most of the Sets. He spoke to them with an ease that I myself did not feel. His professional diplomatic training was evident with the polished manner in which he handled himself. I spoke very little, but chose to listen and to speak only when spoken to. Sacram, gracious and articulate, seemed to please the Sets to whom he spoke. They were intrigued by the subtleties of his polished language. When in the company of these Sets, Sacram spoke in a literary manner. I suppose that was a result of his fondness for literature.

"Most of the men here were trained at the University in Seraph," Sacram said.

"I assumed the Sets would be different somehow," I said, "but they don't seem to be different from other people."

"The main difference," Sacram said,"is they have the social position that comes with wealth. It is precisely their wealth and position that enables them to join the Setro club. "

"So Sacram, how are things in Seraphs," asked one of the Sets.

"Good. We've added several people to the University staff this year."

"The Seraphs, "one Set said, "are impractical in their university training. Honestly, ancient Seraphian poetry is hardly a worthwhile subject to master, don't you think so, Sacram?"

Sacram winched and tried to get out of having to answer the question, but finally, the weight of silence forced him to speak. "While the university training in Seraphs tends to be impractical, it gives the student a specialty with which to teach. On the other hand, the Lats who study in the University of Latipac learn how to manage domas and people, which is a very difficult chore. Both universities are important to the functioning of Setopia."

"I do like the way he dodges the issue," said a senior Set.

"Very diplomatic," replied another.

* * *

After about an hour, I felt comfortable enough to talk with some of the Sets. I cornered one elderly gent who was sitting in a high backed leather chair puffing on his pipe, which let off a most pleasant aroma.

"Hello, my name is Jonathan." I said to introduce myself.

"Name is Erimco," he replied.

"I'm here with Sacram and the delegation from Seraphs," I said.

"Glad to meet you, Jonathan. I like diplomats…use a lot of them in my domas. You may know that I sit on the boards of ten of the largest domas in Latipac."

"That's great," I replied.

"Most people don't seem to realize," he continued," that we Sets have great responsibilities not only to ourselves, and our families, but to the economy of Setopia. Do you know what the economy of Setopia would be like if It weren't for us?"

"No, I don't," I replied.

"Well, if it weren't for us, the people in Seval would be starving to death. The Seraphians would not have any reason to study their books or write their worthless treatises, because there would be no demand for books. The animals in the forest would soon take over what is left of Latipac. They would be all over Latipac pissing on the Lamp posts, and that's what you would have,"

I decided to change the topic and talk about activities enjoyed by members of the Setro Club.

"Do you enjoy hunting big game?"

"Great Sport, hunting," he beamed, "do you hunt?"

“Sometimes.”

"Nothing like a little scare to sharpen a man’s instincts," he said, "I remember once when I was hunting on one of the neighboring islands. We came upon a herd of elephants and just beyond the group was a rogue elephant -- large one he was too. I crept toward him. He did not smell me until I was about two hundred feet away. Suddenly, he got my scent. He spun around and charged. Both ears were spread out so that he looked twice his size, He was enormous! My father taught me how to hunt and my instincts took over. I held my rifle steady and waited. I kept waiting and waiting, it seemed like minutes passed before the beast got so close that I could hear his strained breathing. Then when he was about thirty feet away, I took a bead and fired. He immediately fell dead. He was so close that his head pinned my foot to the ground," His voice trailed off to a moment of silence. After a long pause, he spoke again, "That was quite a kill. I remember it as though it was yesterday, but it was sixty years ago to be exact."

"Amazing,”I replied, "did you have it stuffed?"

"Yes, I had him stuffed the day after I shot him, and then I shellacked him. He now stands in my back yard. Every time I see him it makes my legs grow weak, but he brings back memories of my youth. How I long to be young again."

The old gentleman was pleasant and I enjoyed talking to

him. When I left him, he was puffing on his pipe and reflecting upon the good old days when he was young and hunting wild elephants.

Sacram was talking to a middle-aged man with a thinning head of hair. Sacram introduced me to the man who was Chairman of three banks. His small roundish glasses made him look intellectual. They had been talking about economics and I heard the last part of a question, something about interest rates.

"We set the interest rates," said the Bank Chairman, "and we set the rules. We're Sets, you know, that's what we do, we set things."

All the Sets I spoke with were well educated, articulate, and had grace and social poise. Each seemed to be sensitive and appreciative of art and, each seemed desirous to improve the lot of the common man. Still, I found it difficult to understand how Setopia kept chugging along when these captains of industry were so desirous to improve the poor man's lot. I did like these men whom I found to be gracious and likable. The older men lived with their memories of bygone days. The younger men were interested in politics, the art world, society and the like. What I did notice about this group of men was the presence of leisure in their lives, something lacking in the lives of the other people in Setopia.

These men were at liberty to cultivate themselves in any

manner they chose. If they chose to study philosophy or any other subject, they could do so as long as they wished. They could read as much classic literature they wished without having to worry about a work schedule. Oh, they put in their share of time at the office, but their time was spent giving directions and listening to problems. Seldom did major problems arise because the lower managers, the Lats, wanted to show that they were fully capable of handling any situation, and hoping that a promotion would be forthcoming. These Sets were therefore relieved of the necessity of worry.

As I talked with several Sets, I learned that the Lats – the vast majority of people in Latipac --were not cultured. Their horizons were limited and their days occupied with the details of daily business. They were not aware of writers, or artists, or major thinkers. Office politics dictated to whom they pledged their loyalties. A typical day for a Lat consisted of getting the day's work done efficiently and advancing within the doma. In my country we called the domas, corporations. All a Lat needed do was work hard, keep out of trouble, make suggestions on how to make the doma more efficient. Each Lat was told by the owner of the doma, that if he worked hard and was a loyal worker, he would one day be president, or at least vice president, of the doma.

The Lats had no appreciation of art. They were in many

respects the most insensitive of men. Their natures had made them slaves of the flesh and of physical pleasures and goods. Their minds were not developed. The University of Latipac served only to supply fresh talent yearly for the management of industry. It did not open minds or train its graduates to think. It served instead to instill in its graduates the value of doma life.

The Sets did not to question why Setopian resources belonged to them and not to others. To the Sets, Setopia functioned well and let them live in a style they enjoyed. Often they poked fun at the poor devils who worked for them. The Lats were a class quite distinct from the Sets.

Many of the Sets secretly admired the Seraphians who spent their days engaged in arduous intellectual work developing policy analyses.

The Sets were gracious to one another, and to anyone who came into social contact with them. To the Sets, it was considered proper and gracious to appear charming to those who came into one's zone of influence. Social encounters between people within the Setro Club were done on a peer basis. All were considered equals within the club. As we left the Setro Club, I felt uneasy about my experience there. I had expected them to be harsh, greedy and mean, but I was surprised by how pleasant and charming they were. That contradiction baffled me.

CHAPTER 13

The Tide Turns

The following morning we had an early breakfast and then left to meet Senator Denneck. The Senator was in his office reading a report when we arrived.

"Jonathan, I'm afraid you won't be able to join us in our meeting with Anil," Senator Denneck said.

"I understand," I said, "I intend to visit the art gallery this afternoon while you two are meeting with Anil."

"You'll like the gallery. The modern art exhibit is on the lower level."

"I'll visit that exhibit," I said.

He put the report on his desk and addressed Sacram. "Anil believes the immunities granted by the Treaty of Bodigliani are not valid."

"He signed the treaty. Why does he think it's invalid?" Sacram asked.

"Anil can interpret any document any way he wants. He's the ruler of Setopia."

"Well," Sacram said, "Let's go meet with him."

We left his office and I walked with them almost to the Palace, and then we parted. I felt somewhat left out by not being able to go into the Palace with them, but I realized the delicacy of their negotiations, and realized that Sacram was concerned for my safety. The meeting obviously had its hazards.

I walked to the Setopian Museum of Art a few blocks away and descended to the lower level. On the walls were an assortment of paintings. Most were avant garde forms of expressionism that emphasized the impact of color over form. I remembered an old adage that a civilization is portrayed in its art. Somehow the appearance of this art indicated to me that something was adrift in Setopia and represented a certain hollowness.

Many of the works were nothing more than huge canvases painted with a single color, sometimes with a single brush stroke. They were creative, perhaps, in a minimalist sense. Still, the absolute simplicity and starkness of the works I found strangely appealing, but I questioned how these works differ from those that any other person might produce. Obviously the paintings did not represent a lot of talent, nor a high degree of skill.

Sacram told me talent and genius is different in Latipac than in Seraphs. Talent in Latipac is assigned a monetary value and the artist is rewarded accordingly. The public acceptance an artist receives determines the level of his talent. In Latipac, Sacram had said, each artist strives to sell himself to the best agent or gallery, and often prostituting himself to the favors of the agent or gallery

As I sat on a wooden bench and viewed the works of art, a man with an open shirt, tight fitting slacks and a suave manner displayed one of the paintings to a Set woman. She was obviously from the class of Sets because of her bearing and the amount of wealth displayed by her jewelry and clothing. The salesman showed her a painting.

"This Still Life is wonderful. Look at the colors. Observe the things the artist has hidden in the painting. Look, an olive here, a grape there, and an ant on the grape. However, that's not all. Let me show you how the mood of the painting can be changed by varying the amount of light. Each stroke of paint means something special. It's up to you, Madame, to determine that special meaning."

"It's so clever," said the woman, "I love this piece."

"I must tell you, Madame, in strict confidence, this very artist wandered the streets of Latipac begging for food. All he had to his name was this painting that he had just finished. The gallery purchased it for the cost of a single meal. It was a fantastic purchase." I shifted uneasily in my seat as I listened to their conversation.

"I want to purchase this painting," said the woman, admiring the painting. How much is it?"

“Madame, I will write the price on this piece of paper.”

He handed the paper to the woman who looked at the price.

“Oh my! Very expensive! My husband will be furious, but I must have it.”

"A wise purchase, Madame, the value of this painting should triple within a year. Your husband will be happy that you made such a sound investment." The salesman took her address and other information. Then, two workmen removed the painting.

* * *

I wandered around both floors of the gallery looking at the variety of art that was on display. The quality of art ranged from extremely fine to the ridiculous. I had been in the gallery about two hours when Sacram arrived.

"Anil was in an especially vicious mood," Sacram said, nervously. "The whole deal fell through. I'm convinced that Anil is going to take over Seraphs."

"What!”

"He intends to send more troops to Seraphs. He said the people are getting out of hand in Seraphs."

"That's horrible!" I replied, "what happens now?"

"I don't know, but one thing is certain," he said, biting his lower lip.

"What?" I asked.

"We must act at once."

"What are you planning?" I asked. Sacram flinched. He looked around to survey those in the room. He grabbed my arm and led me from the gallery.

"There's a small park not far away. We can talk there."

We walked to the park and onto a secluded foot path. When we were a safe distance from others in the park, Sacram turned to me.

"Anil arrested Senator Dennek, and accused him of conspiracy. Anil has been watching Dennek for the past year and has been collecting information on the Senator's activities. During our meeting, Anil openly accused the Senator of treason."

"Where is Senator Dennek?" I asked.

"They arrested him and took him away. I don't know where, perhaps in the dungeon below the Fuchsia Palace."

"What can we do" I asked.

"It's time to organize. Will you help us?" he asked. I studied him for a long moment before answering. The seriousness of the situation was evident from the creases on his forehead.

"Yes," I replied,"what can I do?"

"Good. Remember Gloy?"

"Certainly, I saw him in Gloy Park in Seraphs."

"His talks in the park are a front. He's the leader of our resistance."

"Resistance?"

"Yes. He's working with the people of Seval to organize them, but we are still a long way from staging a successful coup."

"Coup?" I asked, "a revolution?"

"Anil is rigid, and the Sets are entrenched. They won't give up unless they're defeated."

"Do you have weapons?" I asked.

"Weapons?"

"Yes, you know, weapons, like guns, knives, etc."

"No!" he exclaimed somewhat disturbed by what I said. "We will use weapons only as a last resort."

"How is the resistance organized?"

"In cells."

"And Gloy?"

"When everyone thought he was in the mountains, he was dressed as a beggar teaching the men how to fight. He wanted

Anil to think he was a mad man. That's the reason he left the university under such strange conditions. He wanted to give the impression that he had lost his mind."

"Then he isn't really the mountain mad man."

"No, he's the main organizer of the resistance."

“I see," I replied, very much amazed, "clever disguise."

As we talked, a couple sauntered into the park near us. Sacram fidgeted as he talked, his eyes searched the area. He was nervous about being overheard. After the couple left the area, we continued our conversation.

"How can we get Senator Dennek released?" I asked.

“He's a prisoner of the state."

"Can't we free him?"

"Unlikely. The prison is heavily guarded."

"Then, how can we get him out?"

"The only way is to free Setopia from Anil's control."

"How?"

"Who knows," he replied, his voice grave. “It's not safe to stay in Latipac. We must leave.”

"When do we leave?"

"Soon," he said, "we'll travel at night, and sleep in the jungle."

"Does Anil know we're leaving?"

"He will before long."

"Just thinking," I said, "Anil knows I'm with you. If he distrusts you, he distrusts me. If you are an enemy of the state, than I am also an enemy."

"True," he replied. "It's not safe for me to return to the hotel. Anil knows the Senator and I are close friends."

"Will they torture the Senator?"

"They torture everyone. Anil doesn't discriminate. No one leaves the prison alive except the guards, and in some cases they too are put to death."

"Gruesome."

"We must put a stop to Anil," he said, clenching his fists, his face contorted with fiery rage. "I served Anil for many years in the Diplomatic corps, but for years, I yearned for the day that I could depose him. Now, that day has come," Sacram said, a catch in his throat. "Anil will enslave the whole of Setopia in a web of intrigue and underhanded maneuverings, unless we stop him. He grows strong from the fears he instills in those he rules. The more terror he inflicts on them, the more fearful they become. The more fearful they became the more powerful he becomes. It's an unending cycle."

"Do you know what Anil plans to do?" I asked.

"Anil is going to send more troops to Seraphs. He doesn't trust the intellectuals. In the past, he tolerated them because the Seraphians produced research papers that legitimized his regime.

Go to the hotel and gather a few clothes and my portfolio. We must leave tonight."

"Where will you be?"

"I'll wait here. Borrow two sleeping bags from the hotel. They're stored in the back room of the hotel."

* * *

I returned to the hotel, gathered clothing, sleeping bags, and a few other things that we would need. As I was leaving, soldiers entered the hotel. I slipped out a side door of the hotel and hastened my steps. I returned to Sacram as quickly as possible.

"Soldiers are at the Hotel," I said, catching my breath.

"We'll hide here in the park until dark."

We walked to a little known area of the park where we could safely hide. There we remained until dark. Luck was with us that night for the moon was in its dark quarter, and a blanket of clouds concealed our departure. We could hear soldiers searching the park and the main roads in Latipac, stopping pedestrians and asking for identification.

Sacram knew a route out of the city through an old drainage channel. Fortunately, he had explored Latipac for escape routes. Set soldiers were obviously searching for us. Any mistake could alert the soldiers to our presence. Our escape from Latipac that night was a frightening experience.

An hour or so later, we had escaped through the drainage channel and were outside the city, a safe distance from the soldiers. Our progress outside of Latipac was slow and difficult. In the darkness, we tripped several time on thick vines growing in the forest. After walking several hours we spread our sleeping bags upon the ground and camped for the night.

CHAPTER 14

The Village Of Seval

The next morning, we set out just after sunrise and walked most of the day. We had no food, so we ate what we could find on the trail, which amounted to wild grapes and a tropical fruit resembling grapefruit. At the end of the day, we arrived at one of the encampments used by the resistance. Much to my surprise, we met the three mule drivers who had led our expedition from Seraphs. That night, we sat around a fire and had a nice chat. They handed us hot coffee in tin cans which we gladly drank.

Most of the men in the camp were armed with knives and machetes. A few had spears and daggers, but for the most part their weapons were primitive, no match for the modern weapons of the Set soldiers. The mule drivers knew the village because they had grown up there. They knew the people, and they knew who was in the movement and who to trust. As they talked, it became increasingly clear that these mule drives played an important role in the resistance. They were intelligence agents for the resistance, and they were very good at their work.

"Have you seen Gloy?" Sacram asked.

"He was here last night," Gimpy said, "he left early morning for Gloy Park."

"Why did he go back to Seraphs?" I asked.

"He has to appcar in thc park cvery so often so the Sets will think he is still in the mountains,"Sacram replied. The Sets have invested a lot of time and money trying to find out who the resistance members are in order to put them to death."

"Are you afraid of the Sets?" I asked Red.

"Na," he replied, "if them knew we fight them, they kill us pronto. We born to fight."

"They be mean," replied One-hand, "they kill anyone get in their way."

"Have more soldiers arrived in Seval from Latipac? Sacram asked.

"Na," Red said, "No more than the normal amount. Why?"

"A friend of mine was arrested and they are probably coming after me as well."

"They kill you if they find you?" asked Red.

"Pronto," responded Sacram, "They like killing."

"Them Sets ya gotta watch," replied Gimpy.

"Red, go into Seval and see if there is an arrest warrant for me" Sacram said.

"They post papers on the walls of our village with pics of wanted men," Gimpy said.

"I would like to go into Seval with him," I said, "I've never been there." Sacram looked puzzled.

"Okay by me, "said Red.

"Be careful," Sacram cautioned.

* * *

We finished our coffee, and departed. After walking about two hours, we stood on a hill overlooking Seval, a village of adobe huts. At the far end of the village were large brick factories with huge smokestacks billowing black smoke.

"This is Seval and there be our work," said Red, pointing to the factories, "We go in now. Don't speak to the soldiers, only grunt."

"You wait her," he said.

I waited in a thicket near the village while he went into the village. He was gone about thirty minutes and returned with burlap clothes.

"Put these on so you look like us," Red said. I put on the heavy clothes. The crude burlap irritated my skin at first, but I eventually got used to it. We saw many soldiers congregated in the shade of a tree not far away. They talked and drank something from a ceramic bottle.

"They like wine," Red said.

Red’s hut was located on the far side of the village which required a twenty minute walk through the streets. We were stopped once by a soldier who wanted to know what we were doing walking the streets during working hours. Red told him that we were working for Latipac as mule drivers. The soldier grimaced but let us pass. When we arrived at the hut, Red's wife and children met him. A red haired boy of two and a blonde girl of about four years of age raced to greet him.

"Did you bring us somt’in, daddy?" each child asked.

He reached into his pocket and gave each a piece of candy he had gotten from Set officials whom he had escorted. Candy in Seval was rare and a major treat for the children.

"These are your kids?" I asked.

The children looked at me in amazement. The driver had to reassure them that I was not one of the soldiers wearing Seval clothing. Still they were not convinced, and eyed me with suspicion.

"It's the way you talk," Red explained, so I began talking like them as much as I could.

"We was just from Latipac last night," I told the family, "and them Sets are after us." This comment prompted each child to withdraw in fear and hold firm to their dad.

"You'll scare the kids," Red said, shaking his head.

"Them Sets not after us, just after Sacram," I said. My comment set them at ease and they seemed to lose their suspicions about me. They asked me a lot of questions about where I came from. I was at a loss trying to explain, so I told them I came from a village very like theirs far off in another part of Setopia.

"You got them Sets too?" asked the boy.

"Yes. Many of them," I replied.

The family finally warmed to me and we had many hearty laughs. The driver's wife brought refreshments, which were meager. I felt guilty accepting the cheese and bread they offered because I could tell from the looks on the children's faces that it must have been all the food in the house. I took only a very small piece of the cheese and a small piece of bread. Red then brought out some wine and poured it into a cup from which we took turns drinking. The children became a little too noisy, so Red told them *grown people were talking! Children should be seen and not heard*!"

Our conversation turned to the resistance, and Red told the children *go outside and play*. "Have you heard ofan order being issued for Sacram's arrest?"Red asked his wife.

"No. not heard of none,"she replied," but I have not talked to friend today. Soldiers act normal. They not on alert."

I felt relieved. At least Sacram was in no immediate danger. As Red and his wife talked about the resistance movement, their eyes brightened and hope shown through.

"First," Red said, "we get rid of all titles. No Sets, no Sevs, no Sers, no Lats. We all equal. We all work. None eats who don't work. We all work."

"That is noble," I replied. He meant every word he uttered. I found his words refreshing. These people wanted nothing more than to be able to live as people and to be able to advance in society in accordance to their talents, not in accordance to where they lived.

"Could we walk around Seval and meet some of the others in the resistance,"I asked.

"Ït be okay now," Red said, "guards not on alert."

"Thank you for your hospitality," I said to Red's wife.

* * *

We left Red's home and walked past adobe huts and through the dusty streets of the village. As we walked past a garbage dump, I was amazed by the poverty we saw. In the area of the dump were undernourished children playing in the garbage, many of them searching for food. Most of the children had swollen bellies and their faces and hands were infected from numerous insect bites. Youthful scavengers were common in the area. They survived by living off discarded food.

"The best food is what the soldiers throw away. They eat well," Red said.

"What causes the wounds on the children?"

"Rats, them sores from rats."

I saw many rats around the garbage that the children were sifting through. The stench of the dump was revolting. Red did not seem to mind the smell, nor the large green and black flies that the garbage attracted. The flies had a painful bite. I brushed the flies off me as best I could. Red ignored the flies. Nearby, other children played a game with circular hoops. They used a stick to roll a hoop down a dirt street, trying to make the hoop go faster than the previous child. I watched the children play for a while and then Red tapped me on the shoulder.

"Must go now," he said, "we go to cell."

"Will Gloy be there?" I asked as I brushed off more flies from my arm as we walked down a dusty pathway.

"Maybe," he replied.

Red entered an adobe hut on the outskirts of the village, then he motioned for me follow him. On the floor of the hut, Red removed a rug and opened a trap door that lead into an underground cave. We climbed down a ladder and into a room of about ten Sevs crowded around a table. Strewn about the table were maps. Red introduced me to the group.

"This is Jona. Friend of Sacrams," Red said.

"Glad to meet you," I said. My manner of speaking also made this group uneasy and they stopped talking and stared at me.

"He ok, can trust him," reassured Red.

I looked around and saw several people listening to a woman on the other side of the room.

“Who is that?” I asked.

“Guinn,” Red replied.

“Oh,”I said and walked over to her so I could hear what she was saying.

"We will use force with force, if necessary to defeat the Sets," said Gwinn. Her long brown hair and hazel eyes gave her a look of intensity. She wore a red madras that covered her hair and wore a gray peasant dress of burlap. The course burlap was indeed the standard wear in the village. Her hazel eyes went well with her brown hair. Her high cheek bones gave her the look of a fashion model, but in Setopia only Lats become models.

The people in the group were vastly different from others in the village. Here was gathered a group of intelligent and dedicated people. They all seemed articulate and not restricted by the limited vocabulary of the other Sevs. They were rebels and revolutionaries and cared little for Set law. Like Sacram before them, they were self-taught. They passed on their knowledge and skills to other Sevs through their cell networks. In the room were books that the members had written as training manuals for the resistance. I was shown an organizational chart which showed each cell and gave its location with a secret code for safety in case the Sets gained possession of the maps.

“You have lots of books here,” I said.

"The place for a Seval is in the factory,” Gwinn said, “we’re self-taught. The more books and knowledge we have the better we're able to act. We don’t like the factories."

"I'm not certain I understand," I said.

"Knowledge is power,” she said. “The more knowledge we have, the greater our power and the more effectively we can accomplish our goal of liberty. Do you understand?"

"Yes," I replied, “I believe I do.”

"Our goal is to rid the village of the soldiers and Set control. Our members have the courage to face death if that is required to liberate our village."

"Are the Seraphians helping liberate your village?" I asked

"The Seraphians are cowards. They sold themselves to the Sets and sold us into slavery. Yes, they have the power to change Setopia. They do not lack intelligence, but they lack the courage to make our nation equitable. They care little for us." Her face flushed with anger. After a moment, she calmed down. "We're having a meeting tonight. Gloy should be back from his trip to Seraphs by then."

"How can you have a meeting without being detected by the soldiers?"

"Our meetings take place in this cave late at night when the soldiers are asleep. They know nothing about the cave."

"How did you find it?"

"By chance, one of the villagers was digging a storage bin in the floor of his hut. He fell through the floor of the cave, and broke his leg. Word spread to the cell captains. They retrieved the injured man. Later they explored the cavern and decided it would be a good place for our meetings."

"Need to go," Red said, "Soldiers patrol soon."

"Pleased to meet you, Gwinn," I said.

"Likewise," she said.

* * *

When we arrived at the camp, Sacram was standing outside a tent and speaking to about fifteen people. He waved when he saw us.

“What did you learn in Seval,” he asked.

“According to people we talked to, you are not wanted by the soldiers,” I said.

“I’m relieved,” he replied.

"My people want to kill soldiers," Red said.

"To kill a soldier is not a victory," Sacram cautioned, "because he will be replaced with another soldier and he with yet another. To kill a soldier is to turn his family and friends against our cause. Killing is wrong. We need to win the soldiers over to our side with truth and wisdom, not with bullets and blood."

"How will that be done?" asked one man.

"By peaceful means," Sacram responded, “we educate the villagers and organize them. That way we act together. It’s more effective than using weapons. We will force our way into the political system of Setopia. Then, we will change Setopia to make it more equitable for everyone." His words brought on a round of hearty applause.

"The Sets must be shown" Sacram continued, “that it is wrong to create poverty through manipulation of economic resources. It is also wrong to have laws that are destructive to the people of Setopia. What we seek are Equality and Liberty!" A hearty round of cheers followed his statement.

"That's like it is!" shouted one.

"Right on, brother," shouted another.

"You got it," shouted a third.

"The Sets use subtle devises," Sacram continued, "to keep the villagers poor and fighting with one another. The most obvious is their refusal to pay the Sevs a livable wage in return for their services. It is not uncommon to see a Sev totally debilitated by the time he is twenty-five years of age. Many Sevs look years older than they are. Of course, the Sets maintain their youthful looks because they have an easy life. It is the people of Seval who are injured and the Sets who are rewarded by economic deprivation. Poverty is a corporate enterprise, and a very profitable one. The interests of the domas and the sufferings of the Seval go hand in hand. Impoverishment and suffering is profitable to the domas. Many of my childhood friends perished because of poverty. I left to get away from the poverty, but years later I returned to Seval. My friends who survived were physical wrecks with broken spirits. We must never lose sight of our goal of economic and political equality."

As soon as Sacram finished with his talk, Gloy entered the camp. Sacram rushed to greet him. The two talked momentarily, and then entered a tent that served as our headquarters. I entered the tent with one of the cell captains.

"The Senator is a good man," Gloy said, expressing sorrow that Senator Dennek had been put into prison. Gloy lacked the psychotic appearance that I had witnessed the first time I saw him in Gloy Park. Sacram and Gloy laughed a lot about old times. Then they discussed the strike.

"If only forty percent of the people of Seval join the movement, we will be successful," Gloy said.

"Do you think that is enough?" Sacram asked.

"Forty percent should be enough to bring the factories to a halt. The soldiers can't arrest everyone."

"When should we strike?" Sacram asked.

"In seven days."

"That's very short notice."

"We have no other alternative. Any further delays will give Anil more time to strengthen his forces. I received word that he is ordering some of the Lat workers into his military. If he learns of our strike, he will send most of his troops here to Sevel. Not good."

"So what do we do?" Sacram asked.

"We need some sort of diversion."

"A Diversion? Like what?"

"I don't know," Gloy confessed."If too many troops show up in Seval, they will overpower us and we will fail."

"Yes," Sacram said, "but when Anil learns of the strike, he will deploy his troops to Seval. That means the Palace will not be heavily guarded. We will enter Latipac and take the Palace and arrest Anil and his generals. That should further demoralize the soldiers. We have propaganda brochures that will hopefully break the moral of the troops and make them question their loyalty to the Sets."

"Here," Gloy said handing Sacram some papers, "look over these pamphlets. Our psychologists in Seraphs designed them."

“Amazing," Sacram said after studying thc pamphlets.

"The people of Seraphs are sympathetic to our cause,” Gloy said.

“But will they help us?”

“The Seraphians will support us, at least in spirit."

"That’s not very helpful," Sacram said.

"The Seraphians are afraid, many terrified,” Gloy said. “They have begun rethinking their loyalties to Anil. Most do not want direct control by Latipac. They helped the Sets in the past simply because they were left alone. Now the situation has changed. Word of the Ser being tossed over the Clift by the soldiers spread rapidly through Seraphs--it had a profound effect upon the people. They are ready to act."

Sacram fell silent for a moment, reflecting upon what Gloy had said. "The time has come for action," Sacram said, "It’s now or never. I don’t want to see bloodshed, but some bloodletting will be necessary because the Sets will not give up until their army is defeated."

"We should use propaganda as much as possible," Gloy said. "The soldiers must be made aware that they are supporting an unjust system. The soldiers will learn that everyone would be better if they lay down their arms and refused to fight. We need to make the soldiers question the morality of their orders."

"I hope it works," I said.

"Just between the two of us," Gloy confessed, “so do I."

Sacram and Gloy examined the names of the potential cell captains until they decided which ones would best serve key positions.

“The people of Seval,” Sacram said, “do not understand that if we act as a group, we will be safe, but if we become fearful groups, the resistance will weaken and the soldiers will win.”

"We need a man like Kram," Gloy said, “to send that message out to the people of Seval. While he was in the munitions factory, he prevented the soldiers from arresting his men. He negotiated favorable terms for his workers who had fallen behind in their rent payments. During the term of his foremanship, he had saved the lives of over fifty Sevs who had gotten into trouble with their Set overlords.”

“Good man,” Sacram said, “We can't let him be disposed of by the soldiers.”

“Where did they send Kram?” Gloy asked.

“He was sent to Detfar yesterday,” replied one of the Captains.

"We must have him back!" exclaimed Gloy. "He is absolutely indispensible to the resistance."

"How can we get him away from the soldiers?" asked Sacram.

"It will depend upon where they are keeping him."

"And if he has already reached Detfar?" Sacram asked.

“I'm afraid if he has already reached Detfar, we won't be able to rescue him." Gloy said.

"Are we too late?"

Gloy thought a moment. "Perhaps, if we could arrange some kind of signal to let him know our plans, we may be able to rescue him."

“It'll be dangerous," warned Sacram.

"An arm band." I suggested.

"Arm band?"

“Yes, if we could somehow manage to get a bright colored armband to him, he could wear it when on the field. Then we could tell Kram from the others. "

"A splendid idea," Gloy said, after a moment’s reflection, "It just might work."

"Get a couple of your best men, and search for Kram," Gloy said to one of the cell captains.

“Yes, sir,” he replied and departed.

* * *

Darkness provided a perfect cover for our rendezvous in Seval as the time approached for our scheduled meeting. Gloy and Sacram gathered their papers, and the three of us departed for the village. When we arrived at the edge of Seval, we saw soldiers were actively patrolling the streets. As an alternative, we returned to the forest and entered the cave at an opening near an adobe wall that had collapsed at the opposite side of the village. We crawled through a small tunnel for about fifty feet, and then came to a wooden ladder that descended some thirty feet to the floor below. A fire in a hearth illuminated the room. About fifteen people were present when we arrived. They were excited when they saw Sacram and Gloy, and their voices echoed throughout the cavern. I wondered if the soldiers above could hear us. Gwinn joined us wearing the same red madras.

"I wondered if you would be at the meeting," Gwinn said, as she joined us.

"I wouldn't miss it,” I replied.

"What will he be discussing tonight?" She asked.

"Time Schedule, I think."

"How's that?" She asked.

"The time schedule has been advanced."

"What?” she exclaimed, “by how much?"

"The strike begins in seven days."

"Seven Days!" she said in dismay. "How are we to get ready in seven days?"

"Don't ask me, but it has to be done."

"'Why is it so urgent?"

"Anil plans to march on Seraphs."

"Oh no!"

"Have there been any strikes before?" I asked.

"Never," she replied "Until Gloy formed the resistance, we didn't even know what the word meant. They're ready to start the meeting."

"We are advancing the date for the strike." Gloy began, as he stood on a large stone near the center of the room. "We received word that Anil is sending troops out of Latipac. We think they're going to Seraphs, but they may be coming here." The announcement was met with moans. "Think Positively," he warned. "We can win if we all think positively. I will answer any questions now. I believe Gwinn raised her hand first."

"I think Gloy is right," Gwinn said."We can win if we convince ourselves that we can win. If we let this opportunity slip by, we may never have another chance."

"She's right," Gloy replied, "but we must convince our friends, our co-workers, and their relatives that it is in everyone's interest to support the strike."

"Who will coordinate the strike activities?" Asked one of the members, "obviously you or Sacram cannot direct them because the soldiers will hunt you down. It has to be one of us."

"We have given that problem a lot of thought," Gloy said. "We need to use one of the cell captains."

“I think Nod would make a good leader,” Gwinn said.

“We agree,” the others said in unison.

Nod climbed onto the rock and stood next to Gloy. He was a large chap for a Seval with dark wavy hair and strong features. He was muscled and his forearms looked like those of a wrestler. Nod was a bright man who knew how to affect a good sentence in order to persuade people. He could speak the lowest guttural or the most polished English.

"We have seven days to prepare for the strike," Nod began, “our plan will succeed only if we can get Anil to overreact and send his troops out of Latipac. Our strike must be non violent. However, if the soldiers became brutal, we will fight back.”

“Thank you Nod,” Gloy said, “the sun will be rising soon. We must adjourn for now."

Gwinn walked to the ladder with other resistance members and disappeared through the opening in the ceiling.

"I'm tired" confessed Sacram.

"Do we return to camp?" I asked.

"Yes," Gloy said, "there's nothing more to do here,"

* * *

Back at camp, I awoke in the late hours of the morning and looked around for Gloy and Sacram, but I couldn't find them

"Where are Sacram and Gloy?" I asked One-hand who sat drinking coffee at the campfire.

"They left for Detfar two hours ago."

"What direction did they go?"

"That way," he said, pointing toward the west.

"Do you know Detfar?"

"Yes, but I afraid to go."

"Will you take me?"

"Much danger!"

"Will you take me there?"

"Yeah," he said furrowing his brow.

"Did the men find Kram?"

"Yeah. They snuck a red arm band to him. We told him to march on the outside of the group, and away from the observation tower."

"Good, let's go."

CHAPTER 15

The Killing Field

One Hand and I left camp and embarked on a long tedious journey through the forest. After travelling about four hours, we caught up with Sacram, Gloy, Red and the others, who were resting and having a light lunch.

“Why didn’t you wake me?” I asked, “I would have gone with you.”

"We didn't wake you because we wanted you to stay at the camp," Sacram said, "but, since you're here, you might as well join us."

We set out together through the forest. Heavy vines seemed to be everywhere as we hacked our way. The broad leafed lower vegetation was especially dense. After two hours of arduous work, Red held up his hand for us to stop. He pointed. In the distance was an encampment.

"That's Detfar," Red said, “no more hacking. Soldiers might hear.”

Smoke arose from an encampment about a mile away. We forced our way through the vegetation without cutting away the vines.

* * *

Much later, we were near a military encampment in a clearing that spread out over a wide plateau. The edge of the thick forest provided cover for us to watch a unit of soldiers involved in training activities. We were close enough to hear and see most of what was going on. We looked for a prisoner wearing a bright arm band but could see none. Two Set soldiers paced back and forth along a barbed wire fence that we thought might be a detention center. All were armed with rifles and dressed in camouflage battle fatigues. Other soldiers with camouflaged uniforms stood guard outside a stone building that looked like it might be their headquarters owing to the security outside the building. An officer wearing metal stars on his shoulders walked outside past the guards toward a group of men wearing red uniforms. He was a large man with determined steps. He was followed by a group of junior officers. As he approached the detention center, the guards snapped to attention and saluted.

"Line up in five columns!" The general ordered. They quickly organized themselves and lined up as directed. The commander stiffened and shouted.

"All right, listen up. You are members of the Armed forces of Setopia. You belong to the state of Setopia. You are soldiers, and I expect you to fight like soldiers! I'm going to turn you into soldiers if I have to break you to do it!" The men stiffened as they heard these words. Their bodies were lean, young and fit. A slight smile appeared on the face of the general. "You're the finest soldiers I have ever seen. You've received days of intensive Training. You're now ready to be sent to the front where you will fight like real soldiers."

"What's a front?" Asked one of the young men. The general walked up to the man and stood face to face.

"Your duty is to do as instructed, not to ask questions," he shouted, "Is that understood?"

"Yeah," the inductee said.

"What did you say?" Barked the commander.

"Yeah"

"What?"

"Yes?" stated the inductee.

"The word is *'Yes Sir'* when speaking to a officer."

"Yes sir."

"I can't hear you."

"Yes sir," said the young man somewhat louder.

"I still can't hear you!"

This time the inductee shouted as loud as he could."Yes Sir!"

"Better! Much better! I'll make a soldier out of you yet!"

"The camp is designed to destroy the will of the young men," Sacram whispered to me. "They have no choice but to follow orders. The promise of being pulled from their poverty and placed in good jobs after their military servicc appcals to these young men. They are told they have enemies, but they never knew they had enemies, other than the Set soldiers, until now."

"How do they program them?"

"They are deprived of sleep and food during training. Then, they are divided into training groups and told anyone wearing a blue uniform is an enemy and to kill the enemy, or the enemy will kill them. Then, on the other side of the Detfar area is a similar camp where they are trained to kill anyone wearing a red uniform. They are all from Seval."

"That's crazy!" I said.

"That's not all," Sacram said, "the recruits on this side are shown pictures of their enemies. Always the enemy is wearing a blue uniform and has a fiendish smile. Often there is a caption on the pictures reading: *Die blue devils, Death to the blue dogs*, or simply *Kill! Kill! Kill!* Men in the camp on the other side of the hill are shown similar photos, but the enemy is dressed in a red uniform."

"How do you know all this," I asked? Sacram shrugged.

"It comes with government service. You learn these things."

“What else goes on in Detfar?”

"Every day the soldiers are taken to a rifle range. There they’re shown how to fire their weapons. Each man is assigned a weapon and instructed in its use. When the commander feels they’ve had enough training, the recruits are sent to the front."

“I been there,” Red said, as an aside, “I escaped to the forest during the march. I watched the battle, and saw many friends die.” As he spoke, a cell captain appeared from out of the forest.

“Kram is on the other side of Detfar,” said the cell captain.

“Did you see him?” Sacram asked.

“Yeah, he’s wearing the red arm band. I know Kram. It was him.”

“Let’s move out,” Sacram said. We returned to the interior of the forest, and quietly made our way to the other end of Detfar. Fortunately we did not meet any soldiers along the route. The going through the forest without hacking away the vines was difficult. By the time we reached the other side, we were exhausted. We decided to make camp a few hundred feet inside the forest. The trees tended to hide smoke from the camp fire, so we made a small fire for warmth. Luckily, Red had brought provisions, or we would have gone without food that night. We were all hungry and tired. Being able to stop and rest was pure exhilaration, and the simple act of leaning against a tree was true pleasure. One-hand broke out a bottle of home brew. We passed the bottle around and soon everyone felt in fine spirit. As soon as we had finished our meal, the old stories began. This time the stories were about Detfar.

Several of these men had gone through the training, and a few had even been involved with actual combat. They knew the screams of men dying on the battle field. The ones that survived escaped into the forest. Some had been shot at by soldiers who called them cowards and deserters as they fled the battle scene.

"I escaped Detfar," One-hand said, taking a sip from the bottle, "I lost my hand during the fighting."

"How did you escape?" I asked.

"A grenade exploded near me and blew me into that ditch on the other side. I lay there until the battle was over. When the soldiers leave, I escape."

"The Set officers devise battlefield maneuvers," Gloy said. "To them, it's like a game of chess. Knowing men's lives are at stake makes their game all the more enjoyable. After all, that is the purpose of Detfar."

“What is the purpose?” I asked.

“To get rid of people in Seval who are intelligent and rebellious, trouble makers to the Sets,” Sacram said.”

“We have many Seval who were trained in combat at Detfar,” Gloy said. “After they escaped, they met up with others in the forest and returned to the battlefield to collect weapons. In time, they amassed a sizeable arsenal. Ordinarily these men would have been killed, but they were able to survive. Their instincts for self preservation were greater than their indoctrination. After escaping the battlefield, they could not return to Seval because they would be arrested and executed. Therefore, they remained in the forest. Many of them became adept at survival and learned to live by their Wits.”

“Gloy, these men are fine soldiers.” I said.

“I organized these men,” Gloy said,”because their skills are indispensible. Living in the forest gave them time to think, a rare luxury for a Seval. In the village they were not allowed that luxury. All their thinking was done for them by the soldiers. Many were punished for using their intelligence while at work in the factories. All my men endured brutalities by the Sets. Now, they are ready to fight back.”

"Our first task is to rescue Kram," Sacram said. "But now, it’s time to get some rest. We have a big day ahead tomorrow."

* * *

The next morning we maneuvered to the far edge of Detfar, and waited. An observation tower surrounded by glass enclosures stood three hundred feet away.

"Take these," Gloy said, taking two pairs of powerful binoculars from a backpack. He handed them to Sacram and me.

"Where did you get these?" I asked.

"One of the men stole them from a Set officer."

With them, we were able to see everything on the field. As soon as the red and blue uniformed troops were ready, a band struck up a marching tune. Troops with the red uniforms moved out first and marched up the incline toward the blue uniformed men. Though the red troops could not see the blue troops because of an incline on the hill, we could see both from our vantage point. After a slight pause, the blue uniformed men began marching. The young men on both teams stiffened with pride and fear as their steps quickened. As the men marched, we saw a man with a brightly colored arm band.

"That's Kram," Gloy said.

"How do we get to him?" Sacram asked.

"One of us has to crawl through that gully," Gloy said, pointing to a drainage area between us and the field.

"Won't he be seen?" I asked.

"No it's low enough that a person lying there won't be seen by either the soldiers or the generals looking down from their observation posts."

"I can do it," Red said.

"Okay, Red, we're counting on you," Gloy said.

Red left and crawled down the gully until he was near where the men would march past. He waited. A short time later the men marched past. When Red saw Kram, he whistled. Kram saw Red and feigned unconsciousness. He dropped to the ground, and rolled into the gulley. Red and Kram lay in the ditch until the entire squad had marched past. Then, they crawled along the grassy gulley and back into the forest to rejoin us.

With each passing moment the blue and red troops grew nearer to each other. Their rifles glistened in the sunlight, as a marching band played on. The troops marched in time with the beat of the drums. They were smiling, seemingly happy to have been selected to participate in the elimination of the state's enemies. They had learned their lessons well, and they knew what the enemy looked like. The enemy of the blue inductees wore red uniforms, and the enemy of the red inductees wore blue uniforms. The rules were simple. If one wearing a blue uniform saw someone wearing a red uniform, he fired to kill. Similarly, when soldiers of the blue team saw red uniforms, they fired to kill.

We watched as the general and several senior officers climbed the steps and entered the observation tower. They were visible to us because we could see them through the plate glass sitting in high-back chairs. The band increased the tempo of the beat and the troops reacted by quickening their steps. A second increase was followed by a third until the soldiers were running at full pace up the hill.

Both teams reached the summit of the hill at about the same time with their rifles leveled. Men from both sides stood still while facing each other. Their faces turned ashen and they stood quite still and merely looked at each other. Both teams seemed flabbergasted and frightened. Perhaps it was because the men wearing the enemy's uniform looked familiar. For a long moment both units stood looking at each other, then the silence was shattered by someone in the rear ranks of the red soldiers who fired shots at the blue. One young man wearing a blue uniform fell to the ground, dead. Then, gun shots rang out on both sides.

Another fellow in a red uniform stood still and ashen. He looked at the enemy. Then, he looked at a small hole in his chest. Blood flowed freely from the wound and drenched his uniform. He clutched his hand to the wound. Then he crumpled and fell dead.

Intense fighting erupted as men fell dead and dying on both sides. Some retreated back down the slope but were shot by Set soldiers as deserters. As the battle progressed, grenades were used by both sides. With each explosion, severed arms and legs flew into the air.

From the observation tower came the heartiest of laughs. The officials seemed to enjoy the battle as one enjoys a rare treat, knowing that it will not last forever. More and more young men lay dying on the crimson field of battle. The battle scene before them was as a work of art. To their eyes it was beauty. Their senses experienced artistic creation that filled their minds and their souls with musical resonances. Madrigals played to their souls as the scene before them lifted them higher and higher into ecstasy.

When there was a lull in the battle, an official gave a grenade to a very young Seval who served as his personal aide. The boy to ran up the hill to throw the grenade into the midst of the soldiers, but before he had run a hundred feet, the grenade exploded sending pieces of the boy's body into the azure skies. A leg detached from the body and the officials watched as it slowly rose until it came momentarily to rest before falling back to the ground.

The scene of the exploding grenade sent the general into a state of orgasmic enjoyment. He laughed so hard and so heartily that he was unable to catch his breath. He turned red and passed out. An aide rushed to him and gave him medical attention.

The battle raged for more than an hour and both sides suffered heavy casualties. Many grenades were lobbed down the hill by the blue side, and thrown up the hill by the red side. The grenades were the most deciding force in the battle, and they were the source of the greatest pleasure to the Set officials watching the skirmish. It didn't matter much which side won or lost. It was the sport of the thing that mattered. The only rule that existed was that no one was to walk away from the battle until all members of the opposing team had been eliminated. So, the battle raged on.

The field of battle was appalling to us. All about the field were the dead and dying young men who had served their country by killing the enemies of the state. The screams of the wounded and dying filled the air. It was as though the very gates of hell had opened and emitted a cacophony of moans and screams that made the most callous of our group cringe in fear and sadness.

Out of the gates of hell roared the sound of guns and grenades. Out came the clashing of metal and the tearing of flesh and the ecstatic cries of the officials. The ground grew more and more crimson as the battle raged onward without end. The moans of the dying and the shout's of the fighters filled the air with the most hideous of sounds. Still the battle raged, and the longer it raged, the more intense it became. The greater the number of men who fell dead and dying, the more intense was the fighting. Each young man knew that if they didn't fight with savagery, he would not live long. Each man fought for his life. The closer each felt the presence of death, the more dearly he wished to live. In the end, all but a few had been slain. When the battle finally ended, only two red uniformed soldiers were left standing. On both sides of the hill lay the dead and wounded. The ground bore stains of battle. Black pot holes from the grenades stood side by side with red stains of blood. The two remaining inductees waved to the general sitting safely behind the bullet proof glass. The official who had given the grenade to the young soldier, descended from the observation tower and walked up to the two men.

"You all did a great job," he said. The inductees looked at each other and smiled,

"They think they now have positions within management in Latipac," Sacram whispered. "It's a promise made to the soldiers if only they killed the enemies of the state. Oh no!"

The officer pulled a pistol from his holster and fired shots point blank at the two inductees who stood momentarily puzzled before they fell dead. Then he erupted with laughter. His laughter was contagious for all the others also joined the laughter that came in orgasmic waves that swept over the battlefield, over the dead and dying. In time the laughter died away, as the officials walked away from the field of battle.

"Did you see that red haired Sev catch the grenade?" Laughed one of the officials.

"Wow! Boom! Hair, blood, guts. Wow! Great!" Said another officer with great excitement. "Did you see the expression on that guy's face when he caught a bullet in the forehead? He just stood there dazed as the blood ran out in a little stream. Fantastic!"

Their conversations faded as they walked away until they were inaudible. We watched the hill in awed silence. None of us spoke. We were horrified by what we had seen. The whole terrifying sequence of events left us nauseated. Before us lay the senseless destruction of countless young men whose only crime had been to be born poor in the village of Seval. These people had no representation in Latipac, and they were sent to Detfar whenever the population became too large. We had seen no deserters. The techniques of mental persuasion were very effective.

"These young men thought they were improving the conditions for their friends, relatives and fellow citizens," Sacram said. "The Sets told them by ridding their nation of enemies they could live in peace and harmony. They were lied to. They were told that the Sets would make their lives better for them and their families if only they would rid the nation of their dreaded enemies. The officials had told them their enemy would rape their mothers and sisters and kill their fathers. The only enemy those young men had were the Set soldiers who instructed them in the tactics of battle and in the use of weapons."

We remained silent for a long time after the officers left the area. We stared at the bodies of the young men who only minutes before bad been youthful and full of life. Now they were carrion for the buzzards that circled in the sky above. We left the forest and examined the fallen men for signs of life. We found only one man who had survived. He had a severe shoulder wound. We couldn't stand to see the bodies being torn apart by the buzzards, so we dug a large trench just inside the forest and made a mass burial. Gloy said a brief prayer. There was nothing more that we could do. Kram had tears in his eyes for his lost comrades.

We carried the wounded man away from Detfar. Our progress through the forest was hampered because the man's wound seemed to open and pour forth blood with each step. We didn't think he would make the journey because of massive hemorrhaging. Only half a mile into the forest he was pale from lack of blood. Red made a poultice from the roots of a local plant and applied it to the wound. It stopped the flow of blood and we were able to continue.

* * *

We finally reached camp late that evening. The inductee was nearly dead, but we gave him what medical care we could. Exhausted, I sat down by the campfire. Guinn was nearby and sat down next to me.

“What was it like?” Gwinn asked.

“Gruesome!”

“All my life, I’ve heard tales of Detfar, but, fortunately, I have never been there.”

“It’s not something you ever want to see. Young men destroyed because they grew up in Seval.”

“That’s what happens if you’re a Sev.”

“I don’t understand. Why do the Sets hate the people of Seval?

“It’s always been that way.”

“What was it like growing up in Seval?" I asked.

"When I was young,” Gwinn said, “my parents, like many parents in Seval, tried to hide the vulgar realities of life from me as much as possible. This delayed the inevitable warping of the spirit and the darkness of the soul that comes from a lack of hope. That's what destroyed many of my friends who saw about them only futility. In time they developed a fatalistic outlook. They felt that they were hopelessly enslaved. They knew only oppression. Reading and writing was discouraged. Many of my friends never made an attempt to learn to read or write because it required a sense of hope and optimism."

"Everyone was like that?"

"Yes, many," She continued, "I had two friends who were very bright and optimistic, but, they lacked hope, so there was no need for making plans for the future because such activities would be senseless. A Seval grabs all the pleasures he can when available. That philosophy has caused many pregnancies in young Seval girls. Throughout their lives, my people face one problem after another. Eventually, they usually end up with a mental illness."

“Everyone in Seval becomes mentally ill?” I asked.

"Not all. Some rise above it. Idealism and dedication to a dream forces them onward even though they face oppressive odds. Many of them were punished by the Sets for their ideals. Some were forced from the payrolls of the factories as retribution for their spirited minds. That is the Set way of breaking an individual. Either a Seval works for the Sets or he goes hungry, or is forced to beg for food on the streets. Fortunately, enough of those spirited Sevals got together and began organizing. They took care of themselves and soon had food processing organizations. They formed secret farms in the forest to provide for those who are dropped from the payrolls. In the old days, before the organization, those who lost their jobs went through a series of events: First they lost their jobs. Then, when their meager savings were gone, they were forced to rely on friends and relatives. In a short time these bonds were weakened by the necessity of the relatives and friends having to fend for their own families. In time these bonds were broken and the unemployed were officially considered outcasts not only by the Sets who wanted to break them, but by their own villagers who saw them as *bums, undesirables and lazy no goods*."

We stopped talking and listened to the insects of the forest, each making its own characteristic noise. The crickets were perhaps the more dominant noise maker closely followed by birds and frogs. The air carried a heavy scent of pine trees and fresh flowers. The whole environment was effulgent with the scents of newly emerging flowers. The sounds of the night were comforting, even though many were strange to my ears. I don't know how long we listened to the forest sounds. Finally, we decided to get some sleep. Gwinn returned to her tent and I to mine.

CHAPTER 16

Headquarters

The next morning we got up early. After breakfast, Gwinn returned to the village. Sacram, Red and I set out for our newly established camp to train those who escaped Detfar. It was very hot and muggy and Red suggested a diversion.

"A water fall near here," Red said, "we cool down."

"How far is it?" Sacram asked.

"Not far."

"A swim would feel great," I said, "so hot today!"

The water fall was majestic and high though it wasn't very wide. The clear swift water bubbled as it gushed past boulders that stood as granite fangs in the water. We had worn shorts because of the heat and we decided to take a plunge. The icy water came directly from snowmelt high in the mountains. We splashed in the water like children and threw water at each other in the basin that had been dug out by centuries of water cascading from the falls. After we tired of swimming, we sat on rocks along the bank.

"Come," Red said, "want to show you what I found."

We followed him along a path that led us behind the waterfall. There, behind the falls was a cavern that extended into the mountain.

"What's back there?" I asked.

"Don't know," Red said.

We went only a few feet into the cavern, owing to a lack of light.

"We need a light," Sacram said.

"I know how to make one," Red said. He left and soon returned with some cattail like weeds that he had soaked in surface tar from a pit not far away where the tar rose to the surface in viscous bubbles. We found a piece of flint and struck it against a hunting knife. With the sparks and a little kindling, we started a small fire. When the kindling was ablaze, we lit one of the torches and returned to the cavern to explore the interior. The cavern was huge. The first room was large and multicolored with a substance resembling mother of pearl. The iridescent walls changed color each time we moved the torch. It was enchanting. As we talked, our voices echoed throughout the chambers. When our first torch burned out, we lit a second.

We continued our investigation into a second chamber that contained a large hole toward the center of the room. We approached the edge with great caution.

"Careful," Red warned, "edges might give way with the weight of a man." We crawled to the mouth of the abyss in order to disperse our weight over as large an area as possible. Our light shown only part of the way down.

Red found a small stone and tossed it into the abyss. We listened for the sound at the stone striking the bottom, but heard nothing. He threw a second stone into the abyss. Again, no sound came from the stone as it fell into the pit. “See, no bottom,” Red said.

We crawled back from the chasm and went into another chamber. Charcoal from a fire, and drawings on the walls gave evidence of former occupants. A small ray of Light entered the chamber from a hole in the ceiling that must have served as a chimney. Scattered about the room were primitive implements, such as flint arrowheads of various size and shapes. We also found stone hammers and a hatchet, perhaps for chopping wood.

"This was probably used by a local tribe many thousands of years ago,” Sacram said. “Our scholars in Seraphs will be interested in exploring this cavern. There might be things buried beneath the floor."

Inspired by the promise of further discovery, we walked further into the network of caverns. The next room was much like the first, but this room had no doubt been the store room because there were crude stone vats that contained the powdered remains of what were probably native grains. The room seemed to have been untouched for centuries.

I felt a tinge of excitement with the knowledge that we three were probably the first people to have entered the cave since the original inhabitants died thousands of years ago. I walked through the room and tripped over something. Red brought the torch and, to my astonishment, I discovered that I had tripped upon a femur sticking up from the floor. We didn't bother unearthing the remains. Instead we explored further into the caverns.

"We could use these caverns as our headquarters," Gloy said, “this would make an excellent well hidden camp. We could store munitions here, safe from the soldiers."

We left the cavern and went back under the falls. Then, we continued our trek into the forest. After walking several hours through heavy underbrush, we arrived at the training camp. Kram was instructing men in tactics of hand to hand combat. When he saw us, he turned the training over to another man, and walked over to us.

"You're doing a fine job,” Gloy said.

"We do the best we can," Kram said

“What do you call your unit?" Sacram asked.

"The Eagles," Kram beamed broadly.

“Why the Eagles?"

"The Eagle represents freedom," Kram said. "We created a shoulder patch to wear on our uniforms." He turned sideways and pointed to a patch on his uniform of an eagle with bolts of lightning in its talons.

"Let me demonstrate some of our combat skills," Kram said. He led us to some wooden benches made of split logs. "Sit here."

"Kram seems in high spirits," Sacram said,

"Attention," Kram shouted, "Alpha team over here on the double." A group of soldiers ran to him. Then stopped in front of us and squared into columns of four. They put their right arms on the soldier nearest them in order to get a uniform spacing, and then stood rigidly at attention.

"Combat teams!" He shouted. The men divided into teams of two each and conducted hand to hand combat. They did so with great proficiency.

"Attach your bayonets!" He yelled. Every other man produced a bayonet, and attached it to a rifle. They then threaten the other team member with a bayoneted rifle. Each man with a rifle was immediately disarmed and thrown to the ground with a heavy thump.

"My men are in good shape," Kram said, "hitting the ground like that doesn't hurt them. The time these men spent in the forest after escaping Detfar toughened them to take the punishment of hand to hand combat."

The combat display was impressive. The more we saw, the more confident we felt of our success. The men were well ordered and effective. After the demonstration, we went into a tent erected near the training grounds. Sacram handed Kram some documents.

"What's this," Kram asked.

"It's a map of the Fuchsia Palace, and the layout of the city of Latipac.

He looked at the maps. "What are these red markings?"

"They're secret passageways,"Sacram replied. "The maps will help familiarize you with the Palace."

"Thanks," Kram said, "my men will need these."

I left Sacram and Kram discussing details of the assault, and stepped out of the tent. Several soldiers were huddled nearby talking and smoking pipes.

"Join us," said one of the men. "Would you like to play?"

"What are you playing?" I asked.

"Mumble-peg," he replied. It was a game played with a knife. The object was to go through a succession of separately sticking each of the three knife blades into the soft ground from various positions on the body.

"I'm not very good at such games," I confessed, "but I will give it a try."

After a few attempts, I got the point of the game, rather it got me since one of the positions was to place the point of the knife blade against the wrist of the left hand while the right index finger is placed upon the top of the knife. The knife is held upright and the object is to flip the knife using both the wrist and finger and successfully stick the blade into the ground so that it will remain upright.

I must have put too much pressure against the knife for the blade penetrated my skin and left a small trickle of blood. Furthermore, it did not stick upright in the soil. One soldier went through all ten positions successfully and thus won the admiration of the others, myself included.

They were a very congenial group, and I felt at ease with them. Each man had a story to tell. One young soldier named Val was quite vivid in his descriptions of his time at Detfar. He had a strong sense of self-preservation and a keen intellect that permitted him to see through the sham of the training sessions. He fled from the field of battle at an opportune moment and survived.

"Did you know about the ravine along the field?" I asked, "that is how we rescued Kram."

He looked surprised and added: "Yes that's how I got away. I looked for a way to escape before the battle. I saw the ditch as we were going up the hill and decided that it looked deep enough to hide me. Since the soldiers were in the rear and I was in the middle and on the outside of my group, I dove into the ditch and lay flat on my stomach while the others marched on. It really didn't matter if I was caught or not, because I knew I would be killed either way, so I had nothing to lose. I lay there for about an hour while the battle raged. I did not dare stir for fear I might be spotted. After the sounds of battle ended, and the laughter of the soldiers died out, I crawled to the edge of the ravine and looked out at the battleground. I did not see any soldiers, so I crawled into the forest. I waited until dark. Then I returned and went to each of the bodies, but found no one alive. I grabbed several rifles and as much ammunition as I could carry and returned to the forest. My first night was rough because I was not used to living in the forest. Without a large knife to cut my way through the foliage, the going was very slow. It was about three weeks before I finally met up with others, like myself who had fled Detfar. There were initially five of us. Eventually, other men escaping Detfar stumbled into camp and joined us until there were about three hundred of us. We couldn't return to the village because we would be shot or returned to Detfar."

“You’re very articulate,” I said, “I thought everyone in Seval had limited vocabularies.”

“We had a lot of time in the forest and so we taught each other how to speak like the Sets. We figured we had to be able to understand them to beat them.”

He had just finished his story when I looked up and saw Sacram waving for me to join them in the commander’s tent. I got up and returned to the tent.

"Have you had any military training?" Kram asked.

"Yes,” I said, “but that was many years ago when I was young."

“We need men with military training to join us in the assault on Latipac,”

"Me?" I was stunned and had never considered such an undertakıng.

Kram laughed and said “Yes, you. Will you join us?"

I looked at Sacram hoping that he would shake his head and that would end the matter, but he did not give any indication whether I should commit.

"It's your decision," Sacram said.

“How can I help?"

"You've been in the Fuchsia Palace."

"Yes. I was there once."

"We have never been in Latipac, nor the Palace," Kram said, "you can us help plan the assault."

"All I know about the Palace I can tell you in five minutes," I replied.

"We need someone who can brief our men."

"But Sacram knows the Palace much better than me."

"Sacram is needed in Seval," Kram said, "at least you've been there and know the general layout."

"Yes," I replied "I will do what I can to help."

"Good!"

I shook hands with Kram as a show of acceptance, then Sacram and I left.

* * *

When we arrived back at our camp, it was in ruins. The tents had been burned and were still smoldering. Our documents lay strewn upon the ground. Utensils were bent and thrown around the camp. Our Mule driver, One-hand, came out of the forest. He had been stabbed in the arm. Blood stained his garments. We rushed to him, but he could only grunt one word, "Sets!!!"

"What happened?" We asked.

"The soldiers were here?" Sacram asked in disbelief. One-hand made a slight nod of his head to say, yes.

"How many of our men were in camp when they came?" I asked, alarmed that they had captured Gwinn. He looked at me and raised two fingers.

"Only two?" I asked.

He nodded and pointed across the camp and in a strained voice said "there." We rushed to the area to which he pointed.

"It's Gimpy," I called out to Sacram."He's dead. He's been mutilated by the soldiers."

"Let's bandage your arm," I said. We retrieved a first aid kit that lay outside one of the burned tents and bandaged One-hand's arm. Gloy and Gwinn walked into camp and stared in amazement at the destruction.

"They were looking for you, Sacram," One-hand said.

"Me?"

"Yes, "Gloy said, "Orders came from Latipac. They have a warrant for your arrest. They must have sent soldiers into the forest looking for you."

"How much do they know?" Sacram asked

"Hard to say," Guinn said.

"This changes things," Gloy said. "We must know if they're aware of our plans."

"How do we know what they found out?" Gwinn asked.

Gloy slowly shook his head. "We can't answer that question until they begin making arrests. Then it will be too late."

"Perhaps not," Sacram replied pointing in the direction of the falls, “We can use the cavern as our headquarters. It’s hidden by the waterfall. We’ll be safe there."

"We need another location, that's for sure." Gloy replied He picked up a bundle of papers and read some of them.

"The soldiers were too stupid to read these papers," he said. "If they had they would know every detail of our organization. Instead they only threw the papers upon the ground. Their stupidity may be our salvation.”

* * *

After burying Gimpy, we searched for more of the papers. Some papers had blow deep into the forest, but we retrieved them as best we could. Gloy, Sacram, and I bundled the papers and departed for the waterfalls.

"Not good," Gloy replied when he saw the passageway under the falls. "We can't have our people going around wet. The soldiers will grow suspicious."

He looked at the top of the falls. "Up there," Gloy said pointing. "If we could divert the flow of the water, perhaps we could enter from one side without getting wet." So, we hiked to the top of the falls and examined the area.

"That boulder," Gloy said, pointing to a large rock lying adjacent to the stream. "Let’s see if we can roll it to the edge of the stream just before the waterfall starts.”

We pushed against the large rock. After several attempts it moved. It splashed us with water as it fell into the stream. We wadded into the stream and wrestled the boulder until we got it to one side of the stream. By placing several smaller rocks near it, we were able to divert the stream flow. We walked to the base of the falls and were pleased with the results. The fall had been diverted toward the center by about one foot. That one foot and a natural crevice behind the fall enabled us to enter the cavern without getting drenched. Pleased with our success, Red lit a torch and led our way back into the cavern.

"The third cavern will do for our headquarters. I especially like the bottomless pit," Gloy said. "With our quarters between the pit and the entrance it would serve well as a defense in the event Set soldiers enter the cavern. If they rush us, many of them will fall into the pit. That could prove to be a natural defense."

"How about the lighting?" I asked.

"We have luminescent lights stored in the mountains near Seraphs," Gloy said. "I'll send someone to fetch them. They will provide good light, but first, we need to make this place habitable with some furniture. Everyone scout around and find things that can serve as benches and tables."

We returned to our previous camp, and gathered pots, pans and utensils, as well as shovels and an ax and brought them back to the waterfall. We split several logs and took turns shaping them with our ax. After a long arduous afternoon, we had constructed benches and a table.

* * *

Later, that night Gloy's aide returned carrying a sack of luminescent lights.

"They work like this," Gloy said, breaking a small vial and pouring its contents into a chamber. Immediately the glass cylinder lit with a bright light. He did the same with other vials and soon our cavern chamber was brightly lit. The luminescent light was soft, and provided welcome relief from the flickering light of the torches.

We stationed one man near the entrance and another person near the pit so as to instruct newly arriving members not to walk too close. The luminescent lights highlighted the natural beauty of the cavern. The iridescent minerals in the walls and ceilings created a beautiful multicolor kaleidoscope that changed colors as we walked about the cavern. We hung a large rug near the entrance so as to keep our lights from being seen by anyone outside.

* * *

Later that day, we left for the village to attend a meeting. When we descended the wooden ladder into the cavern beneath Seval, the room was lit with the same luminescent lights. When most members were present, Gloy arose and clapped two flat pieces of wood together. The talking stopped and the room grew quiet.

"I am surprised by the numerous complaints we've received," Gloy said. "Our Cell captains say the townspeople are frightened, and don't want to risk what little they have. Making our movement broad-based is the key to our success. The Strike cannot succeed unless every man, woman, and child gives his or her support."

"Some people want no part of the revolution," said a small man with a scruffy red beard. "They say if the resistance is successful, then they will join."

"So," Gloy said, "the people of Seval want all the good things from the resistance without risking their own safety. They want freedom, but only at the expense of someone else's life. They want freedom, but only if someone else brings it to them. That attitude is unacceptable!" Gloy's face was drawn and perplexed. He stroked his beard. "I suggest you become better salesmen and be more convincing."

"They won't listen to us," said a thin older man.

"Wait!" Nod said as he arose to Gloy's defense. "All I've heard here tonight is negative. If we allow ourselves to continue like this, we'll fail for sure. We didn't come here to listen to reasons why we will fail. We have a very important mission to gain the political freedom of every man, woman and child in

Seval. We won’t gain independence easily. There will be many obstacles. It will take courage and perseverance. The ones not joining us should know that they will be in greater danger if they do not help us."

"Broad based support! That is the key!" Gloy shouted. “We must gain broad support or the movement will fail. We must show the soldiers and the Sets that we have strength and unity!"

* * *

After the meeting adjourned, we returned to our new headquarters. A fire was burning in a ring of stones arranged into a small fireplace. A small vent hole in the roof of the cavern took smoke from the fire out of the cavern. The cavern air was cold, so the warmth of the fire was pleasant. Someone had made coffee. I got a cup and sat down to drink the warm brew.

“I’m afraid,” said a young man with thin blond hair as he sipped his coffee.

"We’re all afraid," Sacram said. "No one stops being afraid of death. Fear is natural. It's what keeps people alert. Fear saves lives. Bravery can kill."

"Good coffee," Gloy said as he joined us.

“Tell me, Gloy,” I said, “when did you get the idea to revolt against Anil?”

"There are times when an idea is born,” Gloy said. “It’s at such times that revolution occurs. What has happened in the past was necessary because the Forces of the Universe willed it so. When you understand the unity of all things, then you will understand why I formed the resistance."

As he continued talking, I was impressed with the depth and the fluency of his thoughts, and I sometimes found it difficult to keep up with him. But, we were a happy lot, us rebels, during that night as we sat around the fire. Gloy told of the many insights he had obtained through meditation while high in the mountains. After talking with Gloy for a long time, I grew tired and turned in. My bed was made of fern fronds that grew near the falls. Though the fronds were somewhat stiff by themselves, when enough of them were piled on top of each other they proved to be remarkably soft.

CHAPTER 17

Preparations

The next morning, I bid the others good bye and left with a fellow named Trent who served as my guide. He was a young man from the village and an affable chap, though he had a slight limp from an accident in one of the factories that caused him to tire easily. We rested often as we walked to the combat training ground. After a long and arduous hike through the forest, we finally arrived and were met by Kram. He greeted us with a handshake and a toothy smile.

“Ready to begin your training?"

"Ready as ever," I replied.

"Gloy wants you to lead a squadron. That’s why he wants you training with us.”

“Is that necessary?” I asked.

“Yes,” he replied.

"I thought my job was to show the layout of the Palace."

"Look," he said, "once we're in Latipac, we're going to encounter fighting. The soldiers in Latipac are well trained. You'll have a better chance of survival by training with us."

Kram lead me onto the field and introduced me to some of the soldiers. I recognized one of the soldiers, a skinny man named Mot. I had met him on my last visit to the field. I watched others on the field practicing hand to hand combat. I was impressed by these soldiers. They were a rare breed, an elite group. Their training reminded me of the training I had with the Marines. Their willingness to fight for what they believed came from years of deprived conditions that hardened them and made them fit for battle.

"Here's your rifle," Kram said. He handed me the weapon.

"Are you ready to get started?"

"Yes, of course."

My first hour was on the rifle range. We posted targets against trees near the field. The range sessions were broken up into slow and rapid fire sessions. During the slow fire sessions, we fired at the targets at will. During the rapid fire sessions, however, we were to fire two rounds per second. The rapid fire sessions were not as accurate as the slow fire. However, rapid fire would be useful during periods of heavy fighting when we would not have time to take careful aim. The noise on the firing range left my ears ringing, and after firing several rounds in rapid succession, my upper lip bled from the recoil of the rifle.

That afternoon, we alternately ran around the field and did various forms of fitness training, such as push-ups, leg lifts and other forms of exercise.

* * *

Later, Kram pulled me aside from the others.

"I'd like for you to go with me tomorrow night," he said.

"Where?”

“Latipac,” he said. "We're going to survey the Palace and the street layout of Latipac.”

“Intelligence gathering?” I asked.

“Yep,” he said, “we need current information. The officials may have strengthened their guards and placed guns embankments around the Fuchsia Palace. It’s our job to find out exactly what is there and report back to headquarters."

"I see. Who else is going?" I asked.

“Just us,” he said, “it’s too dangerous for more than two. I want you to go with me because you’ve been in Latipac recently.”

“Are we fighting together during the assault?”

“No. I'm leading the main assault. You’re leading a flanking action.”

Kram had the characteristics of a good leader and he had

his men's respect. No one questioned him. From a distance we heard the clanging of a bell. Kram smiled and said "That's our dinner bell.'"

We walked to the mess hall and received food on our tin trays. The food was not very tasty, but it filled our empty stomachs and gave us energy. We sat in front of an open fire and warmed ourselves.

"You're been to the Setro Club, haven't you?" Kram asked.

"I was there once," I said.

"What are the Sets like?"

"They're not bad as individuals," I said. "The main problem with the Sets is their isolation from the people who bear the brunt of their decisions. They don't see the results of their actions."

"Are you telling me they know nothing about their Set soldiers and Detfar?" He asked, giving me a stern look.

"Gloy told me Detfar is more Anil's doing. It fits his style," I said.

"You're telling me our enemies are nice people!" Kram said. "They're responsible for the deaths of the people of Seval just as surely as if they had pulled the trigger themselves."

"That's the way it is."

"When I was a kid," Kram said, "I thought the Sets were

seated on top of the white clouds we saw floating above us. At least that was what we thought as children. We played games and used to imagine our Set overlords looking down on us from their airy offices and peering through the small breaks in the clouds. We used to associate the violence that occurred as being the fault only of the soldiers. It wasn't until I was much older that I realized the soldiers were only following the orders of the Sets. In time, I learned to hate not only the soldiers but the Set overlords as well. All their policies are meant to keep the poor people poor and the rich men rich. Inflation is the worst of their inventions. They can wipe out entire families with the single stroke of a pen and not feel a twinge of sorrow. Have you ever gone hungry?"

"Yes," I said."

“What is the longest period you went without food?"

“I can’t remember,” I replied.

"In Seval, from the time you're old enough to open your eyes, you’re told that you’re another person's property. Every day you see your parents and friends slowly being broken and their hair turning gray far too early, and they lose the spring and the bounce in their steps. Every day you know that you, your family, and your friends are growing weaker while the Sets live free from work and responsibility. It is the Seval who keeps the economy going by the sweat of his brow. It is the Lat who keeps the paperwork going that keeps the factories moving to keep us slaves at our work."

I sat by the fire thinking about what he had said. The fire was warm and light from our fire seemed to stretch far into the heavens. Small sparks flew from the fire and I watched them disappear into the darkness. Sap in the logs cracked and exploded, sending cinders onto the ground. At times, we were showered with an enfilade of sparks. Kram sat silent and spoke not a word.

* * *

The next morning a bugle sounded at five o'clock and woke us up. The men quickly dressed and lined up in formation of perfectly linear ranks and files. They stood rigidly at attention while Kram gave them general instructions for the day. Afterwards, he dismissed them and walked into the chow hall. Breakfast consisted of bacon, scrambled eggs, and a type of gravy with hamburger. After breakfast, I walked back to our cave headquarters.

When I arrived, Gloy and Sacram were studying a map laid out in front of them.

"How was the military training?" Sacram asked.

"Good."

"I understand you're going with Kram into Latipac?" Sacram said.

"That's right."

"How many are going?"

"Just Kram and myself," I said, "why?"

"We've received reports of Set soldiers marching toward Seraphs. We think Anil plans to take Seraphs, and station his soldiers there."

"When will they reach Seraphs?"

"In a few days," he replied, "problem is, he is not sending enough troops to Seraphs. There are still too many soldiers in Latipac."

"When the strike begins in the village, won't he send more troops to Seval?"

"Perhaps, or he might divert soldiers from Seraphs to Seval. If he does that it, we're in trouble."

"We're devising a plan that will ensure he sends most of his troops out of Latipac," Gloy said, "You and Kram are going into Latipac?"

"That's correct" I replied.

"When?"

"Tonight."

"I'd like to go with you," Gloy said.

"What!" exclaimed Sacram, "you can't go into Latipac. The Sets know your face. They will spot you in a second, and execute you."

"Nevertheless," Gloy replied, "I would like to go."

"But," exclaimed Sacram, "if you're caught."

"I understand the risks."

"You're in charge of this operation," Sacram said, "so I have nothing to say. But I do think it's unwise."

"Sometimes it's necessary to take risks."

"But the beard! No one wears a beard in Latipac. You know that!"

"Yes," replied Gloy, fingering his beard, "I wouldn't pass for one of them, would I?"

"You wouldn't get past the gate, unless you shave it off."

"I will never shave off my beard!"

"That is the only way you'll get into Latipac," replied Sacram.

"Kram told me," I began, "that more than two people will not be able to get past the soldiers."

"Yes, Perhaps I'm getting too old for such things," Gloy said, his eyes searching the floor, "more than two people would be risky. I will not go."

"Okay," Sacram said, "we need a plan to divert troops from Latipac."

"Couldn't we increase the number of troops we send into Latipac?" I asked.

"There isn't enough time to train additional men," Gloy

said.

"Hi everybody," Gwinn said as she entered the cavern. I was as surprised as everyone else to see her. She looked impish as she walked to the makeshift table. "What are you two planning?"

"Going over the strike," Sacram said, "how is your work going?"

"Everyone seems happy and energetic. We had good success at getting new members."

"Great!" Gloy said. "That's good news."

"We should get rid of the Lats as well," She said.

"Why the Lats?" Gloy responded.

"Because they keep the Sets in power."

"Young lady," Gloy began, "the Lats have their problems too. Many Lats have their lives destroyed by the Sets who hang illusions before them, as carrots on a pole before a mule, but they never reach the carrot."

"But who cares about the Lats! They're sycophants of the Sets!"

"The Lats are just as victimized by the Sets as the Seval. The only difference is in the way they are victimized. The Lats have it easier but they are used in more subtle ways."

"How can they be victimized?" Gwinn asked. "They go to their offices and are well paid for their work. That's more than I can say for us in Seval. We work at subsistence wages. When we do get a slight raise in wages, the Sets inflate prices so that our wage increases are taken away. You don't see many Lats starving, they live a good life."

"You're wrong," Sacram said, "The Lats are under an illusion that they are serving mankind by managing domas. Most of them suffer from stress."

"Oh poo," she said in a fit of anger, "I don't care what you say about them. I think Lats should be punished just like the Sets."

"They are," he said, "they are punished when they are old and look back over their lives and realize that they have done nothing in their lives but service the doma. Not only are their careers drawing to an end, but so are their lives."

"I wish my family had a chance to retire like the Lats. The only thing they have to look forward to is a bullet from a Set soldier," she said.

"One day soon your parents will be looked after and you and your friends and relatives can have long and satisfying lives," Gloy said.

"Yes, but only after a successful revolution."

"There's a problem," Sacram said. "Anil has sent a large division of troops to Seraphs. We're afraid that when the strike begins, Anil will reroute those troops here and leave too many troops in Latipac."

Got any suggestions, Gwinn?" I asked. She thought a while then said.

"Why not have two strikes?"

"Two?" Gloy asked.

"We could have one strike here in Seval, and another in Seraphs. Two simultaneous strikes would force Anil to deploy all his soldiers out of Latipac." Gloy was shocked by her comment, suddenly his face lit up

"Superb!" Gloy said "Absolutely marvelous! That is ingenious!" He turned to Sacram and said "Do you think we could organize a strike in Seraphs in time?"

"Only if the soldiers don't arrive in Sevals before we're ready," Sacram said.

"But," Gloy continued, "if they had a full scale strike on their hands when they arrive, and the Seraphians refuse to obey their orders. Then, with another strike in Seval, Anil would go crazy with rage. He doesn't have enough soldiers to arrest all those in both Seval and Seraphs. It's a brilliant suggestion."

I looked at Gwinn. She had a marvelous smile that radiated pride in her quick wit and nimble intellect. Her ideas came quickly and effortlessly.

"Gwinn's suggestion has been the best plan to date," Gloy said, "but the question remains whether enough soldiers would be deployed to Seval to leave the Palace defenses weakened enough for us to take it. Our success depends upon their overreacting."

"We must be careful," Sacram warned, "the soldiers might begin a bloody purge."

"The soldiers are cowardly as individuals," Gloy said, "especially when they are not in possession of superior strength. We'll need all the people in both villages to support the strikes, and to do that, we need a liaison between Seval and Seraphs to coordinate strike activities."

"Who might that person be?" asked Gloy. We all looked at Gloy with his long gray beard and weathered face. Gloy was the obvious choice. He was greatly respected by people in both Seval and Seraphs. In Seraphs he was looked upon as a demigod, although many there still think he is a raving mad man.

"I think you're the man, Gloy," Sacram said, "what are your thoughts?"

"It will not be difficult to convince the Seraphians," Gloy said, "they would only need to look at the base of their mountain. The very sight of Set soldiers should be sufficient."

"Gloy," asked Sacram, "do you think you can convince the Seraphians to participate in a general strike? Tell them, we need only to capture Anil and his generals. The Sets themselves are timid and will not be put up much of a fight."

“I know what to tell them,” Gloy said, “I’ve been planning this much longer than anyone here.”

"Gloy, when will you be leaving for Seraphs?" I asked.

"As soon as I pack a few things." he replied in a manner half talking to himself. He seemed puzzled as though he was thinking of many things at once.

"Would you like to go with us, Gwinn?" Gloy asked. Startled, she replied "I think I would be of more help here than in Seraphs. I don’t know the people there, and I doubt that they would listen to anything I said."

Gloy took a few steps away from the table as though in deep thought. Then, he turned abruptly. "Gwinn, find my aides and tell them to bring provisions for a trip to Seraphs."

"Okay," she replied. Then she left.

* * *

Later, she returned with two aides and a mule.

“There’s a pack mule outside loaded with provisions for your trip,” Gwinn said.

Gloy finished putting some of his papers in a leather folder and strapping it to the side of the mule. Then, he left with his aides. Sacram, Gwinn and I stood on the stones just beyond the falls and watched them as they disappeared into the forest.

"We need to meet with Nod," Sacram said

"When?” I asked.

"As soon as he gets here," Sacram said.

"What do you hope to gain from the revolution?" I asked.

Sacram looked surprised by my question,"when we have stripped Anil and the Sets of their power, then we are going to hold a free election in which everyone in Setopia will be able to cast a vote for the candidate of his or her choice."

"But there are already free elections in Latipac," Gwinn said.

"They don't have free elections, they only vote for candidates that the Sets have chosen. If there were free elections, Anil would never have gotten into power. If the people had elected him, they would have the power to remove him. Enough said?"

"Okay," she said.

"It's necessary," Sacram said, "to give the people of Setopia ownership of the resources of this country. As it now stands, one percent of the people control all the assets. The Sets are the one percent. They're the ones who control our lives and our society. The Sets created factories that pollute the environment and make the water in the streams unfit for drinking. They pollute the air of Seval and make it dangerous to breathe. They create miserable conditions in Seval and force the people to live lives of humiliation. There are many changes that need to be made in Setopia."

"We will make the changes!" Gwinn said quite proudly.

"Yes," he replied, "but we cannot change things unless the people want things changed. They also need to be on guard against losing power once we gain freedom."

"Tyrants are always ready to regain power, aren't they?" she said.

"Power hungry people will spend their entire lives waiting for a chance to gain power. That is the reason once we gain freedom we need to defend against new tyrants who arise."

"Have there been many tyrants in Setopia?" I asked.

"Too many,"Sacram said, "most tyrants are sick people. Sick people rise in society because they concentrate all their energies in the pursuit of power. Normal people use their energies over a wide range of activities. That is why top politicians are often the sickest people in the whole of Setopia. They think they're the very center of the universe and Setopia revolves around them."

"Just like Anil," she said.

"Yes, like Anil. Tyrants use *Law and Order* as an excuse to increase their power. Often they are the most lawless, and deprive people of their liberties while promising them law and order. So, shall we get on with our work?" he asked.

We returned to the cavern and began drafting details and schedules for the strike. We wrote slogans and material that we felt might help gain support from the people. After writing for three hours, my hands and brain felt numb.

"When are you to meet Kram?" Sacram asked.

"About six o'clock," I replied, "what time is it now?"

Since none of us used a watch, we were forced to walk out to the sun dial that Gloy had constructed on a large flat boulder. From the markings on the rock, we decided it was about four o'clock in the afternoon. The time for my meeting Kram was near, so I left and walked along a pathway through the lush jungle foliage. Enough people had travelled down this path that the vegetation had been beaten down, so travelling was quick and easy.

* * *

Later, I reached the military camp. Kram was out on the field instructing the men on use of various weapons. He walked toward me when he saw I had arrived.

"Where've you been?" Kram asked.

"With Sacram at headquarters."

"Come into my tent." I followed Kram. He spread some papers out on a makeshift table made of split logs.

"Gloy dropped these off on his way to Seraphs," Kram said, "Looks like we're going to get action all over Setopia. Gloy told me the Seraphians are joining us. It's about time. They've had a free ride long enough. Gloy thinks a strike on two fronts will tax the ability of the Set military.”

“What do you think?" I asked.

"We've got a chance to win this fight. Gwinn's idea to have strikes in Seraphs and Seval at the same time was brilliant. Instead of the Sets fighting a village of illiterates, they’re going have to fight highly intelligent and educated people in Seraphs. The people in Seraphs are very capable of taking over Latipac.”

"I'm glad you're confident."

"Aren't you confident about success?" Kram asked.

“I don't know." I replied.

"If you allow yourself to think that you might fail, then you lose some of your energy on negative thoughts."

"You sound like Gloy," I said.

"I learned from him” Kram replied. “The Sets tried to keep us from learning from each other. They did that by making it illegal for us to congregate in groups, and they made it illegal for a Seval to use more than six letters in a word. You might have noticed that my conversation with you has been in violation of Set law.”

"Your village has come a long way," I said.

"We've been building the resistance for more than five years. Those guys are the core of the resistance. They lived in the forest for years and survived by their wits. They are hardened survivors, and anxious to fight the Sets.”

CHAPTER 18

Reconnaissance

Next morning, Kram and I placed suits and shoes in our backpacks and set out for Latipac. The journey was long and difficult owing to the vines that grew in the pathway. After several hours, we stopped near the dirt pathway leading into Latipac.

"We can dress here," Kram said. "Hide the backpacks and clothing in those bushes over there." He pointed to a grove of bushes nearby.

We put on our suits. I found my shoes to be tight fitting because they had gotten wet from being stored near the side of the canvas tent back at camp. I assumed the leather would eventually stretch back out, but that thought didn't assuage the pain in my feet. We dressed, and set out for Latipac. Our walk through the remainder of the trip was hampered by the darkness and our lack of a portable light. We were afraid using a flashlight would give our presence away to any soldiers who might be in the area.

"How many soldiers do you think will be sent to Seraphs?" I asked.

"Don’t know. Why do you ask?"

"Curious. If a large number of soldiers are sent to Seraphs, there wouldn't be as many in Latipac."

"Don't count on that," Kram said, "Sacram says Latipac is well guarded at all times. Anil would never send enough troops from Latipac to weaken its defenses. Not unless there was an emergency.“

"Like two strikes?" Kram thought a moment, then replied. "That might do it!"

* * *

Later that night, we were on the outskirts of Latipac. The city was well lit and we could see guards patrolling the city gate. To avoid the guards, we used the old concrete storm drain that Sacram and I had used. It had rained recently, and one or two inches of water stood in the lower portion of pipe. We tried to walk on the sides of the concrete pipe, but, still we occasionally stepped into water. As a result, our shoes were wet, and our clothes were damp. After a frustrating trip through the conduit, we entered the park. We hid behind a large grouping of bushes for more than an hour.

"Our clothes are drenched!" Kram whispered with a sense of outrage. "We can't be seen like this. We'll attract attention. Our clothing is wet, and our shoes slosh with each step. Damn! I didn't plan on getting wet! We need to dry off."

"Dry off!" I exclaimed. "That will take hours."

"I know," he said with disgust. "Damn, all that planning and we ruin it all by getting wet. We could have worn fatigues and carried the suits."

"Yes, but we didn't. So, what are we going to do?"

"I don't know," he confessed. "Let's walk toward that steam rising on the other side of the park."

We walked across the park, and past several Lats. Fortunately, no one seemed to notice our wet clothing. We walked across the park to a concrete slab with a metal grill that had steam coming out of it. We stood on the grill for almost an hour. Our clothing dried very quickly although hot air from the vents nearly roasted our legs. After an hour or so, we were reasonably dry, so we left the park and walked down one of the streets.

"Do you remember the way to the Fuchsia Palace?"

I looked around and tried to get my directions. "I think it's that way," I said, pointing to where I thought the Palace was located. I wasn't certain because the buildings looked different than I remembered. We walked for several blocks and concluded that we had gone the wrong direction. We backtracked and returned to the park. As luck had it, a man and woman walked passed us and were talking about a special exhibit at the museum. We noticed the direction they were walking from and went in that direction. After walking a few blocks, the buildings looked more familiar.

"How far are we from the Palace?"

"I believe it's about ten blocks, but I'm not certain," I replied.

"Not Sure! You’re some guide!"

I looked around. I remembered the path I took from the Palace before getting to the museum entrance. After a brief walk, I recognized one building not far from us.

"It's that way," I said, pointing.

"Are you certain?"

"No, but I think that's the way."

"You're a great help!”

“Sorry.”

“We need to walk down the alleys,” Kram said. “It's safer. Not so many people to notice us."

We left the main streets and walked down an alleyway. At the end of each block, we were forced to reenter a street, cross it, and enter another alley on the opposite side. Each time we walked into the well lighted streets, we risked being seen by soldiers or by Lats who might become suspicious and report us. The buildings we walked past in the alley were old and dilapidated. I remembered Sacram telling me it was the lower ranking Lats who lived in the central city, and that many of them lived on the streets. We maintained a constant vigilance in the dark alleyways, least we fall prey to unsavory people. Kram armed himself with a small section of lead pipe that he found near an abandoned building. We did not want to use our pistols due to the loudness of the retort. I walked ahead of Kram. We hadn't gone very far into the second alley when someone came up to me.

"Money or 'ur life," he demanded.

I couldn't see the stranger very well, but there was enough light for us to see that he looked a hideous mess with torn clothing hanging loosely from his thin frame. He looked surprised when Kram caught up with me. He obviously had thought there was only one of us.

"What's the problem?" Kram asked.

"Scuse me fellas," the stranger said, after realizing that he would have to rob two people instead just me. "Ah didn't know they was two of you. You fellas scuse me and I'll be on me way."

"Hold on," Kram said sternly.

"I'm just a poor sole, ah am," he pleaded. "Ah got a wife an yungins. Please, don't hurt me." Kram grabbed him by the scruff of the neck and squeezed the stranger's neck between his powerful hands.

"Ouch," cried the man, "you're hurt'n me."

"I know I'm hurting you," Kram said with a sadistic grin. "I'm going to squeeze the life out of you." He exerted more pressure with his powerful hands. The man's eyes looked like they were going to pop out of his head. A strange gurgling noise came from deep down in his throat. Kram released him and he dropped to the ground. He lay there gasping for air. A short while later, color returned to his face.

"You boy's wouldn't kill me now, would ya?" He asked, trembling.

"I'm debating," replied Kram coolly. "I haven't killed anyone in a long time, and I'm just really anxious."

"Please," said the man, "please let me go. "

"I think I'm going to make mincemeat of him," Kram said as he winked at me.

"P-p-p-please, please don't k-k-k-kill me," he said, stuttering from freight.

"Get up!" Kram demanded. The old man arose and stood shaking.

"What would you have done to me and my friend here?"

"I won't av hurt you'un," he said.

“Indeed," stated Kram firmly.

"Ah only wanted to make his acquaintance.”

"I'm half a mind to fix you so you won't hurt anybody again," Kram said.

"No!” he pleaded, "don't hurt me. I'll help ya."

“How could you help us?" demanded Kram.

"Ah ain't been round long enough to become daffy. Ah knows you' ns wouldn’t be walking down no dark alley, if you wasn' t running from someth’n. Am I wrong?" He asked, studying us. Kram looked at him for a long moment before answering.

"How can you help us?"

"Ah was born in this here city. Born and raised here. Ah knows rna way around pretty good," he said. Kram and I looked at each other. We seemed to be thinking the same thing. Perhaps he could help us, but there was always the possibility that he would betray us if we took him into our confidence.

"There isn't any way you could help us you old alley rat,” said Kram. "You're of no use to us."

“Please,” said the old man, "I knows this city better'n ah knows rna own papa."

"You can't help us. You’re just a tattered old man."

"Yes ah can."

"Can you take us to the Palace?" I asked, feeling sorry for

the old man.

"The Palace?" He replied with a sense of awe. “What you want at the Palace?"

"Never mind what we want. Can you take us there?"

"Ah can take you there, but if'n you's do someth'n bad ah'll be in plenty trouble."

"No more than you're in right now. I could break your neck with one little squeeze of my hand," Kram said. The man backed away a few steps.

"Can you take us to the Palace?" I asked again. He thought a moment, then said, "I’ll do it if'n you's don't hurt me."

“We won’t hurt you as long as you behave," I said.

"But if you don't," Kram said, pulling his .45 caliber pistol from his holster. The man gulped as looked up the barrel of Kram’s pistol.

"Ah understands," he said with a note of resignation. He motioned for us to follow him. He took us down a network of alleyways and through abandoned buildings.

“These buildings will be excellent cover,” Kram whispered to me as we walked. Soon we were at the end of an alleyway a short distance from the Palace.

"There it is,” said the old man. "Now, if'n you' s don't mind, I'll take rna leave now."

"Hold on," Kram said as he grabbed the man's arm, "you'll

stay here with us."

"But ah show'd you's the Palace. That's what you wanted," he pleaded.

“We still need you." replied Kram in a milder tone.

"How heavily armed is the Palace?" Kram asked.

"Ah don't know cause ah can't see well," he replied, "but ah think it's guarded.”

"We're going to have to find their weakest spot," Kram said.

"Weak spot! What you'ns gonna do?" Asked the old man.

"Never mind," said Kram.

"Ah knows all about the Palace," stated the old man with pride.

“What did you say?” I demanded.

"Ah knows the Palace real well," he said with Pride.

"What are you talking about?” Kram demanded, "you’re familiar with the Palace?"

"Better’n that. Ah knows how to get in without going past the guards," he stated curtly with his arms folded across his chest. Kram and I stared at each other in amazement.

"You mean you can get into the Palace without having to go past the guards?"

"Yep,” he replied.

"Show us!" Kram demanded.

"Follow me," he said.

He turned and walked back down the alley. Kram and I stood in awe looking at each other, and then we caught up with him. We retraced some of our steps back down the alley and through one of the old buildings. Then we abruptly changed course and ended up in an old abandoned building near the Palace. One wall of the building had collapsed. Bricks were scattered across the old tiled floor. We made our way across the floor of the building, being careful not to fall through the old timbers. We descended a flight of stairs and found ourselves in the basement near a pile of rubble.

"Behind there," said the old man pointing to the bricks and rubble, "there's a passage. It goes to the chambers of the Palace."

"The torture chambers?" Kram asked.

"Yep."

"Is the tunnel open all the way?" I asked.

"Nah, it's filled with stuff at this end," he replied.

"What kind of stuff?" Kram asked, growing more and more excited about the implications of our find.

"Don't know," he replied, "bricks and stuff. We can look."

After digging through the rubble for more than an hour we cleared away enough of the bricks and concrete to expose an old metal door about six feet tall and four feet wide. With a lot of effort we were able to open the door. It made a loud screech.

“Hope no one heard that,” I said.

Inside, the tunnel smelled of dampness and mold. It had not been opened for a long time. The concrete tunnel was about seven feet high and eight feet wide. At the opposite end of the tunnel, we could see light coming through a small hole in an old wooden door.

"Ah used to come down here when ah was a kid. Ah made that hole with me knife so ah could see the soldiers.”

We climbed over some of the rubble and looked through the hole. Sure enough, we could see the cells and the guards, who appeared to be well armed. We walked back and stood at the metal door at the entrance to the tunnel.

“I wonder if Senator Denneck is in there," I whispered.

"If he is, we’ll find him,” Kram said, “but it may be difficult to find him unless we knew which cell he’s in.”

"Can you draw a diagram of what you remember about the Palace?" Kram asked.

"Yep, I can draw it on the dirt."

Kram examined the map the old man sketched out on the ground what he remembered of the basement of the Palace.

“This tunnel will provide us with an important advantage,” I said. “We can enter the Palace without having to fight our way in from the outside. Some well placed explosives next to the brick wall will create an opening for us to enter.”

“What about the old man?” I asked.

“We can’t afford to let him go,” Kram said, “he might tell his friends, and they might inform the authorities. We can’t take that chance.”

“The old man seems anxious to help us,” I said.

"What you fellas have in mind?" he asked with a twinkle in his eye.

"The less you know the better,” Kram said.

"If you fellas need me help to capture the Palace?"

“What makes you think we’re going to capture the Palace!" Kram demanded.

“Well," began the old man rubbing his weathered chin. "It just seems kind of funny that you two would go to all this trouble if’n ya weren’t.”

"You're going to have to come with us,” Kram said.

"Go with ya where?"

"Outside the city," replied Kram.

“Well,” the old man replied,“ah don 't guess I have any reason to stay here. You fellas got some food out there?"

“Sure," I said, "all you can eat!"

"Sooo, what we wait' n for?"

We closed the metal door and replaced some of the rubble to conceal the entrance to the tunnel. Then we cautiously walked back across the floor, and out into the alleyway. The old man had become attached to us and referred to us as his "*Good Luck Charms*." He kept saying that his "*Ship has come in at last*." and an assortment of odd sayings. We walked back down the alleyway, through the central park and back through the conduit leading into the forest.

"You fella' s sure know your way about the city," he said , "But you fella's don't live here, do you?"

"No, we don't," Kram replied, "I'm a Seval. My associate here is from Seraphs."

"Don't say," began the old man, "a've known a few Seval in me day. I had several old buddies from the village."

"Where did you meet a Seval?" demanded Kram.

"'Why ah used to live on the edge of the city with me folks. When ah was a kid, ah used to go into the forest. Ah meet some of the Seval out there and we became friends."

"What were their names?" demanded Kram.

"Ah don't rightly remember," replied the old man, seemingly unable to remember, which is common for someone of his age.

* * *

We humored Skeeter as we walked back through the forest. The moon had gone behind a bank of clouds and we were forced to find our way in almost pitch darkness. Our progress was slow and somewhat hazardous because we were continually tripping over vines. It was difficult to remain on the pathway because of the darkness, but several hours later we finally arrived back at the training camp, exhausted, sleepy, and hungry.

"Cook!" shouted Kram.

"Yes Sir," carne a reply

"Any food left?"

“Some beef and vegetables left over from dinner.”

"Beef and vegetables!" Exclaimed the old man in anticipation of a warm meal, "ah haven't had beef in years." He turned to Kram and asked, "when we can eat?"

“Right now," Kram replied. '

We walked across camp and picked up our utensils. The old man hadn't used utensils in a long time and he found them awkward to use. He was first to be served, and the cook dished out a sizable portion of the stew.

"That's right, keep on dipp'n," he said to the cook who put food on his plate. The cook gave him the normal helping of everything, but the old man kept saying, "that's it, mate, just keep on dipp'n."We took our food trays to a small table near the campfire. The old man didn’t say a thing. The only sounds we could get out of him were a few grunts in response to our questions.

"More beer," he said as he pounded his tin cup on the table. I took his cup over to the keg and filled it. He ate at least twice the normal amount of food that others consumed. Still he wanted more, so he returned to the cook who gave him another tray full of beef and vegetables. After consuming the second tray, he seemed content and ready to talk.

"What's your name?" I asked.

"People call me Skeeter," he said, "never had a real name.

"Well, Skeeter, how long have you lived in Latipac?" Kram asked.

"Long time," he replied. "Nobody moves out of Latipac, you know. If ya born there, ya die and ya buried there. That place is ya mama and ya coffin. Man, if ya born in the city, that's ya home."

"Do you have family?" I asked.

"Na, me mum and Dad died years ago, when ah was just a pup."

"Sorry to hear that," I said.

"Noth'n to be sorry about. Where we live people die young. Nobody lives long. Either the police gets em, or disease kills em. Ah'm an exception."

"Where do you live in Latipac?" I asked.

"Don't live nowhere. Lately, I stay near the school," he replied, picking his teeth with a sliver of wood he cut from the table. "You remember them buildings we walked past. The one's falling down? Well that' s what it's like round where I live."

"Why do you rob people?" Kram asked.

"Couldn't find another job, but ah never hurt nobody. Tried begging first. The street is cold and real mean. Once ah said to a man and his girl passing by, '*Please sir, can ya spare some change, ah'm awful hungry.'* My clothes were ragged and thin. It was cold that night ah was weak and my brain didn't work well cause ah was starving. Please sir, ah pleaded with them. They stopped and ah saw their scorn. '*You disgusting leach*! *Why should I give you any money*?' 'Please sir,' ah said again 'Cause ah'm starv'n.' '*You wretch*!' he said, '*how can you sink so low! 'Get out of our sight you leper!*' He hit me with his walking cane. Ah got away from him, ah did. Ah went into a corner and wanted to crawl up and die. Well, to make a long story short, ah just had to learn to live with them hard licks cause that's all ya get when you is down and out. Ah never wanted to steal."

"Have some more beer," Kram said, filling Skeeter's cup.

"This here is the best beer a'v ever tasted. On the streets all you could afford is *Rot Gut* beer. Bad stuff – makes me sick."

He arose, stumbled a bit and then lay on the ground mumbling. He smiled and seemed content. He said something about having entered paradise in which the fields were made of beef and vegetables, and the lakes full of beer and wine. He fell asleep on the ground. After we let him sleep for a while, Kram fetched some clothing from one of the tents, and we decided to take him to the stream to sober him up. Once we splashed him with cold water, he revived. He washed, dried off and put on khaki slacks and shirt.

"Them's the best cloths a've ever worn," he said.

"We decided to take you to our cave headquarters and introduce you to our top people," Kram said, "Sacram, will probably want to question you."

"Appreciate you fellas helping me like this," he said, "hope ah can repay ya somehow."

"Don't worry about that," Kram replied, "your information will more than pay us back."

* * *

We returned to the cave headquarters. Skeeter looked around in awe, but he nearly fell into the pit. It was only Kram's quick hand and firm grip that saved him.

"Remarkable!" exclaimed Sacram, after we told of the tunnel and how near to the interior of the Palace dungeon we had gotten.

"A small charge of explosives will clear the door," Kram said, "and our troops can enter the Palace through the basement without much fighting."

"Remarkable!" Sacram said, "We are indebted to Skeeter."

"With his help we can capture the Palace,"

"Skeeter," Sacram said, "We're going to make you an

honorary member of our organization."

Skeeter was moved to tears with Sacram's comment. "Ah don' t know what to say. It's been so long since ah was a member of anything that ah forgot what it's like. Ah finally found me a home," he said tearfully.

"Someone bring Skeeter warm coffee and food," Sacram said.

We sat around the fire and talked of what we had seen in Latipac. Skeeter agreed to assist our forces in the assault on the Palace.

"Excellent!" exclaimed Sacram. "When we succeed, we are going to make you a member of our government. We'll appoint you as a commissioner to help the street people."

"Ah don't know what to say," Skeeter said with a quick smile. "Ah sure appreciate all these things you're do'n for me."

Well, "began Sacram, "we're glad to have Skeeter on our side. Right now, we have to work out details for our meeting tomorrow night. We need coordination between the cells in Seval, Seraphs and Latipac. I've appointed Gwinn to help.

"It's important to capture Anil and the generals quickly," Kram said, "but we can't if we don't know their location inside the Palace. Who can get us that information?"

"We'll never have that kind of information," Sacram said, "Every time I've visited the Palace, the generals seem to be in different locations. We're counting on the generals remaining behind in Latipac and using their couriers to carry dispatches."

"Yep," Kram said, "while the troops are off fighting, the generals will be dining with the plutocrats. I'm going back to my camp. See you tomorrow."

* * *

The next morning a fire was burning in our makeshift fireplace and the ascending smoke disappeared through a hole in the ceiling of the cavern. Gwinn had left early and gone into the village. Sacram searched through papers lying on his make-shift desk. I sat up and rubbed my eyes.

"Good morning?" I said, somewhat groggy from lack of sleep.

"A messenger showed up this morning saying the Seraphians have pledged their support to the strike," Sacram said.

"That's good news,"

"What happened to the folio with our strike schedule?" He asked. "It was here on the table this morning."

"Haven't seen it," I replied.

"I looked through all my papers. It's not here."

"Maybe Nod picked it up," I said.

"Nod!" He said angrily. "I asked him not to take those papers into the village. If the Sets get hold of that packet of documents, it will be the end of us all!"

"I t contains names?" I asked.

"Names, dates, schedules and everything else," he said searching through the papers on his desk.

"Well," he said finally, "we need that information."

* * *

Acting upon Sacram's request, I left and headed for Seval. At the edge of the village, I paused to examine the soldiers patrolling the streets. I felt relieved there were so few soldiers. Still, I used the dusty pathways behind the main street to avoid being seen. I was walking down a small backstreet when I met Gwinn. She looked surprised.

"What are you doing here?" She asked.

"I'm looking for Nod. Have you seen him?"

"He's in one of the huts down the street."

"Sacram needs him. It's important." I said, "I don't want to walk into the wrong building,"

"I'll show you."

She took me down a dusty path that wound through a residential area of small adobe huts. After walking a few minutes, we entered a small adobe hut. Inside Nod and several cell captains were discussing something of obvious importance to them.

"Nod, Sacram needs the briefing papers," I said.

"We need the schedules here with us," he replied

"Why not copy the schedule and give me the folio," I said, "I'll wait while you make a copy."

"Okay," he shrugged, "people in the munitions factory need to know who will be coordinating the strike."

"All their names should be in the folio," I said.

"I'm afraid that we may be betrayed by some pro-set Sevals," Nod said as he sat down to copy names.

"Any of them pledge their support today?" I asked.

"Not today," Nod said. "One woman threatened to turn us in, but I convinced her that she should wait a few days. I told her if we win, there will be no one to inform on, however, if we lose, she will be no worse off. Anyway, Anil will know who started the strike, and who was involved."

"That would be the end of us," I said.

"The end of all of us," Gwinn corrected, "the soldiers will kill all of us."

After copying the information, Nod handed me the papers. Then, Gwinn and I left for headquarters.

* * *

Back at headquarters, I handed Sacram the papers. He examined them and then set them to one side of his desk. "Most of our planning is complete," he said, "Gwinn, have you finished your duties?"

"I contacted all the people I could."

"Well," he said, "there isn't much left to do, but you could draft more slogans."

"What! More slogans?" exclaimed Gwinn. "We've written so many slogans. Why do we need more?"

"We don't," he replied, "but it will occupy your time and give you something to do."

"I don't need any more work!" she said.

"Then, why not take time off and enjoy yourself."

"Great!" she said. She turned to me. "Let's walk in the forest!"

"OK," I replied.

"I know a nice place not far from here. It's my favorite."

"Sure," I replied.

"Enjoy your walk," Sacram said.

CHAPTER 19

Change Of Plans

We walked along a well beaten path toward the field where our troops were practicing. Leaving the main path, we continued down a less used path, one that hadn't been used for a long time owing to the vines covering the pathway. We walked for about an hour before we came upon a clearing covered with soft grass. It overlooked a steep cliff that terminated far below with a waterfall. We sat down on the ledge to rest and looked down at the stream.

"This is a pretty area," I said.

"Yes," she replied, "Setopia is a beautiful place." For a while we said nothing. We listened to the water rushing in the stream below us.

"Courage!" she said after a long pause, "is the one thing the intellectuals lack."

"What do you mean?"

"Intellectuals are cowards! That's how Anil got into power. How can we possibly think they will come through with acts of bravery?"

"Well, it's possible, after all," I said. "They know the soldiers are on their way to Seraphs and will treat them with brutality. It would be suicide for them to back down. They know that the Treaty of Bodiglioni is void. Anil voided it by sending troops to Seraphs."

"I've never had much respect for intellectuals," she said, "in the old days when I was growing up, my family told me of people who lived like gods high in the mountains in a fabulous village with streets of marble and buildings of gold and jewels. They told me the intellectuals could help us and save us from brutality and suffering. But they were cowards. I hated them. I used to lie awake at night knowing that they could help us, but they were afraid. I learned later that Anil, the Sets and the intellectuals in Seraphs worked as a team to keep us in poverty. They used the intellectuals and controlled them. I grew to hate all of them!"

We fell silent for a while and watched the swift white waters of the stream rush downward on its journey to the falls. We were disturbed by an eerie sound that seemed to come from high in the mountains. It sounded rather like the wailing of wind sweeping through hollow rock cliffs, or perhaps the anguish of ancient wooden ships being whipped by raw wind. We turned toward the sound, but it stopped as suddenly as it had begun.

"What was that?" Gwinn asked, startled.

"I don't know," I confessed. Then, we were jolted by a second wave of terror stricken cries.

"It's coming from Seraphs," Gwinn said. "The intellectuals must have seen the soldiers approaching the base of the mountain."

I remembered the video I had seen in Seraphs and the words of Gloy who warned of such an attack. The intellectuals chose to ignore his message and concentrate on their analyses and writings. It was these very intellectuals who were now wailing at the sight of soldiers nearing the base of the mountain.

"It will be another day before the soldiers can get up the mountain to enter Seraphs," Gwinn said, "the only way up the mountain is along a narrow trail along the face of the cliff. It'll take them a while. I hope some of them fall off the trail and die."

The next waves of sounds came more and more frequent until the skies were filled with the cries of the supermen intellectuals of Seraphs wailing at the sight of soldiers approaching the base of their home. No longer could they count on immunity from Anil and his reign of terror by producing research papers justifying the presence of Anil and the Sets.

At last they would know the taste of violence. For years they had enjoyed an unhampered existence devoid of worry. Their only duty was to research and support the most inhuman of political decisions in order to make them seem logical and fair even in the face of the great injustices they created. That had been the duty of each Seraphian to do his duty in an efficient manner, so he could return to his abstract world in Seraphs and live once more the life of the intellectual, isolated from the rest of the island. Only now the intellectuals realized they could no longer remain isolated. As we listened, the wailing grew louder and longer.

"Now they'll learn," she said with a smile, "now they'll learn what it's like to be oppressed and brutalized."

"Yes," I said sadly, "they will soon learn."

* * *

We left the grassy field that only moments before had been serene, and headed back to the headquarters. Somewhat later, we arrived. Sacram and others were outside near the falls listening to the distant wailing. The wailing came in waves that rose to a crescendo, and then fell into low lugubrious murmurs.

"Is the noise from Seraphs?" I asked Sacram.

He looked toward us and nodded. Gwinn smiled and said

"Are the brave intellectuals terrified of the soldiers?" she asked with pursed lips.

"Everyone is afraid of death," Sacram said, "when the soldiers appear, death is imminent."

"Too bad they weren't as concerned for our welfare," she

added.

"Were you concerned for their welfare?"

"Not at all! I don't care what happens to them. They sold us out!"

"I hope one day you'll lose your hatred for the intellectuals," Sacram said."They can be of help to us."

"Like they helped us when we were being beaten by the soldiers, or like they helped us when we were without food or shelter?"

"Things will be different now," Sacram said, returning to his papers.

"What are you working on?" I asked Sacram. "Looks like you've been busy, judging from the large quantity of discarded papers on the floor."

"I've been working on a speech to give after we capture the Palace."

"Do you need a speech for that?" Gwinn asked.

"Gloy will need to address the crowd."

"Yes," she said, "I suppose we do need to have a good speech ready."

Gloy and two aides entered the cave. All three looked weary. "What's wrong?" Sacram asked. Gloy grimaced and walked over to the table and sat on one of the logs we had for benches. Sacram's eyes followed him. No one said anything for a long moment. Finally Gloy took a deep breath and exhaled. "We're in trouble," he began."Anil has sent more soldiers than we counted on and the Seraphians are afraid to resist."

"I thought so!" exclaimed Gwinn. Gloy stared at her for a moment, then continued.

"We organized a small group of Seraphians to resist," Gloy said,"but most are afraid to join the strike. They think if they obey the soldiers, the troopers will go away and things will be as they were. Of course things will never be as they were. It's only wishful thinking. I've tried to convince them that if they don't resist, no one will be immune from the soldier's brutality. Already the soldiers are climbing up the cliff, and the people of Seraphs are wailing with fright, especially the women and children. Several Seraphians want to form a delegation to go into Latipac and speak with Anil about the matter. They think that fighting is for children not for grown men. They think they can solve their differences as gentlemen. They're crazy if they think they can negotiate." Gloy paused to catch his breath. "They'll be murdered before they reach Latipac. I've tried to convince them that their only alternative is to fight and to be part of the strike."

"When is the delegation to leave Latipac?" Sacram asked as he pondered the new development.

"They're talking about leaving this evening," he said, "but they will never make it to Latipac."

"Perhaps all is still not lost," Sacram said slowly "if the soldiers will remain in Seraphs when we begin our action here, we can still capture Latipac."

"But what of the strike in Seraphs?"

"A mini-strike may be sufficient to occupy the soldiers."

"We have enough members for a small strike," Gloy replied, "but the soldiers will destroy them in no time."

"The destruction of a few Seraphians may be our only salvation," Sacram said.

"A bit harsh isn't it?" Gloy asked, surprised by Sacram's statement.

"It might be necessary," Sacram replied, "we're not entering this strike from a position of strength. Strength lies with our opponents."

"Several of those Seraphians are close associates, people I have known for many years," Gloy said, gritting his teeth, "you don't think I'm going to sit by and let them be murdered do you?"

"What would you suggest?"

"If we can't have a strong resistance in Seraphs, then we should have no strike," Gloy said.

"People will die without the resistance!" Sacram said.

"I don't think they will be murdered by the soldiers if they don't resist."

"Gloy, you know very well what the soldiers will do. Face

the facts, the soldiers will murder the Seraphians as soon as they enter the village, and they will continue doing so until they are stopped! You know that!"

Gloy lowered his head. "I'm tired and angry and I say foolish things. You're right. I'm letting my emotions dominate my thinking. We must continue. I must accept that people close to me will die. That is the price we pay."

“We have a meeting in Seval and we need to get ready,” Gwinn said.

“Remind me of our schedule,” Gloy said.

“Gwinn, give Gloy our schedule,” Sacram said.

“Certainly,” she said, “The first strike will begin at the munitions factory. There will to be a fifteen minute delay between strikes at the other factories in Seval.”

“Why the munitions factory?” Gloy asked.

“Our strikes are arranged,” Gwinn said, “according to how badly the Sets need production from their factories. The most important factory produces munitions. Others produce consumer goods, and the last on the list are the food processing plants. Our schedule is devised to hurt the Sets the most while hurting the Seval the least. The Sets want a strong military even if it means destroying Setopia.”

“It’s a shame Setopia has come to this,” Sacram lamented, “we could have been a prosperous island with everyone participating in its prosperity, but that's not the way it is."

"Great power leaves people at the top feeling powerless and threatened from all sides," Gloy said, "the Sets can continually build their military, but they cannot defeat truth and equality no matter how mighty their armies or how great their wealth. Anil caters to the insecurities of the Sets who continually feel threatened by change. Sets feel impotent in the face of change. They spend many hours in conference plotting strategy to rid their society of radicals who bring change with ideas that threaten their positions. The Sets don't realize that change is inevitable. They have the military and will use it to fight us. They can brutalize a few of the villagers, but they dare not brutalize too many because we will attack the soldiers. The soldiers had been briefed about the irrational nature of the villagers, and they know the people of Seval will became like wounded animals if attacked. If the people of Seval no longer fear the soldiers, they will lose the one tool they rely on."

"And they became fearful themselves," Sacram said.

"Yes. Then the soldiers themselves become fearful."

* * *

Later, Nod came charging into the headquarters in a fit of anger.

"What's wrong?" Sacram asked.

"One of the cell captains wants total command," Nod said,

"he tried using authoritarian rule within his cell and started a minor uprising."

"We have enough problems without personality conflicts," Sacram said pounding the table. "Remove that captain and place him under guard until the strike begins least he give away our plans in a fit of anger. Here, take these papers to the meeting tonight."

Nod took the papers and left for the meeting. I returned to my work and stuffed a large sheaf of propaganda papers into a portfolio, the corners of which were frayed and threatening to split under the strain of papers.

"We have little more than spirit to keep us going," Gloy mused, "many of the men are joyful and conduct themselves as though we were about to embark on a venture into a fantasy land in which they are ensured of victory. Confronting the powerful Sets will inevitably lead to violence."

"Yes," Sacram said," but we are sworn to keep violence to a minimum."

"What about the people of Seraphs?" Gloy asked.

"We originally excluded Seraphs," Sacram said, "because they think exclusively of themselves as men of contemplation and men of the intellectual life. They don't care to soil their lofty ideals with reality. They care little for the average Seval who can neither speak nor understand their language. They think the Seval language is primitive, and only used by inferior minds."

"True," Gloy said, "but despite this prejudice, the Seraphians opened their doors to the most intelligent of the Seval with their exchange programs."

"Most of the Sevals in Seraphs," Gloy said, "are only used for research projects or for clerical duties that allow the more senior Seraphians to concentrate on more important things, such as justifying Set policy. *Facts are to be interpreted, and figures can be changed,* is a favorite saying of many an intellectual in Seraphs."

"That expression found frequent expression in Latipac as well," Sacram replied.

"Shall we go to the meeting?" Gwinn asked, "it's late."

* * *

We left headquarters and walked to Seval, taking our time walking through the forest. We entered the underground meeting place, and found many more Seval present than we had anticipated. Gloy descended the wooden ladder and walked to a small pedestal that had been erected for him near the campfire in the center of the room. Sacram walked closely behind carrying a folio of papers. As Gloy mounted the pedestal, the room grew quiet. He briefly looked over the crowd.

"Glad to see everyone," Gloy began, "we have many things to discuss, and I'm certain many of you have things you would like to discuss before tomorrow's strike. Each of' us will face danger from the soldiers, but you must all remember that we are fighting for justice and equality, and for the freedom of Setopia. The strike will begin with Nod's cell in the munitions factory and will progress in accordance with our schedule. "

Gloy paused as the cell captains read the pamphlets that Nod handed out. After everyone had read the information, Gloy continued."As you know, we brought the Seraphians into our strike because we felt they could help us. Anil sent a large number of soldiers to Seraphs. The people there are terrified of the approaching soldiers. We thought it would be a day or two before the soldiers arrived, but they are now making their way up the mountain to Seraphs. We're hoping that the few resistance members we have in Seraphs will keep the soldiers busy until our strike begins tomorrow. I don't think the soldiers will attack when they are aware of our strength. Although the situation in Seraphs is critical, I don't feel that it will make that much difference with our campaign. We will proceed as planned. Kram and his men are ready for the initial assault on Latipac. He trained his men with efficiency and skill. We owe him our gratitude. He formed a first-rate outfit in a surprisingly short period of time. Now that is out of the way, I will be glad to answer any questions." Gloy looked around the group for anyone wanting to be recognized. Most of them remained silent, but Nod raised his hand.

“Yes, Nod.”

"Communicating with other cells will be a problem because after the strike begins, the soldiers will not allow anyone to enter or leave the factory. Trying to find out what is happening in the other factories will be impossible. The soldiers will no doubt seal off the munitions factory, and then the other factories.”

"You’re correct,” Gloy replied, “that is the reason following the schedule will be so important. We spent a lot of time and thought designing the schedule and it will save many lives, if it is followed. After the munitions strike the soldiers will learn of a second strike, then a third, then a forth, and so on until they are uncertain what is going on and are afraid to act without reinforcements from Latipac. They will request more soldiers. That will clear the way for our offensive in Latipac. I have assigned several people to act as liaison. These people will be identified by a red and white arm band. If you are in trouble and need assistance, speak with the people with an arm band. Tell them your problem and they will put you in contact with the appropriate people. For the cell captains, if you have problems, do not come to the command post. The soldiers will have lookouts and scouts and they will follow you. Those chosen as liaisons know how to find their way through the forest without using the paths. They can lose any soldiers that might be following them. Sacram and I will remain at headquarters and will be available to give instructions and receive messages from the various strike sites."

He paused a moment as a messenger whispered something to him. Then he continued addressing the group. "I've just been informed that the soldiers have entered the village of Seraphs. I realize that many of you do not like the Seraphians. We must remember that, all of us are in this together, and what happens in Seraphs will affect us here. The messenger informed me that many of the uncommitted intellectuals have now joined the resistance and are engaging in sit-down strikes. I've been told the soldiers have not acted against these resistors yet. That is good. It means they don't know how to handle the situation and are indecisive."

Many cheers arose from the crowd, but they were quickly silenced by Gloy who raised his hand for them to be quiet. "I can appreciate your enthusiasm," he said, "but we must remember that we are directly beneath the soldiers, and too much noise could carry outside. Be cheerful, but calm your cheers. One more item of importance is the *'buddy-system'*. If a member of your cell is being beaten by the soldiers, help him. The soldiers are brave so long as they have greater numbers. If you see four soldiers beating someone, make sure four others go with you to his aid so there will be five of you. Likewise, if six soldiers are together make sure six others go with you so you will number seven and outnumber the soldiers by one. So long as you outnumber them, they will not harm you. They will wait for reinforcements before they act, so, make certain at all times that you outnumber your opponents."

"That was a marvelous presentation, Gloy," Sacram said as he stood on the rock next to Gloy, "I want to congratulate each of you for a splendid job. You successfully helped built an organization that is strong and resilient. We lost our freedoms to the Sets and Anil. We have as our goal the reacquisition of those freedoms of speech, of assembly, of want from hunger and cold. We have within our grasp the greatest gift any of us could bestow on another human being, the gift of a meaningful life. Not a life of strife and constant danger as we now live, but a life where our children can live free from basic wants, a life in which each of them can develop their talents to the highest degree. A life where the arts and literature will flourish, where subjects are discussed freely, without fear of reprisal. It's up to us to ensure ourselves and our offspring full and meaningful lives. That is why we pledged our lives to liberty and freedom. Powerful men have gained control of our lives and have used us to further their own means. Our village has made the Sets enormously wealthy through the sweat and blood of our people. We have existed as personal property of the Sets for far too long. It is up to us to regain our dignity and control of our own lives. We are dispossessed people who are tired of living lives of quiet desperation. We have worked long enough for distant masters who care nothing of our livelihoods. Distant masters who would rather see a worker dead than sick because a dead worker can readily be replaced. Tomorrow, all that will change. Tonight we live in oppression, tomorrow we live in freedom."

His speech ended with cheering. Gloy raised his hand to silence the crowd. "Quiet! Quit! Please!" he shouted over their cheers. "We must be quiet because the soldiers might hear!" he pleaded. Mention of the soldiers was sufficient to bring the members to their senses, and the cheering subsided abruptly. No one wanted a premature confrontation with the soldiers.

Silence became our security. It concealed our presence from the demons above. Loud noise of any kind was a beast that threatened our existence by alerting the Set soldiers patrolling the streets above us. Silence filled the room. We looked upward as though we could see the soldiers rushing to the cavern with their rifles with sharp bayonets. Fear sprang from the farthermost crevices of the cavern. Had they heard? Are they now coming toward our cavern? Is that clicking noise we hear resounding through the chamber the muffled sounds of soldiers? Paranoia spread through the group like a beast that fed on itself. We were being destroyed by the sounds of our own heartbeats. All in the room turned to Gloy who stood as our pillar of strength and security.

"It's all right, we're safe," he said. The sound of his voice swept away the paranoia which hobbled like a wounded animal back into the innermost recesses of the cavern.

"We're safe," he said again to reassure us. "Are there any questions?"

"I've been told by my cell cap'n," said one of the men, "that we are to ed'cate the soldier while we are on strike. That true?"

"Yes, talk to the soldiers and try to convince them that their own interest is in helping us. The soldiers are just as much a part of the Set oppression as we are. If they can be made to realize that they are just as chained to the Set interests as we are, they will question their loyalties. If we can get just one soldier to join us, we can get others to join. If you can convince him, he can convince his friends, and those friends can convince their friends and so on until we have swung the whole military to our side. Without a strong and loyal military, the Sets can no longer control us, and they can no longer keep us chained in poverty, ignorance and powerlessness."

"How long will the strike last?" asked a lanky older man. "I've been told that it could last a long time, but we don't know how long the strike will last. It could be days, perhaps weeks. Your cell captain has probably told you to bring food and water with you because the soldiers will shut the doors on the factories."

"How should we carry the food and water?" another member asked.

"The best food would be dried food such as biscuits and dried fruit. Water can be carried as well in your lunch pail. Also carry medical supplies. The cell captains have appointed medical personnel. They will be identified by a white armband with a red cross stenciled onto it. Don't rely entirely upon the medical people because their supplies might run out. Carry a small quantity of clean rags and any antiseptic drugs made from roots of plants or leaves or whatever from home remedies you have."

At this point, Sacram turned the meeting over to Nod who joined him on the small stand. Sacram descended from the podium and joined Gloy who was speaking to one of the captains. Gwinn stood beside me in the meeting.

"Are you afraid?" I asked, turning to Guinn. She smiled," anyone who isn't afraid isn't human, or is crazy. Yes, I'm afraid, but you will be in more danger. Are you afraid?"

"I'm not fond of dying," I said. "I try not to think of what might happen."

"That's a good attitude. Accept things as they occurs." she

said.

"Things will be very different soon," I said matter-of-factly.

"Yes, the village will be in upheaval," she replied, "things will be different. Tonight is the last night of the old way. Either our life will be much better, or it will be much worse. If we win, we will be free. If we lose…well, let's not think of that."

"Yes, better not to think about it."

" It would be unfortunate if we remove Anil and the Sets, and after we've accomplished that another dictator takes over, and we're right back where we started: Poor, starving and exploited."

That would be tragic," I said, "but, we must think positive! We are going to win this fight! We are going to secure freedom and equality for you, for your parents, your friends and relatives as well as the Seraphians"

"Don't mention the Seraphians!" she said, "Those cowardly intellectuals! All talk and no action! We're fighting for those cowards who hide in their ivory lofts, and even now they cower before the approaching soldiers and wail far into the night. We're told by the Sets that there is nothing nobler in the world than to be accepted on the exchange program with Seraphs. They tell us that we can become learned and scholarly. I couldn't conceive of myself becoming one of their dastardly lackeys. They are nothing more than decorations for the Sets. They decorate their captors with intellectual jewelry and seductive rhetoric."

It had been difficult for Gwinn growing up in Seval, I thought to myself, witnessing the mistreatment and death of friends and family, but the physical difficulties were not as severe as the psychological difficulties. The scars from the beatings by the soldiers had long sense healed, but the hatred and fear she felt toward the Sets was long lasting and had made an indelible print upon her life. I liked Gwinn, and I could feel a need in her for sympathy. The stage was set for action, and the Seval would not stop until Latipac had been captured and the Sets and Anil were deposed of their power and privilege. My thoughts were interrupted by Gwinn.

"Did you hear what I said," Gwinn asked with her brow furrowed.

"I'm sorry, what did you say?"

"I asked you if you had spoken with Kram tonight," she replied.

"No, but I spoke with him earlier this afternoon."

"Did he tell you about Skeeter?"

"What about him?" I asked.

"He's hallucinating!"

"What!" I said.

"He drank too much and he is seeing things," she said.

"But he is going to guide us tomorrow," I said.

“If he can," she corrected.

"Where is Kram?" I asked.

"I saw him over by the podium," she said.

"Wait here," I rushed over to Kram and told him about Skeeter's condition.

"Oh, he'll be all right by tomorrow," Kram replied, “he just had too much to drink."

"Have you given orders that he is not to have anymore alcohol?" I asked.

"Yes, my aides are plying him with coffee. They will have him on his feet by tomorrow. He's consumed too much alcohol the past few years. His liver is about gone. But, he'll be able to guide us into Latipac and the Palace tomorrow. He says he has a score to settle with Anil.”

“Oh, one thing,” I said, “Sacram says it's our duty to keep Anil and his generals safe until we can bring them to a court and try them for their crimes."

“We’re going to give them the same justice they gave us!” Kram replied.

“I can’t believe what I had just heard you say.” Sacram said. “You’re in charge of the assault, and you want revenge! So many people want revenge. That’s one thing that made me uneasy about the campaign. Too many want to solve personal vendettas against the Sets, but how does everyone solve vendettas without destroying our cause? There are not enough Sets for each villager to satisfy his hatred."

"That's the way it is," Kram said, "the Sets were going to pay the price for their injustice.

"Hatred can be just as destructive as injustice," I said, "so, you kill the Sets, then what do you do with the sons and daughters of the Sets? Are they guilty by association?"

"They tried to kill me!" Kram said.

"I detested the bloodshed I saw at Detfar," Sacram said, "and I could never condone acts of brutality, no matter which side is involved. I cannot condone the murder of Sets any more than I could condone their murders of the Seval. I find the whole idea of revolutions and bloodshed revolting, but there does not seem any other alternative. We must keep the level of violence to a minimum, and that goes for you Kram."

"Whatever you say," Kram replied as he walked off.

Gloy held up his hands to get the attention of all in the room. "Tomorrow is the day we've been looking forward to," Gloy said, "the day of our long awaited strike. Listen to your Cell Captain. He can save your life, so listen to him and do as he says. The strike begins at Seven O'clock tomorrow morning. Nod will lead the strike at the munitions factory. Remember to remain together, and to help each other! Meeting adjourned."

“Are you ready to return to headquarters?” Sacram asked.

"Yes," I replied. “Gwinn, are you going with us?”

"I'm going with Nod,” Gwinn said, “we have some last minute things to go over before the strike. We're first on the schedule tomorrow, you know."

"Yes, I know," I replied, “good luck.”

"You know we’ll be first to get the brunt force of the soldiers."

“Yes,” I replied. That fact bothered me.

"Nod wants me to stay up with him tonight” she said, “I probably couldn't get much sleep tonight anyway worrying about the strike. Good luck in Latipac, and I hope we can meet again under better conditions."

* * *

"When you capture Anil," Gloy warned Kram and me as we walked back to camp," be extraordinarily cautious. He is very cunning. He has an ability to get people to do things against their wills. He has the instincts of a fox, and the cunning of a devil. Beware in your dealings with him. You should place him in a cell as soon as he is captured. Do not permit anyone to speak to him. Be sure and warn the others about him, and order them not to speak to him no matter what happens. Capture him, and place him incommunicado until we can arrange for a trial."

"He isn’t human?" Kram asked.

"No one really knows. It’s rumored that he has magical powers. I can't caution you enough about the man. He is extremely dangerous. Do not talk to him least you fall under his spell as so many others have done before you. Anil is a master of illusion."

“He sounds like a strange person,” Kram said.

"Jonathan,” Gloy asked, “you were in the Fuchsia Palace weren’t you?”

"Yes, I went there with Sacram."

"What do you remember about the Palace?”

"Only that it was impressive," I replied.

"That is the way he chose for you to see his Palace,” Gloy said, “the only way you will ever know the way the Palace really looks is to see it without Anil's knowledge. If he knows of your presence, he'll distort images, and you will see only what he wishes you to see.”

"I saw him as a handsome man who seemed to change into a beast," I said.

"He permitted you to see him as a beast?" Gloy asked, both puzzled and intrigued.

"Yes, and one time he seemed to be alternating between the two. At one time he looked as though he were both man and beast."

"I'm surprised he allowed you to see him as the beast. That

is his true form. Perhaps your being from another world interfered with his ability to project images into your mind. You might be partially immune to his powers."

"He looked like a hideous beast," I replied.

"You may be the only one on the island who can see through his illusions," Gloy replied, "could you detect Anil's facial expressions while he was in the beast state?"

"He seemed diffident. Almost shy, as though he didn't want anyone to see him as the beast. Rather, he preferred that his guests see him as Anil the suave, young, debonair sophisticate. He seemed pained when I looked at his ugly face and the great teeth that occupied his mouth and his huge club fingers," I replied.

CHAPTER 20

The Strike

We reached our cave headquarters and found a runner from Seraphs waiting for us. “The strike so far has been successful in Seraphs,” the runner said, “the soldiers are in a state of confusion, they don't know what to do. They sent a runner to Anil asking for more soldiers. They have never confronted resistance before."

"Listen up, everyone,” Gloy announced to others in the room, “I just learned that the soldiers in Seraphs are confused, and have sent a messenger to Anil requesting more troops. Our plan has worked so far. Tomorrow, we begin our strike in Seval. When Anil and the generals learn of the strike in Seval is occurring in more than one factory, they will send additional soldiers. Kram and his men will be near Latipac when the Soldiers leave. Then they can begin our offensive."

* * *

During that night, we amused ourselves with fireside chats over coffee and sang victory songs throughout the night. All of us experienced a sense of excitement. There wasn't much to do but kill time by amusing ourselves with a card game played with small planks of wood upon which were drawn faces and numbers to make a deck of fifty-two cards. The card game kept us occupied and our minds off the strike.

"Gonna be fun," Kram repeated often that night, "I tell you, it's going to be fun whipping them tomorrow!" We played our games and placed bets with small pebbles collected from the stream. The value of the rock depended upon its color: red for five points, blue for ten, and green for one. During the early hours of the morning, Gloy and Sacram joined us in our card games. We were beaten by their clever hands because they had much experience. Before long, they had all the pebbles and we were forced to return to the stream and grope in the darkness for more stones.

* * *

The next morning, preparations were being made for the long strike. Kram and I left the cave and climbed a tall hill where we could observe events in the village. As the rays of the rising sun illuminated the village, we could see workers in the streets walking toward the factories. Other villagers arrived and were awaiting the opening of the gates to start the morning shift. The binoculars Kram had were very powerful and magnified more than fifty times, so we were able to see things in the distance.

The unique geographic formation of the nearby hills acted as a natural funnel, so we were able to hear much of what was being said in the village.

Many workers showed up earlier that morning than usual. The soldiers seemed to sense that something was not right. They conferred with each other and pointed toward the eager workers waiting at the gates. From our vantage point, we could see Gwinn and Nod standing at the gate of the munitions factory. Most of the workers had cloth bundles that held their supplies.

“Many of the workers,” Kram said, “packed pine needles under their clothing to soften the impact of clubs the soldiers might use when breaking up the strike. We did not see any arm bands being worn, which was good because the bands were to be worn only after the strike began. Nod's crew at the munitions factor was by far the largest. It was important that his people arrive early because they would initiate the strike. Workers also assembled near the other factory gates. As usual, a loud whistle blew at each of the factories signaling the beginning of the work day.

Kram and I left the vantage of the hill and moved closer to the village. We were just outside the limits of the city when we heard foremen and supervisors shouting orders to the workers. Many expletives came from the factories as the foremen spoke to their subordinates.

The workers disappeared into the factories. The soldiers remained outside. They stacked their rifles in triangles and sat down on the grass, laughing and joking with each other. Suddenly, we heard Nod's voice very loud and clear coming from the munitions factory. "Attention! The strike has begun! Sit on the floor!"

Then we could hear a multitude of angry voices. We heard the voice of the munitions foreman confronting Nod and the other members. "Did you hear me? I said get your goddamn asses up! Get up from the floor. I'll kick your asses if you don't." There was a pause in his barking orders, then we heard him again. "I'm giving you bastards to the count of ten to obey my command. If you don't, I'm going to order the soldiers to force you to your stations. I"I'm giving you to the count of ten. One…two…three…four.."

Nod barked out an order: "Stay together!"

The soldiers outside the factories heard the commotion and retrieved their rifles. They prepared to enter at the order of their superior. "Five ••• six ••• " The counting continued and with each count, the voices of the members became louder. Nod's voice was distinctive as he instructed them to *Stay together*!

"Nine." By now the soldiers had entered the factories.

"Ten! Alright, I'm going to give you one last chance. Look over at the door. See those soldiers? They are coming here to break a few heads on my order. I'm giving you one last chance. I'm going to count to five. If you haven't gotten to your positions by the count of five, I'm ordering them in here. Colonel, did you hear that?" He shouted to the officer in charge.

"Yes, Sir!" came the reply.

"One ••• two ••• “The strikers did not move, and their conviction to remain grew more resolute with each count. "Three ••• four ••• I'm giving your one last chance! Five! Guards!" he shouted. The soldiers marched toward the workers. With each step of the soldiers, the workers became more fearful. Each second brought the soldiers closer. The workers consoled each other in an attempt to overcome their increasing fears. The soldiers marched closer and closer. Only Nod remained resolute and unafraid of the approaching rifles.

"Stand your ground," Nod commanded, "Don't let the soldiers split your ranks. Stay together!"

The soldiers advanced until they were near the huddled members, many of whom were shaking with fear. The next few minutes were ones of confusion to us because so many voices were coming from the factory with words of profanity and threats.

Nod's voice was recognizable. The foreman singled him out. "Tell your people to return to their jobs!" he shouted.

"Never!" Came Nod’s resolute reply.

"Guards!" shouted another. We could hear the sound of their heavy boots upon the concrete floor of the factory, echoes of men running to the kill.

"So, you want an example of what will happen to each of you!" Came threatening voice of the foreman. "Then we'll show you what will happen if you do not obey my orders. Guards! Show them what we do to dissenters!"

Nod cried out in agony as they hit and kicked him. With each kick, he cried out in pain, still he implored the others to remain unified. "Remember the strike!" He shouted as the soldiers repeatedly hit him.

Soon, cries of 'soldiers' rang out from another factory foreman. A loud whistle from the second factory broke the angry cries filling the morning air. As soon as the second whistle sounded, the beating stopped, and the foreman and many of the soldiers appeared at the door of the munitions factory. A foreman from the second factory ran to the group who had congregated just outside the munitions factory shouting "Soldiers! The workers are striking!" Clearly, there was confusion within the ranks of the soldiers as they looked to their commanding officer for guidance. Soon another foreman appeared at the third factory's door and shouted "Soldiers!"

"Soldiers! Soldiers!" the foremen shouted, but the munitions factory could not spare any soldiers, for they had a similar crisis on their hands. The soldiers and officials gathered outside the munitions factory. They were speaking in frantic voices.They gasped with surprise and fear. Nothing like this had ever happened in Seval and it had taken them by surprise.

"The soldiers! Use the soldiers!" cried one of the officials.

"Too many of them! They'll kill the soldiers, there's too many of them," shouted one of the foremen.

"Isolate them and kill their leaders," the official shouted.

"Damn people. Nothing but trouble!" said the munitions foreman, "give them a job and look where it gets you!"

"Tie that damn trouble-maker to the wall against that pipe over there," ordered a munitions official as the foreman followed him back into the factory. We could hear the sound of boots upon the concrete. "I'm going to give you people one change to get your asses back to your jobs. If you don't, I'm going to count to ten. If you don't obey my order, I'm going to order this man shot! One…two… three…"

Everyone remained silent. My stomach churned with a deepening sympathy for Nod. I felt sick as I listened to the official counting down the seconds.

"Eight…nine!" came the count. "Are you going to follow my orders?" he shouted. "Ten!" he shouted in a voice filled with anger and violence.

"Very well! Soldiers! Ready, aim, fire!

I remember the retort of the soldier's rifle, and the screams which filled the air immediately following the shot. Even from where we stood outside the village, we could hear the whimpering and crying of the strikers. Still, they would not obey the orders of the official. After the shots, Gwinn shouted, “Don’t let Nod's execution frighten you. He died for our freedom!"

"Another leader! We have a bitch Leader! Another damn trouble maker! Soldiers! Arrest her!" shouted the official. Before she could receive the same treatment as Nod, the troubled whistle of another factory sounded. And that whistle was followed by still another. The officials and foreman again appeared at the door of the munitions factory and looked at the other factories. Again the foreman in each of the other factories appeared at their doors shouting for the soldiers to come to their aid. Soon all twelve factories were involved in the strike. As had been planned, the strikers arose from their sitting positions and walked out the door past the astonished officials. They met each other in the common area which connected the factories. Soon, a large group of strikers were sitting huddled together.

The officials and soldiers stood outside their factories. They were livid with anger, but the wise officials realized that if the soldiers began shooting, the strikers would overpower the soldiers. They realized that the strike was not limited to a few trouble makers, but involved all the workers in all factories.

There was only one thing for them to do. They dispatched their fastest runner with a message to Anil in Latipac. We smiled at each other as the runner disappeared into the forest. We were certain the next phase was ours.

The officials continually badgered the strikers with insults and threats, but the strikers did not give in. They remained unified and refused to work. They also refused to leave the factory grounds, and chose to defy the officials for whom they worked. We were pleased with the initial stages of the strike. We regretted the loss of Nod, but we were pleased with the way the members remained together throughout the terrifying ordeal. The brutality the factory operators chose to show the strikers merely worked against them. The strikers became even more resolute than ever to make the strike a success and to see the factory officials--and the Sets--defeated. They wanted their freedom and victory over the Sets more than anything else.

After growing hoarse from shouting threats and commands, the foremen finally gave up and walked over to where other officials and soldiers were conferring about the situation. Obviously, they needed more troops, but it would be hours before additional soldiers could arrive. The strikers gained renewed strength when they saw the officials walk away, frustrated and beaten. Suddenly, the strikers sang a folk song which was popular in the village. The Seval had never known such power and they felt pride and satisfaction. Confident the strike was going well, Kram and I departed for the military field to rejoin our division and make preparations for our march into Latipac.

* * *

When we arrived at the training field, Skeeter greeted us. "When we leav'n?"

“Soon,” Kram said, “we're waiting until the Set soldiers have time to leave Latipac. Then, we'll enter the city.”

“Yes, Sir,” Skeeter said.

“Taking the Palace through the tunnel is a good strategy,” Kram said “because it would allow a quick penetration into the bowels of the Palace. A direct attack on the Palace will create more casualties, but it will be necessary if the tunnel has been blocked by the soldiers. We need to be prepared in case it's blocked."

“Them soldiers don't know bout the tunnel.”

"Anil might feel threatened by the strike and want to strengthen Palace security," I said.

"Anil won't feel threatened in Latipac,” Kram said, “no insurrection has ever occurred in Setopia, not to mention the city of Latipac."

"No strike has ever taken place here, either, but now we are engaged with major strikes in two of the three major centers of

Setopia," Mot said, "if they block the entrance through the tunnel, that would be a major blow because we would be engaged in a fire fight for hours, or days."

"If they fortify the Palace, their soldiers can hold out for months,"Kram said, "we cannot hold out that long. If our initial assault on the Palace is unsuccessful, then we will be forced to fight a battle for which we are poorly equipped."

"Don't worry," Skeeter comforted, "the tun'l not used for years. Soldiers don't know it's there."

CHAPTER 21

The Assault

Later, after going over many details of our assault on the Palace, I sat outside on a wooden bench. Some of the men engaged in combat practice to occupy their time. Others played Mumble peg, their favorite game. The air smelled clean and fresh, and rays of the sun felt warm. Small streamers of steam arose on the far side of the field, giving the distant edge of the forest a dreamy quality as the trees seemed to disappear into a light blue fog.

"Fall In!" Kram shouted to an anxious group of Seval soldiers. The men rushed to pick up their weapons and other equipment they had stored at the edge of the field and then quickly formed orderly lines of formation. A tall thin sergeant counted the men, then snapped to attention and gave a quick sharp salute to Kram.

“All present, Sir!”

"Everyone ready and accounted for?” Kram asked.

“Ready and accounted for, sir,”

“Forward, March!" Kram instructed. The soldiers moved forward in a neat formation.

"Sergeant!"

"Take over!" Kram instructed.

“Yes, Sir! Hup one, two three….” He barked as the soldiers marched into the forest and disappeared.

Kram, Skeeter, and I collected our weapons and supplies. I placed a backpack full of provisions on my back and strapped on a canvass belt containing cartridges and a .45 caliber pistol. Kram carried explosives in his backpack. We strapped on our equipment and hurriedly caught up with the marching men. Then, Kram took control of the men. Our forced march lasted more than four hours, and when we were in the forest near a roadway Kram ordered, “Formation halt!”

Kram and I scouted ahead of the formation. Kram was a master trail blazer, and a master hunter. He had a keen sense of hearing, and seemed to be able to hear things that were totally inaudible to me. Were it not for Kram's acute hearing, we might have met one of the Set runners face to face, but as it happened, Kram signaled for us to lie under a nearby bush. Soon, a runner came down the trail and disappeared. We waited until he was safely out of earshot, then we continued our march toward Latipac.

“The runner is probably delivering a message to the soldiers in Seval,” Kram said.

The going was tough, and portions of the trail had to be hacked with machetes in order to make passage possible. The intense heat and humidity made us sweat profusely. We lost some of our energy to the heat, and I wondered how it would be possible to engage in a major military action after such a trek through the rain forest.

"We'll rest before entering Latipac," Kram said to me as though he were reading my mind. We continued down the vine ridden walkway. The dense vegetation that we had just cleared seemed to creep back onto the pathway behind us. It didn't take long for the vines to completely recover the pathway.

“How can you tell when you’re on the right trail?” I asked Kram, the master trail blazer.

“I can spot a vine that has been cut within the past year. Our machete cuts produce little scars on the vine that are scarcely visible to the untrained eye. For example, look there,” he said, pointing to a vine lying nearby. I examined it, but could not detect any scars.

“I can’t tell if the vine has been cut,” I confessed.

"It's the angle of growth that I notice first," he said, "when a vine is cut, it doesn't grow straight. It curves slightly."

"Is that how you find your way through the forest?"

"Yes, but we need to blaze new trails because soldiers will be using the open trails. We don't want to run into soldiers."

"No, we don't," I said as the sergeant rushed up to us.

"Two men lost, Sir," the sergeant announced.

"What happened?" Kram asked.

"Somehow they went off the trail."

Too bad," Kram said. "The thickness of the vegetation and the fog that often occurs in this area of forest is dangerous. Men can become lost within a few feet of the trail. The thick vegetation muffles the sound of our voices. A lot of this area is swampy and has quicksand, dangerous animals, poisonous snakes and the like. If either of them yell for help, they will not be heard."

"What do we do?" I asked.

"Too dangerous for a search party," Kram said, "and, we don't have time to search."

"They find their way out?" Skeeter asked.

"They're probably not alive. The swamp provides a quick and certain death to anyone caught unawares. Besides, we can't jeopardize our mission to save two men who should have stayed on the trail."

"The main trail is just ahead," Kram said pointing, "come with me Jonathan, the rest of the men can wait here until the soldiers pass."

“How do you know that they haven’t passed yet?” I asked.

“I don’t,” he replied.

Kram and I walked a little further until we came upon a well used path. Trees had been cleared several feet on either side. Vines and other vegetation had also been removed.

“Has the path had been recently used?"

“Not by the soldiers,” Kram said. He motioned for us to be quiet, then signaled for us to hide in the brush. They’ll come down the trail soon.”

Kram and I hid behind a large fern about fifteen feet from the path and waited. It wasn't long before we heard noises in the distance.

"Soldiers?”I asked.

"Yeah," he replied, "about a hundred meters away."

With each passing minute the sounds of footsteps grew louder. With each second the footsteps produced more and greater vibrations in the ground. As the soldiers grew nearer, my adrenalin surged and my heart pounded. The nearness of such a vast number of trained killers brought all my previous training with the Marines into play as I waited patiently. Finally, the soldiers came into view looking mean and efficient. They marched three abreast with a distance of about four feet between the rows. Each wore a clean pressed uniform. With their rifles resting on their shoulders, they marched past. I worried about

Guinn and the strikers who would soon be confronting these soldiers. We waited, hidden in the bushes, until they passed. When they were a safe distance down the path, Kram whispered, "There can't be many soldiers left in Latipac."

"I hope so."

"Let's go," he said. We returned to the men.

"Attention," Kram commanded, "forward march. No talking!"

We left the forest and entered the main pathway used by the soldiers. It was dark when we arrived at the outskirts of Latipac. Kram led us to the drainage ditch we had used earlier.The rest of us followed in single file. Skeeter walked just behind Kram, but he didn't say much, and remained silent most of the march.

"Pair off!" Kram commanded as soon as the last man exited the pipe. "Run across the park in groups of two. Follow us! Go!"

Kram and Skeeter were the first to reach the other side of the park. I went in the second group. There weren't any Lats or soldiers in the park which was fortunate because the presence of so many troops would have been noticed and reported. We regrouped on the other side of the park. Skeeter led the way to the Palace and we moved in groups of two from alley to alley and from building to building. We went through many buildings and up many dark alleyways. I lost track of where we had been. It seemed we were going through a crazy maze.

“Skeeter, do you know where we’re going?” Kram asked.

“Sure do. Lived here all me life. I’ll get ya to the Palace. Stick with me. I won't let ya down.”

After we entered many alleyways and past multiple building, the men were becoming leery of Skeeter’s guidance. It seemed to them, and to me, that we were going in circles and would never get to the Palace. The men were apprehensive about the assault, and didn’t like having an alcoholic leading them to what might be certain death. Sooner or later, if we continued going through vacant buildings and crossing streets, we were going to be detected.

"Where the hell is he taking us?" I could hear the men saying to one another, "To hell, no doubt," responded another. And even I became uneasy after a while for I had been to the Palace before and I didn't remember it being so far. I became increasingly worried that Skeeter had become lost in the warren of streets.

"One more alley," he said as we followed him to yet another alleyway. Finally, we were in front of the building with the metal door concealing our secret passageway.

“Thar tis,” Skeeter said pointing to the building containing our tunnel.

"Wait here," Kram commanded. "Skeeter, Mot, and Jonathan follow me." We went into the building, down the staircase and examined the entrance to the tunnel. It looked as we had left it. Nothing had been disturbed.

"Hasn't been touched," Skeeter said with assurance.

"How do you know?" Kram asked.

"See that stick," Skeeter said pointing, "Ah put that there on top. If the door moved, I can tell."

"Are you certain that's the piece of wood you placed there?" Kram asked. We were leery that the soldiers might have discovered the tunnel and placed a booby trap to alert the guards of our presence.

"Yep," he replied. He picked up the stick, "See this red paint?"

"Ah broke this splinter off that board over there," he said pointing to a board which had once been part of a wall.

"Okay! You'd better be right!" Kram said, "Mot, get me ten men to clear the tunnel."

"Yes sir."

Mot gathered ten men and set about clearing bricks and other debris from the entrance to the tunnel. With a metal bar lying not far away, they were able to pry open some of the bricks that had been difficult to pull away by hand.

"Lay the brick upon the floor-quietly," Kram cautioned.

Later, with the opening cleared, Kram, myself and several men descended the steps and walked through the long tunnel. We took turns looking through the small opening that Skeeter had drilled as a youth. Two guards in the cell area were playing cards to amuse themselves. We placed explosives against the door.

"We want enough explosives to punch through the wall and to knock out the guards, but not enough to kill the prisoners," he whispered.

"How do you know how much explosive to use?" I whispered.

"Have to guess," Kram replied, "no way to know for sure. We'll close the iron door back at the entrance. That way all the concussion of the blast will go directly into the cell chamber. The bricks and door fragments will act like gun shot. That should be enough to take care of the guards. Hopefully, the tunnel will muffle the blast so it won't be heard above us."

Kram estimated the amount of explosives, placed the detonators and motioned for us to exit the tunnel. He ran a wire back down the tunnel and out through the door well.

"Close the door," Kram said to one of the men, "and put a timber behind it so it will hold the concussion."

We retreated into the alley and ran the wire to a nearby building. Kram spliced the wires and tied them around the contacts on a plunger.

"Stay behind the wall,"Kram commanded. "Well," he said as he readied himself for the blast. This is it!" With that statement, he pushed the plunger. A muffled roar came out of the tunnel. The old building shook slightly and a few loose timbers and brick fell to the ground. We rushed back to the tunnel, opened the old iron door and could see light at the far end of the tunnel. Kram and his men rushed down the tunnel. I remained behind with Skeeter and entered the Palace shortly after the others. The guards lay injured and bleeding from the blast. Brick, wood and mortar were strewn about the room. Kram took the keys from one of the guards. One prisoner was in a nearby cell. He was despondent and looked blankly at the ceiling as he lay on an iron cot.

"Tend to him," Kram told a man acting as our medic, "Mot, take fifteen men and secure the other cells. There should be four or five more chambers in the prison." He pointed to a large metal door just past the cell and said "break through that door if necessary."

We dragged the two unconscious guards down the hallway. A large iron door of one of the cells wasn't locked, and it swung open with ease. We placed the guards into the cell, tied them up and placed gags in their mouths, and locked the door.

A massive ornate metal door served as the main entrance into the prison. Kram and several of us stood behind the door and checked our weapons. Then, Kram pushed open the door. Outside the door, a concrete staircase led away from the cells to the main floor of the Fuchsia Palace. We rushed up the stairway. No one in the Palace seemed to have heard the blast because no one was on alert. I stood directly behind Kram and looked down the hallway. I couldn't see any guards in the main hall. Our resistance troops flooded into the hallway.

Kram signaled for the men to take cover behind stairwells and other objects. I got behind a banister and readied my rifle, but going into such a massive building with no guards gave me a feeling that we were walking into a trap. I was spooked by the eerie quietness. All my training told me we should be in a fire fight with the security forces. But we weren't. *Something wasn't right!*

Perhaps Gloy had been right about Anil's illusions. Was Anil lulling us into certain death? What I saw before me was not what I had previously seen in the Palace. The picture of Anil I had seen no longer hung on the wall in the lobby, nor was there a long-beautifully sculptured hallway leading to Anil's office. There was a hallway, beautifully detailed with statues and marble tiles, but it was not the hallway that I had walked down during our meeting with Anil. What I saw opposite the main entrance was a huge staircase of serpentine marble with two white marble lions standing guard on either side. At the top of the staircase was a large bronze of a Prussian eagle with spread wings. A single eye made from a large ruby seemed to be looking at us. Strange, I thought that no one patrolled the corridor, nor did there seem to be aides or workers. All was strangely quiet. Kram sent five men down each isle on the lower level and the rest of us raced up the marble staircase. We divided at the eagle and paired off on either side of the staircase.

Kram motioned for me to go down the hallway that was nearest me. I stealthily made my down the hallway, but I saw no one. Then, we heard footsteps. I sought cover behind a nearby statue. The sound of heels upon the marble floor echoed down the empty stairwell and throughout the hallway. It seemed a long time before the person came into view. Finally, a guard passed us. Kram grabbed him and knocked him unconscious.

We heard more footsteps. As the person came closer, my pulse increased. I saw a gray uniform, but I hesitated a moment until he passed by me. I leapt behind him and hit him with the butt of my rifle. He moaned and fell to the floor. Two of our men gagged him, tied him up, and dragged him into an adjacent office at the top of the stairs, near the eagle. Kram motioned for me to lead the men with me down the aisle nearest us. Kram and his men did the same on the other hallway. I wasn't certain what we were looking for, but we opened doors and checked the interiors for officials. The rooms were all very impressive with expensive furnishings and thick rich rugs. Each room we entered was vacant. That made me very uneasy. It was unnerving to be in a building housing such important men, but with only two guards.

We regrouped back at the Eagle after securing the hallway. I looked at Kram and raised my hands in a gesture of confusion. He responded in kind as if to say he couldn't understand why there were no officials. Perhaps, Anil was watching us and waiting with his soldiers.

We were uncertain as to where Anil and the generals were located, but we were reasonably certain they would be in a room, somewhat akin to a war room. Of this we were certain because of the large-scale troop movements and the fact that Anil would want his generals close to him. The generals were well known for their propensities during times of crisis to withdraw into their strategic planning rooms and discuss strategy. Gloy had told me that Anil liked the atmosphere of strategic planning, and he often ordered his generals to engage in such activities for practice.

We had secured two hallways, but there was one other we hadn't secured. Our progress down the hall was slow, but without incident. Nowhere did we find either officials or more guards. However, several of the rooms we entered looked as though they had been recently used because the cups of coffee were still warm. Other signs of recent occupancy were present, but nowhere did we find government officials. We had to somehow locate the room where high-level strategy sessions were conducted. Door after door we opened only to find deserted offices. However, as I rounded a corridor far removed from the Eagle, I detected faint voices. I signaled to Kram.

"What is it?" he whispered.

"Voices," I said pointing toward the direction in which they were coming. We made our way down the hallway. As we moved closer, the voices grew louder. We could hear them discussing the situations in Seval and Seraphs. Without a doubt, the voices were those of Anil and his top generals. Our next problem was to discover a way to enter quickly. We came to the end of the hallway. Another hallway turned abruptly to the right. The voices were much louder around the corner, but two guards stood watch outside large wooden doors.

"How are we going to get past the guards?" I whispered.

"The guards," he said.

"What?"

"The guards!" He repeated, "use the uniforms of the two guards we tied up."

The idea seemed like the best we had at the moment. We returned to the room where the guards were bound. We disrobed the prisoners. Kram and one of the larger men put on the uniforms. We returned to the corridor where the two guards stood outside the conference room. I watched from my vantage point behind a marble statue of a woman as Kram and Mod marched down the aisle in the manner of the Set guards. The sound of their boots upon the marble floor echoed down the empty hallway and alerted the guards at the conference room.

"Who goes?" barked one of the guards, pointing his rifle directly at Kram.

"Your relief," Kram replied while walking toward the guards.

"Odd," said the guard looking at his watch, "You aren't due for another hour."

"We're just following orders. We were told to replace the two of you. You're to check with the sergeant. He's down the hall to the right," Kram replied.

The guards were suspicious, but did as directed since he uniform Kram wore outranked them. Reluctantly, they left their station and walked down the hallway toward where we were waiting. We crouched in anticipation. As they rounded the corner we were ready for them. We overpowered them, tied them up and dragged them back to the office where we had the first two prisoners.

Now, we had control of the hallway leading to the conference room. We could hear the generals discussing strategy of conducting war on Seval. We gathered directly outside the conference door. Those inside had not detected our presence, and we had learned from the guards that a new shift would be replacing them in just one hour.

We lined up in groups of two on either side of the double doors. Two men were positioned kneeling in front with their weapons pointing to the door.. They would remain there while the others entered and secured the room. On the count of three, we would open the door and barge into the room.

"*One…two…*" My adrenalin surged with anticipation of what lay on the other side of the door. With the number *three*, we threw open the door and rushed inside with guns at the ready. Within seconds, we had secured the room. The generals and Anil were perplexed. They were so surprised they didn't know what to do.

"Hands against the wall!" Kram shouted.

They slowly arose from a conference table and stood against the wall, as instructed.

“Spread your legs!” Kram commanded.

Anil and his generals all stood with their hands against the wall and their feet spread.

“Make one false move and I’ll kill you!” Kram shouted.

Our men disarmed the generals, tied their hands behind their backs and ushered them into an adjacent room. Anil had his hands tied behind his back, but remained in the main conference room. To my surprise, he recognized me.

"Ah, my friend, we meet again," Anil said.

"Stay where you are," Mot shouted, pointing his pistol at Anil.

"Why the hostility? You are my friends. You are all my guests," he said in a most hospitable manner. He seemed warm and generous, but he was not our host and we were not his guests. We were intruders who had come to conquer his kingdom, and we had come to incarcerate him and his generals and arrange for his trial.

"Don't you remember me? We met one day not so long ago," he said.

"Yes," I replied, "I remember you."

"You may use my Palace in any way you would like. If you are hungry, please, let me have my chiefs cook you one of the finest meals. I have the finest dinnerware. I am at your command. Your every wish is my command. What is it that I can do for you?" Anil said in a calm and generous way.

"We wish nothing from you," Kram interrupted in a fit of rage, "you are our prisoner! We are not your guests!"

"I see," Anil replied calmly, "am I to have any privileges of rank?"

"You have no privileges, and we do not recognize your rank! You are without rank and will be charged with crimes against the villages of Seval and Seraphs, among other charges."

"You have proof of my crimes, then?" he asked.

"Yes, we have proof! The dead bodies of hundreds of our kin and friends you have murdered!"

"My," Anil replied as he stood composed with his hands tied behind his back, "you certainly have me cornered, as the saying goes." In a fit of rage, Kram lunged for Anil, but several of our men restrained him.

"You bloody bastard!" Kram shouted, "I'll have your head before this is over."

“You may have my head whenever you wish it. I am your prisoner," Anil replied in a sycophantic manner with a voice calculated to appease Kram who by now had regained his composure.

“The enormity of your crimes against my people will not go unpunished. Now, if I can have your Excellency’s approval,” he said sarcastically, “I want you removed to another room for interrogation."

"Interrogation?" asked Anil quizzically.

"I want to know your complicity in actions by the Set government."

"By all means, I am pleased to tell you anything you wish to know."

"Escort him into the next room!" instructed Kram.

I followed them into another room just off the main

conference room. We entered a very pleasant sitting room with blue marble floors, pure white marble columns and blue serpentine walls. A large ornate granite fireplace with two small statues of nymphs on either side stood at the far end of the room. A series of metal trophies rested on the mantle.

"Trophies?" I asked.

"Won those while a youth," Anil replied.

“Really?" I replied, not knowing what to say to him.

"Yes. I won them in chess competitions. I was not very good at sports when I younger." he replied. He continually tried to charm us. Never did he lose his temper nor did he let the vitriolic words of Kram anger him. He had perfect control of himself. We seemed to humor him, as though we existed for his enjoyment and he could do with us as he wished at any time. I remember the strange feeling I had while looking into his eyes as we spoke. I felt a strange power coming from his deep dark eyes. I felt as though I lost some of my own control by gazing into his eyes. His eyes were powerful, and his stature, though small by most standards, left me with the sense of a much larger man. A strange power seemed to flow from him with relative ease. His easy manner and high-verbal fluency set him apart from the vast majority of men. He stood in a league all his own. I often found myself wondering if in fact we were not his prisoners. It wasn't until we had been with Anil thirty minutes or so that we suddenly remembered that a relief crew would be coming into the Palace, and we needed to be ready for them.

"Get into the uniforms of the other two guards," Kram said to his men, "Station two men outside the conference room and two more down the hall," One of our men brought Kram his fatigues, so he took off the guards' uniform and put back on his own fatigues. He handed the uniform to one of his men. Four men chosen to act as guards left the room as did about twenty more men who were to hide in the offices near the staircase to subdue the replacement guards.

"Mot, what did the generals say?" Kram asked.

"They're not talking." Mot replied.

Kram and I returned to Anil while Mot and two top aides continued their interrogations of the generals. The generals were saying nothing. Anil, on the other hand was full of information and answered our questions fully and without hesitancy.

"I suppose you think I'm guilty for what occurred in the villages."

"Yes," Kram said, "Exactly right."

"The responsibility is mine. I am chief of state, and anything that happens under my rule is my responsibility. It's only proper that I be punished for the deeds of others who have committed terrible acts while serving under my command."

"How did you conceive of the idea of Detfar?" I asked.

"Detfar?" He asked bewildered, "what is this Detfar?" Kram's face turned red, but he remained calm.

"Detfar! You never heard of it?" I asked.

"Never, what is this Detfar'?"

"It's what you created for annihilating the population of Seval!" shouted Kram.

"I know nothing of this. What is this place you call…what did you call it, Detfar?"

"Is that name so foreign to your ears?" I asked.

"I have never heard of it, and to think that such a horrible thing should have taken place without my knowledge. That astounds me. I will make you a promise that I will investigate this Detfar and I will bring its architect to justice, and I will promise you that the investigation will be thorough, and---"

"It's too late for investigations," Kram interrupted, "you should have investigated Detfar long ago. Before so many people were sacrificed to the sadism of your generals."

"My generals?" Replied Anil. "Tell me which general, or generals, were involved in this Detfar and I will have them executed immediately. You point them out and I will have my men execute them on the spot. I will not have this thing on my conscience. The very idea of such a thing going on under my command without my even being aware of its existence is astounding!"

"Detfar is a field of bloodshed, where friends and relatives kill each other!" Kram said.

"Kill each other?" He asked. "Then the generals were not executing these unfortunate people?"

"No, your generals brainwashed them into thinking they were serving their country by killing each other."

"So, they were killing each other. Then, how can you hold my generals responsible for this thing if they were not the ones pulling the triggers?" He demanded.

"You know what brainwashing is!" Kram stated in a stern voice, "and you know what brainwashing can do because you were the architect of that program!"

"What proof do you have that I was involved personally in this Detfar?" He asked.

"You know everything that happens in Setopia. You have intelligence units which report to you and inform you of all activities in Setopia. You lie when you say you know nothing of Detfar. It was your creation!"

"But you don't understand," Anil protested, "my realm is vast, and my generals powerful. I did not know such things were happening. Had I known, I would have stopped it and punished those responsible."

"Lies! All lies!" Shouted Kram, "admit that you are the creator of Detfar! You and your beloved Sets!"

"Are you telling me the Sets are also involved in this Detfar?" Anil asked. “All the Sets want is to enjoy their profits and live lives of leisure. They do love their leisure and foxhunting," he said with a chuckle.

"Yes, and they love having others support their leisure!" Kram said.

"But that is their privilege. They own Setopia, and what they do not own, they control. I am merely their pawn. I must do as they tell me."

“The generals do nothing without your permission and knowledge!" Kram stated.

"No, not at all,” he replied. “I don't know everything my generals do. Often I know hardly anything. I remember once there was an incident within Latipac where one of my generals was involved in an action that was made public. It had to do with some financial swindle. I must admit my own bewilderment at learning of such things from the public. I should have been informed, but I wasn’t. That is the way things are. I'm not surprised that you find such things difficult to believe. I myself could not believe that such a thing had happened under my command, so you can understand my surprise at this Detfar thing. I am completely unaware of it. You must believe me."

"I believe you had full knowledge,” Kram said, “and you ordered the use of Detfar to keep the Seval from gaining power in Setopia, a devise you created to control the population."

"I tell you honestly, if I had I known, I would never have permitted such a thing to continue."

"Your guilt or innocence will be determined in court, not by us," Kram replied. "The court will determine your sentence as well as your complicity in Detfar and other crimes against the Seval and Seraphians." At this moment, Mot entered the room and waved for Kram to assist.

"Watch him," said Kram, "keep your pistol pointed at him and if he attempts to escape, shoot him between the eyes." With those instructions, he left the room with Mot.

"Will do," I replied. I suddenly found myself alone in the room with this strange man who only minutes before held total power within Setopia. Diffident and sycophantic, his fawning and treachery knew no bounds. I remembered Gloy's warning about falling under his influence. I became aware of Anil's attempt to influence my thoughts. The room suddenly changed drastically and became a type of sunlit courtyard surrounded by marble statues, fountains and flowers.

I fought his attempted intrusion into my mind. I must have been successful because the room changed back to the way it was just as quickly. I attempted to peer through Anil's personal illusion and see him as the beast that I had seen before. I concentrated and soon he began taking on a quite different look.

The charming prince to whom I had been speaking gave way to the beast that had always lurked inside him. Once again I saw the primitive face and large club fingers. Once more I saw the long nose, thick lips and small forehead. He had all the characteristics which belonged to a primitive age. Anil was an anachronism who had managed to outwit time. At another time, he could have taught Machiavelli much about the art and practice of command and the techniques of gaining and retaining power.

Once I had mastered the practice of concentration which enabled me to see through his illusions, I saw a lonely frightened and very ugly man who grew fearful of my own powers. Before me sat the man who had been instrumental in securing power and control from the powerful Sets through his use of illusion. His frailty belied the enormous power he wielded. He looked at me with curiosity. Stripped of his majesty and the beauty of his personal illusion, he had a sullen and not so pleasant smile.

"You surprise me," he said. "No other man on the island can overcome my illusions. Who are you?"

"You should be able to tell."

"Even magic has its limits. You're not from Setopia, are you?"

"No."

"Where then, are you from. There are no other islands outside Setopia."

“Doesn’t matter, you’re our prisoner. That’s all that matters,” I said.

“Are you happy seeing me like this?" he asked lugubriously

"Are you happy?" I asked. Then, for some reason that puzzled me, he started telling me confidential things about himself.

"I was born, a curiosity of nature." he began, “for that reason I was sent away to a special school on the other side of the island."

“Because you were born a freak of nature?”I asked. He looked at me with acute scorn.

"Yes," he replied, "my father was ashamed of me and worried that I would not follow him as Premier of Setopia. After all, who would follow, as you say, a curiosity of nature? Nature was cruel to me."

"Did you attend school with normal kids?" I asked.

"My classmates mostly seemed to be normal kids, but they didn't like me. They called me names like monster, ugly, monkey. I was very unhappy."

"What did you study in school?"

"The normal subjects like history, economics, politics and so forth. It wasn't until later that I met a magician high in the mountains who taught me to project imagery."

"You are very good at that."

"I grew better with practice. When I learned that I didn't have to be ugly anymore, the whole purpose of my education changed. I learned that the scores of books I had read were of little help in preparing for my future. My desire to be accepted rested with my skills. I was to become President of Setopia when my Father died, you know. The sorcerer taught me that all life is an illusion. We must learn to live with illusions. I learned my own ugliness could be changed. After all," he continued, "what we see are only pieces of reality. Reality is just illusion."

"You learned to project illusions so that others wouldn't see you as a freak?"

"Freak! That's very blunt," he said, but then continued. "I learned that I had a natural talent for illusion which I could use at will. It took years to master. It's talent that needs nurturing and constant practice, you know. Finally I became a master of illusion."

I continued questioning him about many of the earlier experiences in his life. I learned that the affront he received from others about his ugliness had left an indelible mark on him, and he constantly tried to compensate. He had developed his powers of illusion to such an extent that he projected himself as a very handsome and charming young man. With a powerful mind and iron discipline, he secured a supreme position of command. His ugliness I did not find revolting, but it made one feel sorry for this dwarf of a man whose hands and features were out of proportion to his stature.

“Why do you support the Sets?”

“The wealthy people?”

“Yes, the wealthy Sets.”

"I felt comfortable around people who had wealth and all the accoutrements of wealth, such as education, estates, and social position. They were the only people I knew. I have never known poor people, and I did not find myself sympathetic to the problems of the poor. I rather saw their low social positions as resulting more from their own incompetence and laziness."

"Would it have made a difference if you had known poor people or intellectual people like those in Seraphs?" I asked.

"Who can say?" he began, "I might have been more sympathetic if I had grown up with them. I don't really know, but I do know that when I became the leader of Setopia, I had an obligation to the people and groups that had made my transition to power possible. I knew that if I did not satisfy their desires and needs, I would not rule very long. It is necessary as chief executive to cater to the desires of the powerful because they're the ones who can keep me in power. I knew they also had the power to create a military coupe in which I might be assassinated.”

“Did that happen to your father?”

“No, but I learned from my father that one must constantly cater to the powerful. It is not the weak and poor who determine a ruler’s longevity in office, thus, it is not wise for the chief executive to cater to the poor who lack wealth and power."

"Wouldn't it be morally right to see that the poor have reasonably good lives? After all, they are also under your command?"

"This thing called morality. You have only an outsider's view of morality. Morality is whatever is expedient. Morality is whatever keeps me in power."

"Bit harsh isn't it?" I asked.

“Perhaps, but the executive who caters to the powerless does two things: First, he displeases the people who can help him; second, he can never please the powerless for whatever the executive does for them, they will inevitably end up biting the hand that feeds them. It doesn't make political sense to appease the masses. On the other hand, it makes good political sense to appease the rich and powerful. If I attempted to appease the Seval, how long do you think the Sets would let me remain in power? After all, the Seval are the people who produce the wealth that the Sets reap. If I attempted to cut off their supply of workers, how long do you think they would allow me to remain in the Fuchsia Palace?"

"You appeased the sets," I replied, "but you did not appease the Seval. Look at your current position. You're the prisoner of the Seval, and you will be tried for crimes against the villages of Seval and Seraphs. By aligning yourself with the powerful, you created the very forces that have destroyed you. You're a marked man. You angered too many Seval for the tribunal to allow you to live. You've been the focus of their anger. They think you are responsible for the murders of their sons and daughters, and it is you they feel is responsible for their poverty and all the diseases and ailments that poverty brings. I think it would have been safer for you to have made concessions to the Seval, and to the Seraphians, rather than the Sets."

"Perhaps," he replied, "I am a doomed man, but not because I made a wrong decision to support the powerful. I am a doomed man because the forces of nature, and of history, have turned against me. I have known for quite some time now that the old system that had worked so well in the past was giving way to something new. I had known that the old rules did not seem to apply as well as they did in past years. Of course, I had often thought of making concessions to the Seraphians. Their tasks here in Latipac were little more than finger exercises to keep them busy with trivia. The Seraphians are well suited to trivia. Give them a long and complicated problem and they will become so engrossed that they never comprehend the real issues.

Of course, we used them because it was expedient to do so. Any man would have done the same. I am only guilty of being in the wrong place at the wrong time. That's the ultimate joke."

"A Joke?" I asked. "You're guilty of all the agonies you have inflected on the Seval and Seraphians of Setopia. Their anger will be your accusers, their fears will be your jurors, their anguish will by your judge, and their lost loved ones will be your executioners. You had a chance to change Setopia and to make it more just, but you decided against it and instead chose to reinforce injustice. You will pay for your choice."

"What I did was necessary,"Anil continued, "that is the nature of power and command. Had I chosen other actions, Setopia might have collapsed, the population would be hungry and begging for food-which most are not doing now. They would be much worse off. My actions were in the best interest of the people. I have always tried to give the greatest amount of good to the greatest number of people. I have created a high standard of living in Setopia. If the people only knew the good inside of me they would not wish for my speedy trial and execution, they would build statues to my memory. They would have marble plaques in the streets commemorating my services. They would remember me with only the kindest of thoughts. Without my guidance the economy of Setopia would crumble and chaos would reign."

"How can you say that?" I asked, "only the Sets benefited from your actions and policies. Your actions were beneficial to only one percent of the population. They were not beneficial to the remaining ninety-nine percent."

"How's it going?" Skeeter asked as he stuck his head into the room.

"Fine," I replied.

"Our people got them guards," he said.

"Any problems?"

"Naw, no problems," he replied as Kram re-entered the room.

“We prepared a cell downstairs for Anil,” Kram said, “we need to place him in confinement as soon as possible, but first, I want to talk to him. Alone!”

We left the room while Kram spoke to Anil. What they talked about I don’t know. After about fifteen minutes, Kram opened the door to the conference room. He looked tired and angry.

"Get the prisoner and follow me!" Kram ordered.

"By all means, incarcerate me immediately!” was Anil's angry retort.

We left the room and went down into the basement and into the prison cells. A special solitary confinement cell had been created for Anil out of rugs and others items hung on the bars to block anyone from seeing him.

"No one is to speak to Anil without my permission," Kram warned, "if I catch anyone speaking with him without my personal authorization, I will have him arrested and confined pending court marshal. Is that understood?"

“Yes, Sir,” came a few murmurs.

* * *

We placed Anil in a cell hidden behind rugs that were taken from an office. As he was going into the cell, Anil turned to me and said, "I enjoyed our talk. Perhaps we can speak again. We have much in common, you and me." Kram pushed him into the cell, closed the door and secured the lock.

As I walked away, I saw the friendly and familiar face of Senator Dennek. He recognized me and rushed forward to shake my hand.

"Didn't think I would see you again," I replied.

"Those people had me scared as hell,” the Senator said. “I didn't know if Sacram would be able to get me out. Anil had me facing treason charges. Where is Anil?"

"He’s in there," I replied pointing to the curtained cell. Dennek took a quick look into the cell. "I understand there is a general strike going on in Seval and Seraphs."

"That's right," I said, "the strike seems to be going well. Anil sent a large number of soldiers to Seval. I'm not certain how they will fare when the soldiers arrive."

"That's not good," he replied, "perhaps we could get Anil, to issue an order for the soldiers to lay down their arms."

"I've already tried that," Kram said, overhearing the Senator's remark. "Anil refused to call off the soldiers, and the generals also refuse. They say their men will soon return, recapture the Palace and free Anil. They think we're marking time, and our time is running out."

“What if we sent their commanders a false message from Anil, ordering them to lay down their arms?” I asked.

“Mmmm. Not a bad idea. Who would be the messenger?" the Senator asked.

"We have two captives in a cell in the next cell block. One is an aide to Anil," Kram said

"Let me speak to them,” Senator Dennick said, “they should know me from my frequent visits to the Palace. Perhaps I could convince them to relay a message."

"It's worth a try," Kram replied. "Follow me,"

We followed Kram into the next cell block. He opened the cell containing two young men. They were both in their early twenties, both frightened and willing to do anything to be released from captivity.

"Which of you is the aide to Anil?” Senator Denneck asked.

“I am,” replied the well muscled dark haired man.

“Will you deliver a message to the commander of the soldiers in Seval?"

"What is the message?" He asked.

"You are to tell the commander of the Seval division…What is his name?"

"Captain Regers," The other man in the cell replied.

"You tell Captain Regers that we have captured Latipac and the Palace. Tell him that his commander has ordered him to lay down his arms and surrender to Gloy in Seval. Tell him that if they attempt to return to Latipac, we will be forced to destroy the Palace and dispose of Anil and his generals. Tell him that the Sets have been placed under house-arrest. Tell them their best alternative is to surrender. Will you agree to deliver that message?"

"Yes, but I'll need documents with the seal of Anil. They won't honor my word,"

"Are you familiar with the wording of such documents?" the Senator asked.

"I've carried many orders. I could write one myself," said the aide.

"Will you write one for us?"

"What do you want it to say?" He asked. "That Anil and his generals have been captured?"

"Yes. That’s right." The Senator said.

"Get me ink and paper.”

One of our men went upstairs, and soon returned with the appropriate supplies. We worked out a rough draft, which the Senator picked up and read.

“Needs a little polishing,” the Senator replied after reading the document. “We need to make a few changes.” After a few modifications and word-smithing, we had a neat and official looking document.

"Looks right," replied the Senator, "will you deliver this to Captain Reder?"

"It's missing the seal of Anil," the aide replied.

"Where does he keep the seal?" I asked.

"The seal is on a ring he wears. He presses it against wax which he places on the document."

"I noticed he wore a ring," I said

“Get that ring," Kram said. We returned to Anil’s cell and opened the door.

“Remove your ring,” Kram demanded.

“No! The ring stays on my finger.”

"Give me your ring or I'll cut it off!" threatened Kram.

"Why force me to remove a ring that has been on my finger for many years?" he said holding the ring upward so that everyone in the cell could see. “The only way you will get this ring off my finger is to cut it off."

"Then we will cut it off!" Kram replied angrily.

"Please," replied Anil composed and without fear, "Give me the document you wish authenticated and I will place my seal on it."

"You will do that?" Kram asked.

"Of course," replied Anil, "a condemned man has no choice in such matters, does he?"

"No," replied Kram, "he doesn't. I'm glad you decided to cooperate."

"Then bring me your document."

Kram got the document and brought a candle. He lit the candle and waited for the wax to melt. Then he poured melted wax onto the corner of the document.

“Press your ring against the wax,” Kram ordered. Anil did as ordered and his majestic imprint showed the royal seal of Anil which was used on every official document in Latipac.

"Will that suffice?" Anil asked.

“Yes,” Kram said as he examined the seal. Then, we returned to the aide who would deliver it. Kram showed the document with the seal of Anil.

“You’ve seen these documents before, does this look official?”

"The seal is authentic," he replied after examining the

imprint, “but, it’s on the wrong side. The seal is always on the lower left, not the lower right. This document would not be accepted.”

"Anil tried to trick us," said Kram angrily. We returned to the cell and Kram shoved the document into Anil’s face. “You tried to trick us.”

"You asked me to apply my seal, and I did so. It was you who chose the position of the wax, not me. How can you say I tried to trick you?"

"You should have told us the seal was in the wrong place!"

"I would have told you, had you asked," Anil replied.

This time Senator Denneck drafted the order on new parchment. After a few minutes, we had another document. We returned to Anil’s cell, lit a candle once more and poured wax onto the document in the presence of Anil.

"I am asking you once more. Is the seal in its proper location?"

“Yes.”

“Put your seal on the wax!” Kram ordered. Once more Anil pushed his ring into the wax and left an impression.

“Is this document official now?” Senator Denneck asked.

"Yes," Anil replied, "it looks fine. No one could tell that it was obtained through extortion, not even my generals--"

"Who are imprisoned!" interrupted Kram.

"Indeed, and are they being provided for?"

"Until their trial," replied Kram.

Senator Denneck handed the document to the aide who stuffed it into a folio.

"Go with him," Kram instructed one of his men. "Make sure he delivers the message. If he tries anything, you know what to do."

"Yes, Sir!"

"We're not certain the commander of the Seval division will acknowledge the order but at the moment all we could do is wait," Kram said. "We have no defense should the soldiers return to Latipac. They can easily retake the Palace and we would be prisoners of Anil and his generals. We tried to convince the aide that we had many more men than he saw in the Palace."

"The Colonel will no doubt question him about our strength, and in learning that we were so few, they will decide we could be easily defeated," Senator Dennick replied.

"We only have a short time to establish defenses around the parameter of the city," Kram said. "We need to place explosives along every point of entry within Latipac. We can eliminate some of the opposition before they enter Latipac."

"Sir," Mot said, "we found explosives in one of the store rooms in the Palace."

"Good. Take several men and place explosives along every

entrance point in Latipac. Also place explosives around the Palace."

"Yes, Sir." Mot and several other men left the cell area and disappeared through the large iron door.

"I'm surprised at Anil's cooperation," I said to Senator Denneck.

"Perhaps, we can get him to do what Sacram and I discussed earlier," Senator Denneck said.

"What was that?"

"We want Anil make a public announcement that he is a captive and the domas are to declare a national holiday with pay."

"Will the Sets go for that?"

"Don't know. We need to talk with the Sets over at the Setro Club."

"Are you going to talk with them?" I asked.

"I think Sacram would be a better choice," Senator Denneck replied. "He has good rapport with the Sets. But where is Sacram?"

"He won't be back for two or three days," said one of the men.

"Great!" Kram replied. "We need to talk to the Sets and Sacram is unavailable."

* * *

Everything about the Palace I found confusing and chaotic. None of us knew from one minute to the next what needed to be done and we reacted to events more than controlling them. I suppose that is the way of provisional governments. Nothing is structured and chains of command and control are lacking. Perhaps it was our lack of organization that Anil found amusing. Every time I saw him or had a chance to speak to him there persisted a slight smirk as though he found amusement in our chaotic state of affairs. Perhaps he was merely waiting, knowing that our ineptitudes would be our downfall.

Anil was a cruel man, to be sure, and one to whom human life was without value. He knew Setopia very well and was an expert in ways to perpetuate that system. After all, he had studied the art of statehood for many years.

Anil viewed the Sets as one might view a favorite pet. They were to be pampered and taken care of. One could not toss them into the perils of the night with good conscious for such an act would go contrary to one's sense of avuncular pride. Their respect and admiration for Anil were tinged with fear. That was the primary reason that a feud never developed between the Sets and the occupant of the Fuchsia Palace because one was necessary for the orderly existence of the other. Both blocs of power existed in a perpetual stalemate, and each benefited the other. Now, things would be different.

CHAPTER 22

Negotiations

The Sets had heard of the overthrow but were not in immediate communication with us. We assumed they didn’t want contact with the provisional government. Such an act would acknowledge our existence, and by doing so they would be relinquishing their own power. The realities were somewhat more straightforward because we had already captured the Palace and they had already lost their power. With both Anil and his generals in our custody, the Sets could do little more than refuse to acknowledge our existence.

“Senator Denneck,” Kram said, “I would like for you to head our negotiation team with the Sets.”

“I was elected by the Sets," Senator Denneck replied, "to represent them in congress. They would consider me a traitor if I negotiated for the provisional government.”

“Senator,” I said, “Anil arrested you for treason and he might have had you executed. You owe no loyalty to the Sets.”

“You’re right,” Senator Denneck said after a moment of

reflection.

“Will you head our team?” Kram asked.

“Yes, what do you want me to do?”

“Establish contact with the Sets at the Setro club. Present them with our terms and conditions, and then await Sacram's arrival in Latipac. Sacram will negotiate the final terms.”

“Do we have talking points?” the Senator asked.

“Yes, here,” I said handing him a three page document outlining our terms.

* * *

Senator Denneck, Kram, myself and twelve other men left the Palace for the Setro Club. When we arrived, several Sets stood under the veranda outside the entrance. As we approached, they disappeared into the building only to reappear with other members of the club.

"What do you want?" Shouted one member.

"We have come to discuss terms," Senator Denneck shouted back.

"Who do you represent?" Asked another.

"The provisional Free Government of Setopia. I have been instructed to offer you a negotiated peace. Will you negotiate?"

"No!" Was the sharp reply. "Your government does not exist! Only the legal government of Setopia exists. You acted in violation of our laws.Your government is not legitimate! You are criminals, all of you! Go away and leave us alone!"

We continued walking toward the Setro club. Standing near the entrance were several defiant club members. Kram instructed seven of the soldiers to remain outside and told five to follow us. We walked past many members who sneered at us as we entered the club.

Inside, we found a group of frightened Sets confronting a situation they had never had to face before. Most of the Sets were visibly worried about their safety and future. Others were bemoaning what they considered to be a sorry state of affairs. Still others were castigating Anil for allowing us to take the Palace.

"Who is in charge here?" Kram asked forcefully. There was no immediate answer. The Sets merely looked at each other. The policy within the walls of the club had been of equal among equals. There were no leaders, and no single person was in charge. However that status changed rapidly when a middle-aged man with graying hair stepped forward.

“I suppose as President of the Setro Club, I am the one you need to talk with,” said the club President.

“Mister Greyson,” Senator Denneck said.

“I suppose you have joined these renegades, Mister Denneck,” said Greyson.

“Yes, I have decided to join them.”

“Too bad Anil didn’t take care of you when he had the chance.”

“I have come to present terms of surrender," Senator Denneck stated bluntly.

"To what group are you presenting your credentials?"

“To the class of Sets to which the exclusivity of this club admits no others. I am presenting you with terms of cooperation with our provisional government."

"We do not negotiate with criminals! You have no legitimate government. You and your compatriots are nothing more than base contemptible riffraff. Do you think that by merely walking into this club that we would recognize your legitimacy?"

"We’ve taken the Palace. Anil and his generals are our prisoners. We are the government!" Kram replied.

"And the army? Have you conquered the army? Of course not! We’ll wait until the army returns. They will hang the lot of you!"

I found myself angered by his arrogance and by his refusal to recognize us as a legitimate government. They saw us as rift raft, and in many ways we felt like rift raft for we had no real organization. I was uncertain myself and this group felt immensely superior to us. However, behind their remarks lurked a fear of our power. They were frightened because they knew we had taken the Palace. They wished to play for time. In bits of conversation I heard the words Seraphs and Seval spoken angrily and in connection with Anil's stupidity to deploy so many troops as to weaken the defenses of the city. They clearly blamed Anil, for their current distress, and many swore to remove him from office and to install someone more competent.

“We were pledged,” Kram said, “to make sure you Sets never have power in Setopia again. I don’t think you fully comprehend your position. You can adhere to your conservative and reactionary philosophies and pretend that change has not taken place. You care little for the misery and poverty that you create in Seval. Poverty and misery are strictly lower-class ailments to you.”

"How long do you think you can control Latipac?“ Mr. Grayson asked, “You lack experience in government. How do you think you could possibly run a government as complex as ours?"

"I have no interest in running the government. That is not my job," Senator Denneck replied. "My task is to present you with an ultimatum.”

“You can either cooperate or be incarcerated. The decision is yours," Kram stated. Kram’s words brought a gasp from many members of the club standing within hearing of our demands.

“It’s outrageous for a non-Set, to enter this club and make

such demands of us!” said one man in a yellow jacket standing to one side of the President. "Why the very thought of it is revolting!”

“We came here without intent to harm,” Senator Denneck said. “Sacram will be here soon to present our final terms.

"What are your terms?" Mr. Grayson asked

"That you recognize our government.”

“And why should we?”

“You don’t have a choice,” Kram said, “either you recognize the provincial government, or we toss the lot of you into jail.”

“Outrageous!” Said the man in the yellow jacket.

“What are your other conditions?”

“That you give the Lats a day off with pay. After all," Senator Denneck continued, "your domas, the corporations, would be disrupted with the transition of power anyway. Our concern is that the economy not be disrupted."

"To hell with the economy!" Came an angry retort from a club member wearing a tuxedo.

"If the economy is not preserved," Senator Denneck warned, "a great depression will ensue and drastic measures will be taken. We are offering you the chance to participate in the economic growth and health of our government. We welcome you as a part of that government."

"But not as leaders," replied Greyson.

"Not true, some of you will remain in important social and economic roles. Others will--"

"Who will determine who remains and who goes?" Interrupted Greyson.

"That will be worked out later when Sacram arrives." Senator Denneck replied.

"That will stifle initiative," Greyson said, "and the government will bungle everything, the economy included. You know how bureaucrats are, they'll mess up everything."

"It isn't necessary that leaders own the organizations they head." Kram said.

"Hell, how can they control an organization if they do not own it?" he asked.

"The leaders of our provisional government will select the leaders with certain qualities," Kram said. "Those lacking those qualities will not be allowed into leadership roles."

"Then, your government will be like the government of philosopher kings?" Greyson asked.

"Yes, but our government will be composed of elected leaders, not of kings. We will have special schools to select and train those most qualified to rule."

"That will stifle initiative and drive," replied Greyson, "profit motive is the only important motivation. Without it, society will crumble into decay."

"Those qualified to rule will be qualified by virtue of natural talent," Kram said.

"You talk nonsense!"

"No," Kram replied, "we're talking about your surrender."

"Surrender! One moment you're asking us to cooperate with you, and the next you're asking us to surrender, as though we were your prisoners. Believe me, we will never become your prisoners, we will die first!"

"Our good friend Sacram will negotiate the final terms." Senator Denneck replied.

"I respect and admire Sacram, but I cannot imagine his having joined a bunch of rebels."

"Gloy is also with us," Kram replied.

"Gloy! Of course! Gloy is perfect for joining the rebels."

"Can we count on your cooperation?" Senator Denneck asked.

"I'll need to confer with our membership," he said.

He walked to the back of the room and motioned for others to circle around him. There was a brief discussion that resulted in much shouting. I could not hear what was said, but after about fifteen minutes, the President returned.

"We will close our corporations, the domas, but only for one day," he replied.

“What day do you want our domas shut down with pay for the workers?”

“We’ll let you know,”Kram said.

"We will honor your request for a paid holiday. I personally do not care to pay people who do not work."

"You and the other members are paid for not working." Kram said. The President looked at Kram with disgust.

“We own the domas. We put our wealth into the domas. If we did not do so the Lats would have no jobs, and with no jobs they could not support their families."

"With the domas, you received wealth created by the Lats, the Sevals and the Seraphians."

"Seraphians!" Greyson exclaimed, "We subsidized the Seraphians. What did they do for us?"

"They made your Set policies seem logical, complex and moral," Kram said.

"They helped simplify our operations to the people," he replied.

"The Seraphians complicated matters to make them more confusing,” Senator Denneck said, “you used first-rate research to obfuscate issues."

An artery on Greyson’s neck swelled as his face flushed. After a moment, he regained his composure and said. "Had we not invested in our industries, the state of Setopia would have returned to a primitive state of nature in which there are no laws and only the strongest would survive. You seem to be lacking in fundamental academic training in economics. I think you would do well to return to the university so that your incorrect views might be rectified."

"The truth is," Senator Denneck replied, “that your formal economic training does little more than obfuscate economic issues and makes them unduly complicated so that the average Lat, or Sev cannot understand what’s going on in the economy around him."

"The Lats, the Sevs, all of them benefit as the economy improves, you know that. There is a trickling down effect which tends to improve the lot of those at the bottom."

"That’s never worked! Those at the bottom live in misery and disease," Kram replied.

"It’s their own fault. If they weren't so lazy they would have more money. We Sets are the job creators. We are getting nowhere with this discussion," Greyson replied with increasing frustration.

"You're right,” Senator Denneck said, “so, you agree the domas will close and all employees will be given a day off with pay?"

Greyson stared at Senator Denneck without speaking. Then he looked at the others who had their heads bowed and stood looking listlessly at the floor. Several of the gentlemen nodded to him, and he replied, "Yes, we will close our businesses, and we will pay our employees for not working. If that is the wish of the new government! We will cooperate as fully as possible. We shall see which society has the better system. I personally predict that your government will be bankrupt and the economy in chaos within the year, however, we don't seem to have a choice in this matter."

* * *

When we returned to the Palace, Mot met us in the front lobby with a sheaf of papers in his hand and great frustration in his voice.

"We must get Gloy to help us organize," Mot stated despondently, "I've never seen such a sorry state of affairs. This revolution is chaotic with no planning, no structure, nothing! Everything is done on the spur of the moment. We can't plan anything!"

"What's the problem?" Senator Denneck asked.

"I have to tell everybody exactly what to do. Nobody seems to be able to act without being told precisely what to do. Haven't our people every heard of personal initiative? I'm constantly occupied with our members asking me what to do. I tell them to guard the prisoners, or to clean up the mess the blast caused. Most of them don't listen to me and do as they wish anyway. They only do as I say if they wanted to do it in the first place."

"You should tell them to do only what they want to do, then there would be no insubordination," I replied somewhat humored by Mot's distress. He was tired and dyspeptic.

"You should get some rest," I said, "we'll hold down the Palace."

"Maybe you're right." He sat down in a nearby chair. "I thought our revolution would be different!"

"Get some rest," I advised.

* * *

Nothing much happened during that first night. Kram set up shifts so that our people could get some rest. Many of them were dead tired from the long march and from the day's activity. After stationing guards and assigning shift changes, Kram and I walked back to the cell block adjacent to the one in which Anil was incarcerated. Inside the cells in the second block were the top generals and aides who we had captured in the briefing room. They were mostly asleep though two were still awake. They gave us looks of hatred as we passed by, one spat at us.

At night, the Palace was frightening in its lonely silence. Only the occasional moan of someone sleeping disturbed the dusty silences of the cell blocks. I left through the main hall and walked outside. Several of our soldiers stood guard in various parts of the garden and gate house. I reentered the Palace and walked down the hallway then returned to the cell block. I found Kram sitting up in his bed.

“Problem sleeping?”

“Yeah, I slept a little, but not much. I keep thinking we’re in deep trouble. Keep thinking the Set soldiers will return and recapture the Palace. You know what they will do to us.”

“Try to get some sleep.” I said.

* * *

The next morning, I took a walk outside the Palace through the garden enclosed by the high iron fence. Near the guard house was a group of Lats. They were looking through the fence eagerly awaiting information. When they saw me, they shouted questions.

“What has happened?”

“Who is in control?”

“What’s going to happen to us?”

"What about Anil? What has happened to Anil?" shouted one.

"He will be tried in a public court as will his generals and all other people guilty of crimes against the people of Setopia." I replied.

There were more questions than I could possibly answer. At the first opportunity, I walked away from the fence and away from their questions. A small pathway led away from the fence into the garden of the Palace. I followed the path and entered a beautifully kept garden with neatly trimmed hedges and pebble walkways that contained a multitude of flowers and shrubs. Marble statues of what looked like ancient Grecian heroes adorned the path. I found the tropical garden full of exotic vegetation and colorful birds. After an hour or so of reflection, I decided I needed to talk with Anil.

* * *

When I arrived at Anil's cell, he was sitting on his cot. I unlocked the door and entered.

"How did you sleep?" I asked.

"I slept very well. Thank you for the accommodations. A nice rug hung over the bars which gave me privacy so that I could sleep without being watched like an animal in a cage. I thank you for that."

"You seem very cheerful considering your circumstances," I said.

"One should always s be cheerful, "he said," one cannot always have everything his way."

"You seem almost as though you're happy that we're here."

"Your group interests me for several reasons not the least of which is the fact that I can sympathize with your struggles"

"How can you sympathize with us? We are your

opponents."

"Not at all. I consider you and your group to be my guests. You may have the use of my Palace with my compliments."

"We have the use of your Palace without your compliments." I replied.

"It might make you happy to know that I agree with what you are doing and I welcome you into my home."

“I don’t understand,” I confessed, “you're our prisoner, but you act like a gracious host. Why?”

"My dear friend," he replied, "I am not acting. I am sincere in my wish that you enjoy your stay, and I do enjoy groups such as yours. Some men take an interest in animals, some in real-estate, and still others take an interest in collecting things. I take an interest in things political. You probably think I must be interested in money and privilege, but you are wrong. I have little interest in commercial things, and I find the whole concept of profits and all that rubbish somewhat revolting. Men often perform jobs that are contrary to their own interests, and in some cases, men do things that are downright distasteful to them personally, but they must perform because that is what they are being paid to do.”

“And you supported the Sets at the expense of the others in Setopia.”

"I supported the Sets because they placed me into office to

help them. I serve them and establish policies which help them expand their enterprises and create more profits. After all, that is what they exist for, to make profits. It's a game with them. They don't need the money. The average man could not spend in a lifetime as much as the average Set makes in a single day. After they have achieved a certain standard of living, such as admittance into the exclusive Setro club, everything else becomes a game. They buy and sell businesses. They venture into real-estate merely as a game in which they see who can pull off the biggest scheme and get away with it."

"Scheme?" I asked, "what do you mean?"

"They play a game with the people of Latipac and get them to do things they wouldn't ordinarily do?"

"Their schemes are fraudulent and serve only to fleece the people," I said.

"There are many such plans and schemes that they use. The Setro club is the garden of such ideas. From the club have come some of the grandest schemes."

"Why are there no laws preventing such a things?"

"My dear man, laws are made by the powerful to protect their interests. They are not made to protect the powerless. In Latipac, the Sets have lots of fun with their games. It proves very valuable to their wealth. Many have made fortunes on a single scheme. All they have to do is hire the slickest and most convincing salesmen. Then they have me stamp their papers to make them look official. When the people see my symbol on the documents, they immediately believe the scheme to be honest and true."

"When the scheme is fraudulent!".

"That's correct," he replied, "it's my job. I have no other alternative. I must help them."

"That's immoral!" I said.

"Immorality! Now we come back to that tyrannical word. Haven't you learned yet that where money is concerned and vast wealth is at stake, there exists no morality. Morality consists in staying ahead of the next man. It's about survival in the financial jungle. After all, if one were a lion among lions, he would be foolish not to act like a lion. If one were to act as a lamb, wouldn't he be in immediate danger of being killed by a large hungry lion?"

"As chief executive, you owe your subjects protection from the beasts," I replied.

"But, you don't understand. The people are being taken care of. The strong always use the weak, and In Latipac, it's the Sets who have the strength and power. Right is on the side of might. That is what Setopia is all about, might makes right. I didn't make up the rules. I only see that they are obeyed."

"What about the enemies of the Sets?" I asked. "How are

they dealt with?"

"Oh, they are dealt with in the manner in which any enemy is dealt with."

"With or without a trial?" I asked.

"We do have our courts. Of course, they were given a trial."

"Were the trails fair?" I asked.

"Fair? Is it fair to me to have enemies who dislike me and refuse to honor me? People I have never met? Do you know what' it's like having people hate me because I represent authority and for no other reason? Of course we gave them trials."

"How were they executed?" I asked.

"Oh, you know, the usual methods, hanging, shooting, dragging or stoning. Crimes against the state are dealt with slowly. Simple street crime like stealing is usually dealt with by a quick and speedy execution."

"Who do you reserve for the torture chamber?" I asked.

"You know about that?" he asked.

"Yes," I replied, "I saw the chamber."

"Oh," he said, "It depends upon the crime. High crimes are treated with severe methods."

"Like the torture chamber?"

"That so called Torture Chamber' is only used for high

crimes."

“The lesser crimes are met with quick death," I said.

"You should spend some time here as my guest and I will show you our marvelous system of justice."

"I don't think I would care to see it," I replied.

“Why don’t we--” His sentence was cut off when Kram entered the cell.

“You’re not supposed to be in here. Orders are orders,” Kram said,” and you’re not to speak with the prisoner.”

“Sorry,” I said, “I shouldn’t have come in here.”

“You should follow Gloy's advice and keep our contact with Anil to a minimum!” Kram cautioned.

CHAPTER 23

New Government

Later that week, I was reading our draft of the speech that Kram wanted me to review when a cry rang out from the courtyard. Kram and I rushed outside. We had just arrived at the Gatehouse when two high ranking military officials of the Set army stepped from the guardhouse to confront us. Kram and I froze in our tracks. We had been afraid that this would happen and our wildest fears had come true. Anil was right, he would soon be back in command. We hadn't had time to fully react when Sacram appeared from behind the soldiers.

"I want to introduce you," he said with a broad smile, "to Colonel Sven and Captain Regers of the Set Army. Sending a messenger with an official document from Anil was brilliant! All the soldiers lay down their arms. The resistance members spoke with small groups of soldiers. They explained that the soldiers' interests lay in joining the new government. They told them about the medical care and the benefits that such a government would give them and their families. Many were resistant at first and rejected the idea of '*giveaway'* programs. It didn't take long to convince them that a giveaway program already existed in Setopia with the sole beneficiaries being the Sets."

"Did you convince them?" I asked.

"Yes, truth works wonders," Sacram replied.

"The Sets at the Setro club are awaiting your arrival," I said. "I think they're ready to negotiate."

"There won't be any negotiations," he replied, "they are going to work like everyone else and benefit like every other citizen. They will no longer be a privileged lot. I've been thinking the large mansions of the Sets could very easily be converted into government office buildings and shelters for the needy. Also, I think the name Setopia should be changed to something else. We should change everything that reminds us of the former state."

"You've been doing a lot of thinking," Kram said.

"Gloy and I did a lot of talking during the past few days," Sacram said, "I'll explain what we have talked about later. First, I want to speak with Anil."

* * *

We continued to the cell block and Sacram went inside. Kram and I remained outside. I couldn't hear all of what was being discussed, but from what I heard, he discussed with Anil the possibility of Anil becoming part of the new government. After about an hour, Sacram reemerged from the cell.

"Jonathan, Kram, come with me. We need to talk."

"About what?" Kram asked.

"The form of our government. Gloy is waiting for us in the main conference room."

We walked up a winding staircase that led to an ornate conference room. It was furnished with posh furniture, crystal chandeliers, and expensive rugs on blue marble floors.

"Please sit down," Gloy said as we entered the conference room. I sat in a carved wooden chair of dark oak and looked at the long ornate table of dark wood in front of me. A young scribe with small round glasses sat to one side of Gloy prepared to take notes.

When we were all seated, Gloy began. "We've been tasked to draw up a constitution that will cement our values for all time. My scribe will take notes that we can later develop into a formal constitution. I would like your thoughts on how we should structure our new government since the two of you helped bring about our success. Sacram and I have discussed at length the form of government we would like. Is that right, Sacram?"

"Yes."

"We think," Gloy continued, "that our new government must be a cooperative venture, but it cannot stand long if it does not satisfy the needs of the majority of its people. The Lats are brainwashed into thinking that their best interests are satisfied by working and constantly striving to get to the top. It is a policy that is designed to make people sick because the government has given them an illusion of an opportunity that they do not in fact enjoy. People should look upon their government for guidance and protection. The government policies should be in the interest of all the people, not just the wealthy."

"Can such a government exist?" I asked.

"Government must look after the interests of its people, or it cannot last," Sacram said, "Anil's government ruled by repression. It serves to perpetuate those already in positions of power."

"Like the Sets?" I asked.

"Yes, like the Sets. Government must exist to help the people and to improve their lives. Anil's government enslaved the people to corporate interests. The domas should do nothing more than serve the needs of society. At present, the domas are fiefdoms in which the workers are little more than slaves. The priorities in Setopia are inverted."

"But, surely," I said, "if the government regulated the domas and controlled who ran them, the government would not need to own the domas. What if the domas were organized as worker cooperatives in which the people who worked also owned the domas through ownership of stock that is given to each citizen. The citizens could elect a board to run the domas and all would share in profits through dividends paid by the domas on a fair and equal basis."

"What we want," Gloy said, "is a government of the people, by the people and for the people. Anil's government was a government of the Sets, by the Sets, and for the Sets. The average citizen was little more than chattel to be used by the Sets in the procurement of wealth. The government must own the domas."

"If an elite of government managers is created," I asked, "what will keep them from misusing the power to enrich their own lives at the expense of the average citizen, much the way the Sets did?"

"They will be schooled," Gloy said, "in the methods of dialectic and meditation. When they see that their own best interests are derived by using their talents to improve society, they will act accordingly."

"What will cause them to act in the best interests of the people?" I asked.

"Because they will know that the best interests of the citizens are also their own best interests. Do you understand?" Gloy asked.

"I don't think so," I confessed, "after all, what is to keep them from thinking that they can immensely improve their own lot by impoverishing the lives of others? "

"But you don't seem to understand," Gloy said, "the rulers we select will be men of noble minds who are trained to know that their own highest interests are achieved by improving the lives of all the citizens. I can envision sidewalks full of artists, the parks full of poets and writers, the corporate offices being utilized cheerfully for the good of society. People produce cheerfully when they feel it is in their own best interest to do so."

“What if the rulers act like the Sets do now,” Kram asked.

“When people are aware,” Gloy replied, “that their efforts are rewarding people who are not contributing, then they will be full of dissatisfaction and rebellion. In such a society only repression will serve the rulers, for they are not ruling in the citizen's interests but in their own. In such societies, the average working man is nothing more than a government statistic which is used in computing profits and the gross national product. In such societies, the gross national product is the only measure of economic success even though it causes the state to float on a sea of turmoil."

“If the rulers serve the people,” Sacram said, “the citizens will benefit through benevolent and democratic government.”

“Exactly,” Gloy said, “by knowing their government serves them, they are more willing to work, and the hours they do work will be more productive and cheerful. Men are happiest when that which is most noble in them is developed. The noblest thing in a man is his mind. It is the mind which separates man from the lower members of the animal world. When man develops his talents and creativity to the fullest, only then is he happy. When government serves to create the conditions wherein man is freed from the slavery of a dull job and the game of corporate ladder climbing, only then will he begin to find true happiness. That should be the chief priority of our government."

"But," I asked, "won't the citizens feel anger when portions of their wages are taxed? I'm told that many workers here in Latipac are angered when they receive their paychecks and learn that much of it goes to the government."

"Not at all," Gloy replied, "financing of our government will be based upon a consumption tax. A citizen will be taxed only in proportion to what he buys."

"But a consumption tax will punish the poor more than the rich," I said.

"A consumption tax," Gloy said, "will not punish the poor if we level incomes so that everyone's incomes are within a fairly narrow range. Food and shelter will not be taxed. The more someone buys the more taxes he pays. Our government will help those who need help in proportion to their needs. Those at the lower end of the social spectrum who need the most help will receive the most help. Those at the top who need the least help will receive very little aid from the government."

"That is almost opposite to the way Setopia works," Sacram said, "yes, the government of Setopia rewarded those the most who needed it the least, and it helped those the least who needed aid the most."

"And the new government will serve the highest instincts in man?" I asked.

"Our government will create the conditions," Gloy continued, "by which people might develop their highest talents. When they have achieved that, there will be no need of government because each person will know that his own best interests lie in treating other citizens as he himself might wish to be treated. By behaving equitably toward others, a person inspires equitable treatment from others toward himself. Of course, one would be naive to assume that all citizens will behave well. There will always be some who will want to usurp power and misuse the laws in pursuit of personal gain. However, by creating conditions for man to learn and reflect on his nature, he will come much closer to becoming a benevolent being."

"And Setopia will become a land of utopia and bliss?" I asked.

"Not exactly," Sacram added, "first of all we need to get rid of the name Setopia. I think the name is dreadful. We will use another name in referring to our island. But you are right in our attempting to bring out the best in our people."

"I've often thought," I said, "that when the state owns the means of production, a non-democratic government develops which does not respond to the people. Do you see that danger?"

"Ownership by the state is nothing more than the sum ownership by all the people," Gloy explained. "Each citizen has a share in the means of production. Each person benefits in good times, each suffers in bad times. Our government will be a cooperative in which ownership is by the people, and the benefits are distributed evenly across the whole of the population. There will be no unemployment because as the population expands, we will expand the means of production to create new jobs. Jobs in medicine and agriculture will be created to accommodate increases in population. Methods of birth control will be freely taught and appropriate contraceptive devises given the citizens so that they will have only children that they want. There will be no unwanted children haunting the streets at night. We will create day-care and child centers to care for children who are now neglected. We will teach them skills until they are able to earn their own way. Our government will be like an extension of the family, a family that cares. A Parent would not let his child roam the cold streets would he?"

"No, "I replied, "but seizing assets by the government doesn't work very well."

"Then, what would you suggest?" Gloy asked.

“Like I said, all the assets should be turned over to the provincial government, but those assets would then be issued to the domas. Furthermore, the government could issue stock in the domas to everyone in Setopia on a fair and equal basis. The surplus assets of the domas could be returned to the people through dividends, or quarterly payments.”

“What would be the role of government, then?” Sacram asked.

“The government will regulate the domas. Our provincial government will use its resources to help our people,” Gloy said.

"What about the small shopkeepers and the merchants?” I asked, “what if they want to keep their profits, and inflate their prices?"

"Inflation will be viewed as any other crime by our government,” Gloy said, "the initiators of inflation will be punished the same as one who robs another on the streets. After all, inflation is only robbery twice removed. It’s a form of greed which periodically sweeps the nation, and draws the creative energies away from the people. It's a cancer which gradually spreads through the land and destroys all it touches."

"But how can you control greed? Isn't it inbred in all of us?" I asked, being somewhat skeptical of Gloy’s idealistic vision.

"Greed,” Gloy continued, “is a base instinct not greatly

different from that which requires toilet training in childhood. The child is gradually taught that there is a place for such things and they are not done in the streets on in the living room of one's home. Greed can also be overcome by proper training. If, initially, the parents, and later the leaders of society, teach the people to value those who lack greed, peer group pressure can be used to reinforce the positive attributes. Later, as knowledgeable adults, they will learn that greed is an aberration which will only weaken society and make men worse off. They will see that it is wrong for a whole society to perpetuate the existence of a few who make no contributions. They will know that inflation and other tools of greed only serve to disrupt society and make people worse off. We will emphasize man's positive traits in our new society. We will strive to develop only the positive side of man while discouraging the negative side of man such as his greed, his cunning, his antisocial behavior. Each will learn to function on the highest level to which he is capable."

"But, what about those people whose natural talents are not so great, and those who are deficient from birth?" I asked. "How will they fit into this society."

"The same way as everybody else because their happiness will come from developing those innermost traits which are most desirable to society. They might be good painters or sculptors. It isn't necessary that they be gifted. There is a place for everyone in our society. But the gifted will not be idolized because that would only create unhappiness in those of lesser talents. The most gifted would receive pleasure in using their gifts to help the less fortunate. There will be no social stratification."

"How long will it take to achieve those goals?" I asked.

"Not in our lifetime," Gloy said, mournfully and with a distant look in his eyes. "I'm afraid. It will take many years to undo the damage and negative conditioning that greed and antisocial strivings have bred into our people. As children, people can be taught and trained to behave in whatever manner is desired. However, once they reach their teenage years, their personalities develop. They are somewhat like damaged earthenware that has already been baked. Before it hardened, the earthenware would be shaped into whatever its creator wanted, but after the clay has hardened and the fire has been applied, the earthenware becomes brittle and fixed in shape. One has to either accept the product or reject it, but it can never be remolded. The first generation of our government will be the most difficult because many of these people are hardened and cynical. It's too late for them to develop their inner talents which would have made them happy and productive. Instead, our society is inundated with these unfortunate people. We can do little more than tolerate them and try to absorb them."

"Will a national health program be met with anger and

resistance from the medical profession?" I asked.

"The doctors under the old system had become specialized and greedy. The hospitals would not accept patients, nor would they treat them unless they paid for the services in advance. Babies could not be born in hospitals unless the parents had prepaid medical expenses. Doctors were charging their clients unreasonable fees for their services. By specializing, the doctors could more nearly take advantage of their clients. Each doctor was specialized so that one admitted the patient, one took the x-rays, one read the charts, and the like."

"Another example of greed?" I asked.

"Yes, among others," Gloy replied. "A psychologist in Seraphs created a profile for Setopian doctors. He found that their psychological profiles were the same as those of salesmen. The focus of a salesman's life is making money and becoming more Set-like in their living habits. I think his research says a lot about the quality of people attracted to the medical profession in Setopia. They are attracted primarily by the promises of wealth. After all, a seriously ill patient will not quibble about price of services when he is dying. One would think it a quality of the medical profession that they be benevolent and people oriented, instead they take advantage of desperate people. That is another Set trait they have chosen to mimic, like gods to be worshiped and admired."

"The government must be a part of the people," Sacram replied, "and the people a part of the government. No more slums and poverty, but no more wealthy people. All will be making similar wages within a broad band of wages, depending on skill levels involved."

A long pause ensued during the meeting in which no one spoke. Finally, Sacram turned to Gloy. “We need to meet with the Setro club. We’ve discussed this enough, don’t you think, Gloy.”

* * *

We walked from the Palace and down the street leading to the Setro Club. As we approached, we could see Sets standing outside the club, awaiting our arrival. We were welcomed to the club by an elderly Set gentleman with an ornate cane of carved wood with a silver handle.

“That’s president Greyson,” Kram said, “he’s the man with the silver handled cane.

“Yes, I know,” Sacram replied.

“Sacram, so good to see you,” Mr. Greyson said, I know Jonathan and Kram, but who are the others with you?”

“You’ve no doubt heard of Gloy,” Sacram said.

“I’ve heard a great deal about Gloy," said Greyson, "we’ve heard much about the prophet of the mountains."

"I too have heard much about your Setro Club," Gloy

replied. "Is it true the sun rises and sets on this club?" His question brought a murmur of laughter through the strained atmosphere of the club.

Greyson took us into a small ornate room to the side of the main hall. We sat down in posh leather chairs. The initial conversation between Gloy and the president had nothing to do about the resistance movement or about the capture of the Set government, but centered more on finding common ground.

"I hear Seraphs is lovely in the fall," Greyson began, "I am told the aspen turn golden shortly after the first frost."

"Yes," replied Gloy stroking his beard and falling into reverie," many a day I awoke in my camp to the beauty of the golden aspen and the heavy dew hanging languidly from the leaves. The sun creates a multitude of colors as its rays go through the droplets of water."

"So, Gloy, what did you learn in your years in the mountains?" Greyson asked.

"I learned of the violence that one man does to himself by doing ill to another, especially by acquiring great wealth."

"What do you mean?" he asked, "surely one man can increase his wealth by not doing ill to others."

"One who owns too many material goods does so at the expense of his psychic health. He injures himself and he injures others by pursuing self interest."

"I would think self-interest is important," Greyson said.

"Self-interest is a blight which spreads throughout the land cursing all the inhabitants because a few powerful men care little for the interests of others. All is one, and one is all. If you understand this you will know that by hurting another person, you are hurting yourself. We are all members of Setopia. When people do ill towards others, we begin to see slums in the cities, high rates of crime and unemployment, mass dissatisfaction and the like. If men followed their natural inclinations toward benevolence, there would be no crime or wars because there would be no poverty, no uneducated people, and no slums. Materialism has harmed Setopia more than you can imagine."

"So you say," replied Greyson."I haven't seen any evidence that our members are responsible."

"Deep down inside yourself, do you not sense that you have created the problems of inequity and social injustice?" Gloy asked.

"No," he replied, somewhat indignant, "neither I nor the members of this club, created those slums. If it wasn't for our activities, there would be many more people out of work, and more slums. We put people to work. How can you criticize us for putting people to work? We are job creators, not slum creators!"

"You could have put more people to work."

"Hell! That's impossible! There are too many people to put

everyone to work, besides it is bad policy to put everyone to work. If the workers become too satisfied, it's bad for business."

"So Setopia rewards those who go along with it?" Gloy asked.

"Hell yes, it rewards those who are loyal, and it damn well should! And it will destroy anyone who tries to screw it up! I don't like people who screw with my domas. Makes me damn mad!" Damn fighting mad!"

"You don't describe a very good society," Gloy said.

"It's better than having wild dogs running through our streets pissing on our streetlamps!" Replied one elderly gentleman who was standing behind Greyson.

I couldn't help being amused by the old gentleman's similar remarks at an earlier meeting.

"I don't believe you understand your position," Gloy said, somewhat ruffled by Greyson's remarks, "we're not asking you to make concessions. We're demanding that you do so. We have declared the Set government illegal and its laws null and void. We have control of the Palace and Anil."

"We have control of the army!" Greyson shouted," and they will soon be in Latipac!"

"That army," Gloy continued, "has pledged its support to the new government,"

"Preposterous! I don't believe that for a moment."

Gloy signaled to an aide who stepped outside and brought in the colonel who had been in charge of the Seraphs expedition.

"Let me introduce Colonel Sven," Gloy said. "I believe you know him?"

"Is it true?" the president asked, astounded, "Have you joined the enemy?"

The Colonel looked briefly at the president then replied, "Yes, but they are not our enemies."

"The whole Set Army has gone over to the enemy government?" Greyson asked, astounded.

"The Army has pledged support to the new government," the colonel replied.

"We are returning Setopia back to the people," Gloy said.

"Damn bad!" Greyson slumped back into his chair. "What has happened? Where did we go wrong?" he murmured to himself.

"That's it, turn the city into a menagerie of animals that will be running wild, there'll be no government at all, only anarchy!" said an indignation old man in the back of the group

"All members of this club must relinquish their assets and turn them over to the new government," Gloy said firmly. His eyes glared into those of Greyson.

"You don't know what you're asking," said a startled Greyson, "the whole economy will collapse. Your government will never work. Only private ownership works. You can't turn the production assets over to the government! How about the medical system, and the education? You're going to turn this nation into a state of anarchy. The people will never stand for it! They will never support your government!"

"I'm going to give you a chance to speak to the citizens of Latipac tomorrow in the park. You will tell them they have nothing to fear from the new government."

"Never!" he shouted, "I'll not assist you, nor will any member of this club!"

"Then you leave me no alternative. Guards!" shouted Gloy. Two large men carrying rifles entered the room and stood at attention. "Either you cooperate or I will have all of you arrested! I'll ask you only once more, and I want you to think very carefully before answering. Will you cooperate with our government?"

The president slumped in the chair. His face was ashen as he buried his head in his hands. A short time later he raised his head, "Yes," he said in a voice barely audible, "we will help your government."

"Tomorrow," Gloy said, "I am speaking to the Lats in central park. I want you there with me, and I want you to tell everyone there that the Set industries have been nationalized, and that we are forming a cooperative government in which every citizen will have a part ownership in the domas. All people will benefit in good times, all will suffer in bad. However, all will be better off than they currently are."

"You will have whatever you want. We no longer have control. But, I am curious. What will your government do with us? Are we to die?"

“You Sets killed many people,” Gloy said. “You Sets deserve to die, but you are fortunate in having a benevolent government. You will not die, but you will no longer be wealthy men. You will have to work like the Lats and the Seval and the Seraphians. There will be no privileged class. Everyone will work. "

"Sounds idealistic," retorted Grayson.

"There will be emphasis on the arts,” Gloy said, “and on the things of the mind. Citizens will be encouraged and allowed to participate in their government. There will be no slums or any of the other social ills that you Sets have instilled in society."

"How long do you think your government will exist? Your government will collapse with widespread revolution within the first year, if not, then during the second."

"Our government is dedicated to the improvement of society,” Gloy said, “that is the premise from which all other policies will be derived. That will be manifested in our constitution and in our parliament. The elected members to the parliament and our laws will reflect this philosophy."

"I wish I could share your idealism. I've been too long in the world. I find your philosophies naïve," Greyson said.

"You may find them anyway you wish. I'll expect you in the park at ten o'clock," Gloy replied.

CHAPTER 24

Acceptance

A Speaker's platform erected near the center of the city park stood under a large oak tree. Several chairs and a podium stood on the stage. The air was crisp, but pleasant and a slight wind rippled through colorful banners placed along the platform. I met up with Gwinn as Sacram, Gloy, and the President of the Setro Club, Mr. Greyson, ascended the stairs to the wooden platform. As the Setro President walked up the stairs, cheers arose from the crowd. More and more Lats entered the park. An air of excitement filled the park. Silence fell over the crowd as Greyson arose to speak.

"I have been asked to speak to you today," began President Grayson,"by representatives of the new Provisional Government. All of you are aware by now, that a revolt occurred in which our government was overthrown." He paused as a murmur arose from the crowd before continuing. "The new government is currently in control of the Palace, the City of Latipac as well as all of Setopia. I am told this new government will be a better government. The leaders of the new government say it is a better government for the Lats and the Seval and the Seraphians. The only group the new government does not support is the Sets who are being divested of their belongings and being relegated to the level of the average man. I have also been told that we will benefit from learning how the common man has to live, I am told that it will make us better citizens and that we will become more sympathetic to the plights of people less well off. The impetus of the revolt did not come from you. All of you were loyal workers, and I want to express my gratitude to each and every one of you for allowing me and my family, my friends and my associates to serve you. I want to thank each and every one of you for your support and loyalty. I now relinquish title and command to the representatives of the new government, one of which is an old and dear friend whom I cherish and wish all the best in his efforts to establish a new government. I now turn the podium over Sacram, my good friend and representative of the new government."

Sacram arose and walked to the podium. For a long moment, he did not speak, but merely looked over the crowd assessing their mood. "Friends, fellow citizens," Sacram began, "I bring to you today the realization of a dream. Today we stand on the threshold of human possibilities. Today we stand on the brink of the possible, on the brink of a new humanism in society and government. We do not wish to separate government from society as it has existed in the past. Rather, we wish to make the citizens an active part of the government. We wish to implement what is good and right for society. Ours will be a society of people, a government that exists for the people. We will not again be a people who exist for the government. "

As Sacram spoke, I noticed a change in the mood of the crowd. Each had a stake in the new government. The Sets publicly pledged support to the government. The Sets had also pledged to relinquish their vast holdings to a public trust which would be managed by those in government. For years, the Lats had worked for the Sets in a symbiotic relationship in which each existed as a small cog in a large machine. It was from the more senior Lats that the greatest criticism of Sacram and the new government emanated. I could hear some of their criticisms. It was these men who occupied the executive suites in the domas, and it was these men who were nearest to the Sets.

By far the great majority of Lats were in favor of the new government, or at least it would seem so by their demeanor. Within minutes after Sacram began speaking, optimism swept through the crowd, and by mid speech, they were openly cheering. Their government would no longer be based upon the premise that might makes right. Instead, it would be based upon the premise that each man has a right to the same rights and privileges as any other man, and it is each man's right to seek redress in the courts or to take complaints to the new government. It is the government's job to listen to these complaints and to act on them. The Lats were receptive to the idea that they too could become members of the community of Seraphs, and the Seraphians could become members of the community of Lats for there would no longer be discriminatory titles and barriers separating them. It had been a useful device for the Sets to keep the people separated and distrustful of each other. Portraying each division of Seraphs as an enemy of the other was a devise the Sets used to divide and conquer. The Lats were a fearful lot, and fear could be used by the Sets to produce desirable actions. Most lats were conditioned to accept Set doctrine unquestioningly. The Sets controlled by fear, but fear is dispelled by intelligent inquiry. That was the message Sacram was delivering.

“Our domas will be reorganized as worker cooperatives in which each citizen has an ownership. It will be the workers who select, hire and evaluate management and vote on issues important to the doma. The highest paid executive will not be paid more than eight times that of the lowest paid employee. That is how we will abolish inequality in Setopia. Each citizen will benefit in good times and suffer in bad. We are all in this economy together. Also, a consumption tax will be placed on all goods purchased rather than having an income tax. The Sets enjoyed the income tax because they paid virtually no income taxes due to tax-loopholes. Income taxes are to be abolished. Governmental revenue will come from a gross consumption tax which taxes everyone more equally since income will also be more equal; however, professionals and others who have trained many years should enjoy benefits not shared with their lesser trained counterparts. This was seen as an injustice since long years of hard work should not go unrewarded." A murmur swept across those in the park as his words sunk in. "A council of the wisest men," Sacram continued, "will be created as a permanent part of the government. They will guide the policy of our new government. Next, we will rid ourselves of the name Setopia because that name does not create an image of equality."

The ideas put forth by Sacram fell on receptive ears, and the Lats became more eager by the moment until they were openly joyous at what they heard. The prospect of a full and meaningful life struck chords within them and the notes bore sonorous themes which excited them.

"Ours will be a better society in which all people will participate and all will benefit. We do not like the trickle-down-economics that the Sets defended as being a healthy part of free-enterprise and one which purportedly improved standards of living. I will not go into great detail about the new principles which will drive the new government, nor will I engage in moralistic prognostications of all the things the new society will give to its members. I will say, however, that each of you must contribute for the new government to function. With those words, I conclude my speech."

A drone of conversation filled the air as the excited Lats discussed their new Setopia. They were eager to begin working toward the new society, though many wondered how their own lives would be under the new government.

* * *

The following day, a great feast was prepared at the Palace to celebrate the new government. Many of those people who had participated in the strike in Seval travelled to Latipac and joined in the feast. Others came from Seraphs. A few, but not many, of the Sets joined in the festivities. Long tables were filled with the finest meats, salads, vegetables, and deserts. Water buffalo, considered a delicacy by those in the lower valley, was on the menu as was leachy stew, made from a plant grown in the highlands. There was beef from cattle in the plains, venison and pork from the forest and many other types of meat and vegetables. The culinary skills of the chefs were the finest in all of Setopia and the meals they provided were divine.

CHAPTER 25

Departure

Gwinn sat with me at the table enjoying the meal, but my thoughts were not about food nor the new government. My thoughts were about my family and old friends in the United States. I wondered how I could return to my home in Washington, D.C. I felt myself apart from this cheerful group. This was their island nation, not mine. Gwinn must have noticed that I was day dreaming, for she asked, "What are you thinking about?"

"My home and my family."

"Are you anxious to leave us?" she asked, somewhat hurt.

"No, but someday I must attempt to return home."

"Aren't you happy with us?" she asked.

"Yes, but I miss my family."

"Oh, I wanted to tell you something.The other day I was walking along the beach and saw something that might interest you," she said, a twinkle in her eyes.

"Oh," I replied, “what was it?”

"A boat,” she said, “one with a little house on top.”

“A boat?” I asked astounded,"where?" My interest was now aroused because I knew she might have discovered something that could take me away from this island.

"Not far from here,"she said, "it looked as though it had been washed up on shore by the high tide."

"Was it damaged?"

"There was a large hole in the bottom. I'm afraid it wouldn't do to travel with, it would sink immediately without a doubt."

"Would you show me where it’s located?"

“Of course, when do you want to see it?” She asked.

“How about right now?”

"Now? Shouldn't you remain here and enjoy the feast? Besides, Sacram or Gloy might need you."

“I doubt they need me," I replied, “please show me the boat. We've finished our meal."

"My, you are eager," she replied.

“How far is it to the boat?”

“Not far. It’s on the shore."

“Let’s go,” I said as we got up to leave.

"Gwinn and I are going to the beach," I said to Sacram as we walked past his table. “Anything you want me to do before we leave?"

He paused a moment, then replied, “no, we can manage. Have fun. Oh, by the way, Alita wanted me to give you her best wishes.”

“Is she coming to Latipac?” I asked with a spark of hope.

“No. She is staying in Seraphs, but wanted you to know her thoughts are with you.

“If you see her…” I said.

“Yes?”

“Just give her my best regards.”

“I will.”

* * *

Gwinn and I left the banquet and headed for the coast. We walked about thirty minutes before I could hear the sound of surf breaking upon the beach. A short distance more and I could smell the salt air. We climbed down a pathway along a rocky cliff about a hundred feet high. Soon, we stood on a beach of white sand that extended for a long distance in both directions. Seagulls soared above us in the rose colored evening sky. Sandpipers ran up and down the sandy beaches near the rocky cliffs. I felt wonder and excitement at being on a beach again. I was overjoyed.

We climbed to the top of a small knoll overlooking a section of the beach that spanned far to our left. In the distance alongside the water lay the hull of a boat that had drifted into the estuary at the mouth of a river. In an uncontrollable fit of emotion, I ran the half- mile or so to the beached boat, unaware that Gwinn had fallen behind. An overpowering sense of homesickness overcame me at the sight of the small blue and white boat that lay on its side partially covered with sand.

Most of its paint had weathered away by the incessant pounding of the surf and some of its fiber glass was splintered around a hole driven into its side by a rock. Fortunately, it had drifted into the waters of the estuary where it had been protected from further damage. I climbed aboard and entered the cabin. I found the compass to be operational. Other items of navigation, such as a sextant were also intact. After a while, Gwinn caught up with me.

"You ran very fast," she said panting, “I couldn't keep up with you.”

"Come aboard," I said, offering her my hand, “but watch your step." She climbed up the sloping deck and entered the cabin.

"I've never been on a boat before," she said.

"I think I know who sailed this boat," I said, "it was a British guy I met in Seraphs."

“I heard the owner’s body washed ashore a few days after this boat showed up on the beach," she said.

"Must be a crew member," I replied, "I met a fellow from Britain who said his boat ran aground. Said he lost two of his crew members. This is probably his boat."

"Where did you meet him?"

"He was in a cell next to mine in Seraphs. They shipped him out somewhere. Don't know where."

"Can you sail this boat?"

"No. There is too much damage. Anyway, I'm no seaman."

"But you sailed to our island didn't you?"

"I sailed in the air," I replied. Gwinn looked confused. "I flew in a plane with wings that flew through the air like a bird. This boat has sails and uses the wind to move over the water."

"I don't understand," she said, "you can fly like a bird?"

"No, not like a bird," I said, knowing that she would not understand, so I changed the subject. "There's a lot of damage to the boat, but I think the navigation equipment is okay."

"What good is this equipment if the boat won't float?"

"I can use it if I built a raft."

"A raft?"

"Sure. I could tie several logs together and sail out there into the open ocean."

"Can you do that?"

"Yes, but it will be difficult. It's one thing to navigate in the open ocean, and another to navigate raft near shore with rocks and other obstacles."

"I'm glad you found our island," she said.

"So am I. I like the people here. But I need to return to my own land. I have a family waiting for me. They probably think I'm dead."

"I've grown fond of you," she confided as she turned away and looked through a porthole in the side of the cabin, "I'll miss you if you leave."

"I haven't left yet."

"No, but one day you will leave. You'll build your raft and sail away."

"Yes, one day, but not today. Perhaps I'll live here until I'm old and gray. I might even become a member of the Council of Wise Men."

"You would make a good wise man."

"Thanks, but there are better men on the island than me."

"That's not true," she said," I think you're just as bright as any of the intellectuals of Seraphs. Gloy and Sacram always spoke very highly of you. They should know. They've been in contact with the best of the intellectuals. You should have confidence in their judgment."

"I feel honored to be held in such high esteem. They're the most brilliant men I've ever met."

"How do you think all this will end?" she asked.

"What?" I asked,

"Do you think the new government will survive?"

"I don't know. At least they're trying."

"What is your country Like?" she asked.

"My country is very big, and it influences most of the rest of the world. If there are good times in my country, there are good times around the world"

“Are there Sets in your world?"

"No. In my country, everyone is equal under our constitution."

"That would be nice having everyone born equal. I would like that for Setopia."

"I believe you will have equality," I replied.

"Gloy and Sacram are idealists and visionaries,” Guinn said. “The Sets have lost their wealth, and they are now just like everyone else, but they really aren't like everyone else, they're different. I don't know if they’re born different, or they became different. I'm skeptical. I think the Sets will regain power. They’re very clever. I don't think they will ever treat us as equals.”

"Perhaps," I replied, "but Gloy and the other leaders will design the new government with checks and balances to prevent the Sets from once more controlling Setopia. He wants the educational system to instill in the citizens a sense of fairness and he wants it to screen potential office holders and to train them early in the virtues of office. If their education is successful, they will take their posts in government out of a sense of duty to society, not because they wish to gain in some way. They should want to leave government as soon as their services are completed. Government should be an obligation or a duty. That is the way Gloy wants it to be."

"Men are selfish creatures by nature, and I don't think that any amount of education will rid them of their animal natures. Ideals are not worldly things," Guinn said.

"You've been around Gloy too long," I said." You're becoming a philosopher."

"I've been thinking a lot," She said "In my village of Seval, the Sets considered imagination to be wrong because it make us dissatisfied with our work in the factory. For that reason, imagination was discouraged. I lived in a world of fantasy. I couldn't stand the rigors of factory life, and I was appalled by the filthy conditions of Seval. My imagination helped me sooth the pain of living."

"I'm glad you saved your imagination," I said, "because I'm not certain what you would be like without it. That is one of the qualities I admire in you. You have a fine imagination, and you're very pretty."

She blushed but said nothing. She looked vacantly out the

small porthole in the side of the ship and watched the white caps on the breakers in the Shoals just off the coast. "Would a raft be safe?"

"Nothing floating on the ocean is safe."

“Oh,” she said looking a little sad, "it's getting late, and the others might be worried. We should return to Latipac."

"Okay, but first help me remove these instruments. I want to place them in a safe place in case the ship is washed back into the ocean.

"Where can we store them?"

"I don't know," I said, “perhaps just inside the forest."

"Will they be safe there?"

“I think so. Hand me that bag of tools,” I said pointing to a small canvass bag I had found in one of the drawers."

We removed the compass, the sextant, maps and other items that I felt would be useful. The tools I knew would be of use so I took them as well. I wrapped the compass, sextant, maps and tools in a canvass bag we salvaged from the boat, and placed them in a cavity under a boulder, then covered the opening with rocks and other debris to hide our stash.

* * *

When we arrived back at the Palace, the sun was just setting and the distant skies had the color of bright vermillion. It looked like a fire raging just over the mountain peak. Sacram and several of the others were in the main conference room of the Palace working on details of the new government. Their conversations had to do with a list of possible candidates for the Council of Wise Men. Gwinn and I sat down and listened to their discussion.

"The problem, "Gloy said, "is that prejudices are passed on from generation to generation. If the Lats are given a chance to sit on the committee, their votes would be cast for those who swear to give them more of what they grew up with."

"Like Set rule?"

"Yes. They grew up under set rule and their natural inclination is to do as the Sets wish."

"We're not talking about having a committee composed entirely of Lats," Sacram said,"of course there will be lats, but there will also be Seval and Seraphians. We need to have a balanced committee. This idea of you and I choosing who will sit on the Council of Wise Men strikes me as being anti-democratic."

"Anti-democratic, hell!" retorted Gloy, "what would be democratic about the Lats selecting people who are pro-Sets? What they would propose would benefit the few the most and the most the least. Can we afford to take the chance of our government being oppressive and anti-democratic? Isn't that what we've fought against all these years?"

"Yes," replied Sacram, "but we must be aware that you and I picking members of the council would result in an undesirable precedent!"

* * *

In time Gwinn and I tired of their arguments. We left the room and went outside into the garden. As we sat talking, my thoughts continually left the garden and our conversation and brought me back to the raft and the possibility of my being able to return to the United States.

"Aren't you listening to me?" said Gwinn angrily, "I've been talking to you and you don't seem to hear what I'm saying. Are you bored with me?"

"I was thinking about building a raft."

"A raft! That's all you've been thinking about all evening. Don't worry about the raft. If you want to leave us so badly, we'll help you build you a large raft and you can sail out to sea. Is our island such a bad fate,?"

"I like everyone I've met on Setopia, but I want to go home."

"You may not be able to return to Setopia if you leave. Besides, what if you don't find this fog you speak of? Will you float about in the sea and drift so far out that you can never return? What would you do then?"

I thought a moment. Her question raised anxieties in me,

for I too had considered the possibility of losing both worlds and being lost and dying at sea.

* * *

The next few weeks I was occupied with building a raft, with the help of many people. Kram was very helpful in building the raft. “The sap in this tree will keep the logs from becoming saturated with water,” Kram said, pointing to a particular gray tree with very slick bark. Kram was not only an expert woodsman, he was also a fine carpenter. With the help of Kram and others, we cut logs in the forest, and stripped the bark. Together, we dragged the logs to the water’s edge. Placing them side by side, we secured the logs with coarse rope procured from the Palace and made wooden pegs from a very hard ironwood that grew in the forest. We drove the pegs into the logs to secure them and cut a hole in the center of the raft for the mast and lashed it with ropes. Then, we drove ironwood pegs into the mast and decking to give the mast greater strength.

“Fifteen logs across the beam should be enough,” Kram said.

Midship, we constructed a small cabin and fitted the logs with dovetail cuts so they would stay together in rough seas. Into each of the dovetail notches we drove ironwood pegs to reinforce the fittings. Many days later, our raft began to look more and more like a seaworthy craft with a fine looking midship cabin.

The cabin looked like a small replica of the type of log cabins used by pioneers back in my country. We built a drop leaf table which swung on wooden hinges from the cabin wall, and constructed an assortment of shelves with small wooden bars on the side to keep things from flying off the shelves when the raft pitched with the waves. We also secured to the deck two wooden chairs from the Palace. The rudder we made from ironwood and secured it to the deck logs.

“This raft looks like a fine vessel,” Kram said as we were putting the finishing touches on the raft.

“She’s a beauty,” I said admiringly.

"What kind of flag will you fly from the mast?" Gwinn asked amused by the tall pole attached to the mast.

"I don't know."

"Fly the flag of your home country. That way, they will recognize you and rescue you quicker," she said.

"Does the new government have a flag?" I asked.

"No, “she replied, "it hasn't, but we soon will have one. That will be my first task. I will design a flag with an emblem that will properly display the qualities of our new nation."

"Then you should have in your flag the emblem of Fraternity, liberty and equality," I said.

“Yes, I like that, Fraternity, Liberty, Equality.”

“Will people in your world come here when they learn of

our island?"

"I don't know."

* * *

As the weeks passed, the new government established many of the ideals of good government. A consumption tax was levied upon the citizens to finance the new government. In such a manner, thrift was encouraged because tax was paid upon money spent, not on money earned.

The commercial organizations were no longer incorporated, so their charters were changed to serve as workers cooperatives. The concept of the doma was abandoned, and the whole of the new nation became as a cooperative in which all benefited equally, and all worked equally. As I walked through the streets of the new Latipac, a great number of artists and poets filled the parks. Most people were smiling and laughing. The incidence of crime disappeared. People were happier and more civil to one another.

As it turned out, many of the members of the Council of Wise Men were Seraphians since they were the intellectuals. Such people are greatly needed by society. The council was composed of men who possessed a rare blend of men of action and men of contemplation. In that way, they were able to think in terms of the ideal while being able to engage in the vigorous activities of political life. The council was charged with proposing imaginative and innovative social schemes to benefit its citizens. Their recommendations would receive the full force of the government and would be implemented upon approval by the parliament which would be composed of the most courageous and benevolent people.

The schools were responsible for educating the citizens in their duties as citizens, and they would receive encouragement in allowing their imaginations to caress the distant limits of what would be good for society. The schools would not rigidly enforce social classes as they had in the past. There would no longer be the destructive class distinctions which had crushed so many children under the old system. Children would wear the same uniforms to school so they would concentrate on their studies rather than participating in a fashion show. The former Setopian society had fed on such ills because it helped perpetuate the Sets.

Conditions in Seval also vastly improved under the new government and people working in the factories were much happier. They were now working for their own interests, rather than for the interests of their set masters since they were now part owners of the factories.

At first, many were suspicious of the new government. Gradually, however, as the Council of Wise Men was established, the citizens learned that the government provided them with better health care, employment and living conditions.

Under the new system, work days and hours were greatly reduced. Resources were now used to build public houses, better parks, safer buildings, and the like. Soon, the people learned that good government can exist for them and their children and their children's children. They learned that good government was common sense government.

The old government had not acted in their best interests, and their former government officials had only been interested in serving the narrow self-interests of the Sets. Once the people understood the uniqueness of their new government, they rejoiced. Many felt a great weight lifted. Gaiety filled the streets of the city, and merriment filled the parks. The citizens bonded into a coherent whole and each strived diligently to perfect the ideals of humanity.

* * *

After many weeks of arduous work, the raft was finished and stood partially floating at the edge of the ocean, moving easily with the advancing and receding waves. At last, it was ready for its maiden voyage. When the day of my departure arrived, Gloy, Sacram, Gwinn and many of the others gathered on the shore to see me off. Parting was painful and my heart was filled with sorrow. Many of my friends wished me to remain on the island, but I had other responsibilities that propelled me forward.

The raft had sufficient provisions of food and water for more than two months. Ten fifty gallon drums of water stood lashed to the deck timbers. A compass was also securely lashed to the deck. I looked at the compass and saw the needle pointed north and away from the island. I felt that was the direction I needed to go in order to to seek out the magnetic fog that might let me return home.

It was a heart wrenching moment for me as we pushed the raft out into the water. I hopped aboard and the raft slid gently out into the blue waters of the lagoon. I set the sail and, as it filed with wind, my heart sank as I watched my friends disappear into the distance. I waved to them until I was far out into the ocean.

The first few hours were the most difficult as I watched the island of Setopia slip into the distance and disappear. When I no longer could see the island, I sat down and read a book to pass the time. For many hours, I listened to the waves splashing against the raft. The waves beat a soothing rhythm. Occasionally, I caught sight of a fish or sometimes a dolphin. Funny, I thought, how simple things can occupy my mind and entertain when there are no other distractions. Many hours I entertained myself by watching seagulls that had followed my raft. However, one day they disappeared when I was far out into the ocean.

Then, my mood changed as I became aware of my need for survival. I focused on charting a course toward where I thought

Bimini lay in the distance. The charts and the sextant I salvaged from the wrecked sailboat were enormously helpful. However, I didn't know how much I could trust either the maps or the sextant because I didn't know for sure where I was located and if I was still actually on the Earth. Strange, I thought, not to be sure what ocean or sea I was floating in. Still, I studied the map and tacked a course of North by North West, toward the area from which I had originally entered the fog. For my meals, I cooked on a small alcohol stove that I salvaged from the wrecked sailboat. The meals were relatively tasty and attracted many a sea bird to my raft. During the first few days at sea, the waters were relatively calm and I often found myself wondering if I had fallen asleep and only dreamed about my adventures in Setopia.

It was during the afternoon of the third day of the second week that a storm quickly came upon me from the west and swept my raft many miles off course. I dropped the sails so the strong winds might not tear the masthead from its anchor, and lashed them to the deck. Large waves pounded my raft throughout the day, dashing the cabin with blown spume that left a salty residue on my face. Squall winds echoed throughout the cabin and sent ocean spray over everything and drenched anything that wasn't covered. During the night, the storm intensified. Two of the outer logs of the deck tore loose from their ropes and floated away into the darkness along with some of my provisions. Fearful that more logs might be torn loose, I fought the wind and rain to secure all my remaining provisions and lashed them to the center deck logs. Then, I lashed myself to the deck. The storm intensified and tore away more of the outer deck logs. For hours I laid strapped to the center of the raft holding the ropes that were attached by pulleys to the rudder, trying to keep the bow of the raft pointing into the storm. Throughout the night the winds howled and waves tore at my raft. During the middle of the night, a large wave inundated the raft and tore away a part of the cabin. By morning, the storm subsided and the ocean was calm. As light from the rising sun appeared over the horizon, I saw a large part of the cabin and most of my provisions had been lost to the storm. I rushed about to secure what was left of my raft and lashed the logs back together as best I could. Then I set about to rescue what water and other provisions I could find. Fortunately, one barrel of water bobbed in the water off the port side of the raft. I threw a rope over the barrel and managed to drag it aboard. The main mast and the canvas I had lashed to the center part of the raft had somehow survived the storm. I ran the canvass up the mast, but there was no wind to set my sails.

That afternoon, a thick fog descended on my raft that exerted enormous pressure on my body. I felt as though my eyes would pop out of their sockets. My compass again spun freely as it had before in this devilish part of the globe. For several days I floated aimlessly in the thick soupy fog, and became more and more disoriented. The forces that caused my compass to spin also influenced my mind. Many images appeared to me as though I were watching a play. At first, the images were fleeting diaphanous demons that appeared and quickly disappeared. After a while, they took on more corporal forms that seemed real. As the apparitions appeared through the mist, they seemed to speak with mournful sounds. Their images were scarcely distinguishable from the fog, and appeared in many vibrant colors. One image appeared through a magenta mist and spoke with a voice that seemed to come through the millennium of time. I did not know if I was dreaming or awake as I spoke to the colorful visages appearing in the haze that engulfed my raft. One appeared as an elderly man with a long flowing beard and white hair. He spoke with a melodious voice, sweet and soft, with a resonate voice that reverberated through the fog. I must have lost my mind, for suddenly all around me appeared a panorama of beautiful scenes of lost cities. The melodious voice continued until the vibrations from his voice sent me into a state of delirium. For many days, I floated on the raft surrounded by the all-inclusive fog. I consumed all the water I had managed to rescue from the storm. There was nothing left. Lacking water, I lay on deck in a state of delirium. One day, while delirious and close to death, my raft slipped out of the fog. I don't know how long my raft drifted in the sun drenched ocean because my thoughts were jumbled.

I heard something strange off in the distance. With great effort, I lifted my head and saw a large ship heading in my direction. At first, I assumed it too was an apparition. It wasn't until I heard a loud fog horn that it seemed real. The vessel had orange stripes along its side. Exhausted, I lay back down and closed my eyes.

Soon, a U.S.Coast Guard cutter pulled alongside my tattered raft. Two men jumped onto the deck of the raft, but I could not understand what they were saying. I tried to put on the halter, but lacked the strength. They strapped me onto a harness and transported me through the air and onto the deck of the Coast Guard vessel where I was rushed inside to a medic's station. Days later, after I recovered my strength and was no longer delirious, the Captain asked me many questions about my origins and how I came to be floating on a makeshift raft in the middle of the Atantic. I tried to answer his questions and to explain about the plane wreck, about Setopia and what had happened on the island, but to no avail. The Captain repeatedly told me I had suffered a concussion from the plane crash and the place called Setopia does not exist.

Made in the USA
Middletown, DE
27 March 2018